THE NATURE
of
DISAPPEARING

ALSO BY KIMI CUNNINGHAM GRANT

These Silent Woods

Fallen Mountains

Silver Like Dust

THE NATURE

of

DISAPPEARING

A NOVEL

KIMI CUNNINGHAM GRANT

MINOTAUR BOOKS
NEW YORK

First published in the United States by Minotaur Books, an imprint of St. Martin's Publishing Group

THE NATURE OF DISAPPEARING. Copyright © 2024 by Kimi Cunningham Grant. All rights reserved. Printed in the United States of America. For information, address St. Martin's Publishing Group, 120 Broadway, New York, NY 10271.

Ellen Bass, "The Thing Is" from *Mules of Love*. Copyright © 2002 by Ellen Bass. Reprinted with the permission of The Permissions Company, LLC, on behalf of BOA Editions Ltd., www.boaeditions.org.

www.minotaurbooks.com

Designed by Gabriel Guma

The Library of Congress Cataloging-in-Publication Data is available upon request.

ISBN 978-1-250-90761-5 (hardcover)
ISBN 978-1-250-90762-2 (ebook)

Our books may be purchased in bulk for promotional, educational, or business use. Please contact your local bookseller or the Macmillan Corporate and Premium Sales Department at 1-800-221-7945, extension 5442, or by email at MacmillanSpecialMarkets@macmillan.com.

First Edition: 2024

10 9 8 7 6 5 4 3 2 1

For those of you who are in a wilderness

He found him in a desert land,
And in the howling waste of a wilderness;
He encircled him, He cared for him,
He guarded him as the pupil of His eye.

—DEUTERONOMY 32:10

The National Wilderness Preservation System is a network of over 111.7 million acres—more area than the state of California—of public land comprised of more than 803 wilderness areas administered for the American people by the federal government. These are special places where nature still calls the shots. Places where people like you, with an appetite for adventure, can find a sense of true self-reliance and experience solitude.

—THE U.S. FOREST SERVICE ON ITS DESIGNATED WILDERNESS AREAS (SEPTEMBER, 2023)

ONE

SMOKE tinges the world white. It swallows the spired treetops and narrows the canyon ahead. It erases altogether the majestic gray faces of the Obsidians, shrouds the valley, slips up the ravines. Emlyn stands midstream, the river lulling at her thighs, pressing her waders tight.

A shadow overhead, a flash of dark. In a moment it swoops to the water, hard and fast. A bright splash as it hits the surface, then it lifts, flapping higher, its catch secure in its talons. Osprey. Emlyn looks at the client, clambering ahead and sloshing upstream, and wonders if he sees it. Some people, they feel the trout in these waters belong to them and not the birds, and Emlyn has a feeling the client is such a person.

John Thomas is his name, and he seems to hold it against her that the wildfires in California are ruining the cerulean Idaho skies promised on the company website. Earlier, as they'd loaded gear into the truck, he'd waved his hand toward the gray-white space in the distance where the Obsidians hid, veiled in smoke, and, frowning, said, "I thought there were mountains."

He'd arrived fourteen minutes early in an Aston Martin Vantage, teal with a yellow pinstripe down its hood. Emlyn had tried not to stare, which is exactly what a car-loving person like herself was wont to do, and exactly what a person who drove such a car expected people to do. She'd tried not to eye the handcrafted Oyster bamboo rod, which she knew carried a price tag of forty-six hundred dollars, though, in the end, she couldn't keep herself from commenting. And she'd tried not to look too hard at him, John Thomas, maybe ten years her senior but glowing with good looks and vigor, a shining example of how money could prolong youth. He'd climbed out of the Aston Martin, extended a smooth hand, and flashed her a winning smile. "I've heard great things about you," he'd said.

To her relief, she'd delivered. Well, that and they'd been lucky. Luck was always part of the story. She'd set him up with a hopper-dropper—the hopper peach with Sharpied dots on its underside, the dropper a zebra nymph, both of which she'd made herself—and the man had caught a fat, glimmering brown trout in a public stretch of the Salmon, early in the day. Later, and to his great delight, he'd taken a small bull trout in a tributary on the Henning Ranch, where Emlyn had permission to fish. She'd cited statistics about the odds of such an accomplishment and snapped a slew of photos before returning it to the cold water.

This is good work, guiding, and she knows it. Spending day upon day where she feels most at ease, in the wild, in a place she is sure is the most beautiful stretch of land in the country, if not the world, and most of the time, she loves it. On the river there is no humdrum, no watching the clock. There's splendor, there's variety. Clients of all sorts come to her. Some have never held a fly rod and, enamored with all those gorgeous descriptions in books like *A River Runs Through It* and *The River Why*, want to give it a whirl. She remembers that initial impulse herself, watching her father wade into the water as she sat along shore, knees tucked. Seeing him squint and lean and then set the hook and begin to reel it in. How the fish fought, how her dad didn't rush, but took his time bringing it in. "Can I try?" she'd asked, and he'd grinned and waved her to the stream. The water cold and soaking through her tennis shoes. She was a girl, then. Eleven. But still she remembers the desire, the sense that she could not just sit on the bank any longer.

And so, when these clients with their intrigue and curiosity pay the shop their mind-boggling fee to spend the day learning, Emlyn gladly accommodates them. She drives them up 75 in her truck, past Selborne hot springs, where the thermal water rises from the earth and spills hot down a golden hillside into the Salmon. She swings left to the dredge ponds, where the client has plenty of room to learn a backcast, and where the trout have been stocked so thickly they swim fin-to-fin, darkening the clear water. She doesn't mind those days. She doesn't mind the days when the client is an equal, someone who simply wants knowledge of the area, access, some recommendations on which flies to try. Sometimes, though, there are John Thomases: entitled jerks who are simply checking off a locale from a list someone posted on the internet. People who don't really love that feeling, how the rest of the world can blur and disappear when you are on the water, but who are after something else, something less. And today is one of those days.

All morning she's been trying to find a word for him. It is something she does, identify one word to summarize a person—one solid, shiny word that really captures someone's essence. Deep down she wants to believe that people are much more complicated than a single word, that perhaps a person doesn't really have an essence at all, but rather essences. Or that maybe a person could be one thing, but then change. Even so, it's a game she plays. But, try as she might, she has not yet come up with John Thomas's word.

HE insists on lunch at the Sunny Creek Lodge, which is fourteen miles south of where they are now. Emlyn doesn't want to eat lunch with John Thomas, but unfortunately, this is part of the gig. Schmoozing, chatting, making the client feel like he is sharing a day with an old friend. It's the one part of the job that Emlyn really considers work, and the one part she is not particularly good at. More often than she wishes to admit, this is noted in the survey that clients are asked to complete after their day with each guide. She's aloof, she isn't friendly, she is awkward. She can't really deny any of those things, but still, it stings to read them, and on more than one occasion Oliver, her boss, has asked her to try just a little harder, please. And she does try, she really does, but that tendency to hold everyone and everything at arm's length, to view the world through a lens clouded with suspicion, is so deeply ingrained in her that she isn't sure she will ever be any different.

In the zip pocket of her chest waders Emlyn keeps three things: her Dr. Slick offset nippers; a bottle of Gink; and the emergency flashlight her dear friend, Rev, gave her for Christmas her first year in the valley. Now, she runs her palm over the pocket, feeling the shape of each item beneath the nylon. A habit. She drops her hands to the river, grazing the water. Like always, her left ring finger tingles in the cold. An old wound, a reminder of the past. Though she is finally in a place where she doesn't think much about that old life, sometimes the finger will remind her of all that she had, once. And all that she did not.

Upstream, John Thomas has managed to reel in yet another fish, and he is struggling to hold it in his left hand, the right hand gripping a phone out at arm's length, taking a photograph of himself. When he releases the fish, she raises a hand, and he starts making his way back downstream to her.

The air quality is poor today, "unhealthy" in the words of the National Weather Service, and on days like this Oliver requires his guides to keep a close eye on the clients, who can easily feel the effects of not only the smoke but also the elevation. "We don't need anyone keeling over on the river," he has told the staff, "not with the closest hospital eighty miles away." She's had John Thomas out on the water for hours now, since dawn, and it is nearly noon.

He splashes closer.

"Cuttie?" she asks.

"Yeah," he says, grinning. "Big, probably twenty-five inches."

Oliver's words scuttle through her mind. *Try a little harder.* "Nice," she says, forcing a smile. She swings her long braid over her shoulder. Even from fifty yards away she could tell that the fish had been much smaller than that.

THE Sunny Creek Lodge doesn't take reservations, but there is a tiny booth on the south corner that Roxy, the owner, is usually willing to save for Oliver's guides, if they call ahead. It's an ancient, run-down place that leans to the side, its log and chinking still hanging on from a previous century.

Even on a weekday, lunchtime in summer means a line is snaking its way out the door and into the gravel parking lot. Roxy and two seasonal employees are bustling their way through a dining room crammed with too many booths and tables, red trays propped on their shoulders. Two more employees are in the back, grilling burgers and slicing French fries from big brown bags of Idaho potatoes.

For lunch John Thomas orders a veggie burger topped with jalapeños and figs. He snaps a photo of the plate with his phone and then asks Emlyn to take one of him as he grins, holding it between both hands. He scowls at her bison burger with a pejorative eye.

Emlyn excuses herself from the table and walks to the counter to pay the bill. She glances at the small television, mounted in the corner above the bar, muted during lunch hour. A fast-food chain alerting its patrons of a widespread *E. coli* outbreak. Summer storms pummeling the Midwest. A white headline at the bottom of the screen: MISSING? PAIR OF #VANLIFE STARS GOES SILENT.

Emlyn pulls her phone from her pocket. She messages Oliver and tells him they'll be back soon. She hands Roxy the check and two twenties, then dumps the change in the old mason glass tip jar. She tucks the receipt in her pocket to turn in later.

And then the television flashes a snapshot of a familiar, gorgeous blonde, leaning against a towering arch in Moab, smiling, a red beanie atop her head. Another photograph: the woman again in the same red beanie, huddled next to a thick, brown-haired man, both draped beneath a bright plaid blanket, the Tetons looming starkly in the background. Emlyn goes still. Then a final photograph, the woman, sunglasses on, standing in front of a gray Mercedes camper van, holding a cast-iron skillet brimming with a glorious array of vegetables.

A chill rolls up Emlyn's spine.

Janessa?

Just last week, her old friend had called while Emlyn was out hiking. They'd chatted for a few minutes—small talk, which was their custom these days—and then Janessa had shifted gears. "There's something I need to tell you," she'd said, right as Emlyn had come to one of the many inevitable spots in the area that lacked cell coverage and the call had dropped. Hours later, when Emlyn again had service and called back, it had gone straight to voicemail. She'd left a message, but in the days since, she hadn't given it much thought.

The room hums with lunchtime din: forks scraping plates, a baby slapping her hands on the tray of a high chair, a woman laughing at the corner table. "Turn it up," Emlyn wheezes to Roxy, though the news has trundled on.

Roxy frowns and leans closer. "Sorry, what?"

Emlyn flaps toward the television, hands shaking. "The news, can you turn it up?"

Roxy slings her towel over her shoulder and searches behind the bar, sliding glasses, clinking bottles. Now, on the screen: some senator, embroiled in a scandal. When Roxy finds the remote, she holds it toward the television, turning up the volume. A patron close by looks over his shoulder and hollers to turn that garbage down, please; he is trying to have lunch in peace.

"Did you catch the story?" Emlyn asks Roxy. "The missing couple. Did you hear, did you get the names, anything?" She lifts her Buff and dabs her neck.

Roxy dries a glass and flips it upside down. "Sorry."

"How about earlier? Before lunch? The story about the missing couple."

"No, kinda busy here," she says, eyebrows raised. (Roxy's word: *plucky*.) But, looking closer at Emlyn, she tilts her head. "You all right?"

"What?"

"Here, sit down a minute." Roxy gestures toward an empty stool.

Emlyn waves her off, searching the scrolling ticker for details. It can't have been her, she reasons. The pictures flashed quickly; she had maybe four or five seconds to look. And it's been years since she's actually seen her old friend. *Friend*. Is that the word? Yes, of course. In fact "friend" was almost too flimsy a word. They'd been more. Confidantes, allies, sisters.

And then they'd been less.

They'd drifted apart, Janessa had moved away, they'd had a falling-out. All of these things were true, and yet they didn't really explain what happened. Nor has Emlyn ever been entirely sure of the order in which those events occurred. She has her suspicions, of course. She has her regrets. How many times has she lamented over the ifs: if things had gone differently, if Tyler hadn't left her in the woods, if only she'd listened to Janessa from the start, if, if—

Emlyn had hoped the two of them could make amends; she wanted to rebuild. From her point of view, that's what the two of them were in the midst of doing, now. After a period of silence, she and Janessa had started to call each other on occasion. They sent each other birthday cards and funny Valentines. Janessa had mailed her a Christmas gift: lip balm, fancy tea, cookies in a beautiful tin.

But things had never been the same, since that summer, five years ago.

Emlyn reaches out and grips the red countertop.

John Thomas rises from the booth, scuffs his way toward her and stands far too close. "Ready?"

She blinks, struggling to reorient herself.

He flashes a wide grin at Roxy. "The burger was exquisite," he says, and then checks his reflection in the mirror behind the bar.

"Patronizing," Emlyn says aloud, the word swimming to her ("condescending; demonstrating a pompous attitude toward others").

"What's that?" John Thomas says, turning from the mirror.

Flustered, Emlyn points to the television. "That reporter," she tells him.

ON the drive back to the fly shop, John Thomas scrolls through his phone and moans about the poor reception. He talks again about his bull trout and the enormous cutthroat with which he'd ended his day on the water. Emlyn tries to listen enough to seem decent, but her mind whirls and burns.

They were two separate stories, she tells herself. Janessa isn't missing, Janessa wouldn't live in a van, Janessa wouldn't post pictures for the whole world to see all the intimacies of her life.

Well. Maybe she *would*.

There's so much about Janessa's life Emlyn doesn't know anymore.

When at last they pull into the parking lot back in Heart, Emlyn climbs out of the truck and shakes John Thomas's hand. He asks for a photo with her, which she's sure he'll post online, tagging the fly shop. Oliver lives for these moments—his business has boomed since a certain movie star tagged the shop two summers ago, a fact that the guides are reminded of every June. Emlyn wants to refuse. She's never liked the notion of people documenting their lives (and, in turn, hers) for the world to see. But, remembering that there will be a client survey, that she will have an employee review next month, she agrees. She leans her head close to John Thomas's and forces a smile while he snaps a picture, and then says, as sincerely as she can, "I'm glad we could do this."

TWO

AFTER what had happened with Tyler, after death had licked at Emlyn's door and she'd leaned close and then finally decided to pull back, the deal she made with herself was to break things off entirely. A clean, cold, shattering severance. There was no middle ground, no standing between that old life and her new one, a foot in each world. The only thing to do was to slough it off entirely, every last inch of it, and try to piece together some new version of herself. She did not tell Tyler where she went. She did not answer phone calls from him or any of their mutual acquaintances. She did not do any online searches of his name. She did not think of him or the life they'd had together at all. Well, she tried not to. She wasn't that far from where they'd lived together—an hour-and-a-half drive— and she was even closer to his family's cabin at Patten Lake, where they'd spent holidays and weekends. But if she wanted to build a new life for herself, the first step was setting boundaries, and those boundaries were strict.

With Janessa, Emlyn had made an exception. If it hadn't been for Janessa, Emlyn might be dead.

Now, as she sits in her truck in the fly shop parking lot, Emlyn unlocks her phone and types Janessa's name into a search engine. Immediately the headline from CNN appears, and she clicks on the story. The same images from the diner television fill her small screen. Emlyn stares at the photographs, absorbing the terrible reality: it is indeed her old friend. Dread lodges in her throat, the phone trembles in her hands. The story is brief. The "beloved social media starlet" has been silent for nearly a week, and friends and family have not heard from her. That's all. Emlyn dials Janessa. The call goes straight to voicemail. She hangs up and begins scrolling through her list of recent incoming calls. Oliver, Rev, John Thomas, Oliver again. There. Janessa. She counts the days and realizes it's been exactly a week since that dropped call. Anxiety churns along her skin. She drops the phone on the seat beside her, starts the engine, and heads home.

HOME, for the moment, is six miles up a dirt road that begins four miles north of town. She has been here for a while, in her Airstream, and the truth is it's beautiful, and she'd like it if she never had to leave. She takes a very quick shower and then fills the kettle from a plastic jug. She lifts the front of the bed and pulls her Mathews bow from the storage compartment and hauls it outside. From the cabinet she plucks an enamel mug, blue with white specks, and makes a cup of tea. Is there something she should do? Call the police? Post her contact information in the comments on the CNN website? She turns off the stove, leaning against the small dining table, dunking the tea bag up and down and watching the colors bleed into the water.

At some point during the afternoon, a wind drifted in from the north, lifting the smoke and carrying it southward, and now the sun hangs bright in the sky. The Obsidians have reappeared: black, austere, rimmed in white. The colors emerge in the valley, green and gold, and the light catches the world aglow.

With her tea, Emlyn steps out of the Airstream. She scans the topography, searching. A habit. This is home, now, this wild and magnificent landscape, and there is little here that scares her. Wolves are around—she saw one once, on a trail camera she set up for hunting season, and she hears them often at night—but they are scarce and elusive and pose no threat. Black bears are not uncommon, but they can be spotted a long way off here in the sagebrush, and she is always careful not to leave any food out. Mountain lions, though, are a different story. Attacks are extremely rare, she knows that, but still.

The same breeze that swept the smoke from the valley now whips at the trailer's awning. She wraps her fingers around the mug, breathes in the sagebrush, and slumps into a collapsible camp chair. She picks up her phone and sends a quick message to Janessa: *Are you okay?* She clicks send, then puts the phone and the tea on the steps of the Airstream. She takes her bow from the case. Twenty yards away, she has a target set up. She stands, feet shoulder width apart, and draws back. Her fingertips graze the side of her mouth. All summer she's been practicing, building up her strength to be able to pull the recommended fifty pounds. She's guided hunts before, but for the first time since she arrived in the valley, she drew a coveted elk tag, which means she can hunt them herself this year. Her heart is set on harvesting one, or at least being strong enough to give it a try. An elk could feed her and Rev for the year to come, and the idea that she could do that, that she could in some small way repay Rev for all she has done over the past three years, has motivated Emlyn to work hard since the snow began to melt.

SHE'S still on her first round when she hears it: the distant roar of tires crushing gravel, the heave of the engine as it climbs the ridge. A vehicle. She turns and watches as a cloud of dust lifts in the distance, billowing upward. Hikers, maybe. There is a trailhead a mile past her. Or possibly campers, looking for a good spot with privacy and a view. She nocks another arrow, pulls back, exhales, shoots.

At last a white Jeep emerges from around the bend, and it slows and pulls over in front of the Airstream. Varden. Hands on the steering wheel, he raises his pointer finger. *Decent* is Varden's word, and not in the sense of "passable" or "tolerable"—which does not suit at all—but "marked by goodness, integrity, and honor." That definition summarizes Varden perfectly.

"Emlyn," he says, climbing out. He is in his usual Forest Service attire: stiff dark green pants, stiff gray-green top, his name printed in gold lettering on a name tag fixed to his pocket.

"Varden," she says, smiling.

He leans against the Jeep and folds his brown arms across his chest. "How many pounds you pulling?"

"Forty-six. Not enough yet."

"That's good. Real good." He takes his hat off and sets it on the hood. "You'll get there, I'm sure. You set your mind to something, nothing can stop you."

Her heart hammers at the compliment. "Thanks."

"You still doing your push-ups?"

"Sure. You?"

He nods. They started doing them together, last winter. "Looks like a good group," he says, gesturing toward the target, where four of Emlyn's arrows have landed in a tidy, tight circle.

She sets the bow in the case and picks up her mug of tea. "You want a drink?"

"Thanks, not today."

"Well, I know you didn't drive all the way up here just to say hello."

Varden takes a deep breath and wipes his brow. "No."

Emlyn knows the real reason, and she feels sorry to be doing this to him again, making him correct her. She knows it's the part of his job that he likes the least—policing, enforcing—and she knows he feels especially awkward about it because it's her.

"Been too long, Em." He shakes his head. "Got people complaining."

"Who's complaining?"

"You've been here almost a month, Emlyn. Limit's ten days now. You know that."

She rolls her eyes. "Almost a million acres of wilderness, and still people can't mind their own business."

"Well, maybe if you'd picked some hard-to-reach place with no view, nobody would even notice. But this spot, it's desirable." He steps away from her and turns to look at the soft, rolling hills just below, and then the sprawling valley, gold with the setting sun, and the stark and startling Obsidians beyond all of that. "Which I know is why you picked it. I don't blame you. Best view this side of the summit. But still. There are rules. How do you even stay out here so long?"

She shrugs and looks beyond Varden at the hill that rises higher and higher, the game trail that winds west and out of sight. Every Wednesday after dark she hooks up the Airstream and hauls it down to the national forest dump station to empty and fill her tanks. And no, she does not leave the required ten dollars in the little metal box next to the hose.

"I don't like this any more than you do," Varden says.

"I know."

"Bring it down to Rev's place for a while. She'll always make room."

Rev is what everyone calls her, though Emlyn knows her real name is Ruth, and she isn't even a real reverend, just someone who's always willing to listen and pray—at least that's how she explained it to Emlyn, long ago. Ever since that first winter, Emlyn has spent the coldest months down at Rev's, in one of the cabins that sit empty after tourist season.

"I'll be down. Soon."

"She misses you." He kicks a stone. "So do I."

Varden rents one of Rev's cabins year-round, and Emlyn loves winters with the two of them. She loves how they took her in, no questions asked, how they folded her right into themselves, back when she was alone and adrift and nearly dead.

"Anyhow, you'll move?"

She looks at her watch. "Tomorrow. Is that all right?"

Varden nods. "That'll do." He turns to go. "They stocked Tatum Lake a few days ago, with a helicopter. I might hike up, wet a line. You want to come along?"

Varden loves her, maybe. And she loves him, too, or wants to, but the truth is that she's a mess, and she isn't worthy of a man like Varden. From a distance, he cannot see this, but if she lets him get close enough, he will. And then he will leave her. In a kind way, yes. He would make it about himself, or some external detail. But she knows it would be because of her. If there's one thing her twenty-eight years have taught her, it's that there are people in this world who inspire loyalty and devotion, and there are people who are forgettable and leavable. She is the latter. A stepping stone, a place marker, a seasonal employee. This is what will happen. This is what always happens. And, though she can bear many things, Emlyn cannot bear to lose Varden, and then Rev, and this whole community that circled around her like matron elephants when she had nothing.

"I think I have to work," she says, which is a lie.

"I'll keep asking, you know," he says.

"Will you?" Her voice sounds hopeful, she hears it. Maybe a little desperate. All the things she wants out of life seem to flare before her like a lighthouse gleaming across dark water. Trust, closeness. Babies. Boisterous mealtimes, Christmas mornings, picture books on the couch. Does Varden know that, lonely nights in her camper, she has secret fantasies of those things with him? Does he catch that flash of desire in her voice? Embarrassed, she looks away and plucks another arrow from the quiver. She steals a glance as Varden climbs into the Jeep. He is handsome, and so very good, and she wishes she could figure out a way to break through the walls she has stacked around her heart. She wishes she could let him in.

Varden shrugs. "Until you say not to." He climbs into his Jeep and starts the engine. "Always good to see you, Em," he calls, and drives off in a cloud of dust.

SEVEN YEARS AGO

THE first time Emlyn meets Janessa is at Bumpy's Diner, two towns south of the Pennsylvania college where she is a sophomore. Emlyn comes here because (1) she will not encounter the unbearable fraternity boys who run rampant at all the eating establishments in town, (2) she will not encounter the even more unbearable sorority girls, and (3) the pancakes are delicious and cost three dollars. Once a week, she gets on her bike and treats herself to this diversion. Francine, the owner, knows her by now, and allows her one-dollar cup of coffee to be bottomless. So, three dollars, plus a one-dollar cup of burnt coffee, plus a one-dollar tip. She wishes she could leave more, considering how long she camps out in her booth, but it's all she can afford. She rides her bike home in the dark, which is unwise, maybe, but the autumn air rushing at her cheeks, the feel of her heart thudding during the final hill that leads to campus—it is her only escape from that gorgeous, glittering prison, the only time each week when she can feel at ease, and she embraces it.

On this October night, two men whom she can only presume to be locals glide into the diner. Francine pours them coffee and tells them to behave, then disappears into the kitchen. Only one other person is here this late, a young woman in a Carhartt jacket at the far end of the diner. When the men attempt to strike up a conversation with Emlyn, she does her best to seem absorbed in her studying, picking up her highlighter. When one slides next to her in the booth and the other wedges his large body into the seat across from her, panic surges through her. They reek of alcohol and motor oil.

"Whatchya working on?" the one next to her asks. He reaches out a blackened finger and smudges the open page of her textbook.

She cranes her neck, searching for Francine. "Homework," she says. Outside, her bike leans against the building, right below her window, and with a sick feeling she realizes that maybe the long nighttime rides back to campus are even more unwise than she thought.

"Hey," a voice says, and all at once the woman in the Carhartt is standing at the table, backpack slung over her shoulder. A ball cap is perched on her head, her hair hidden. "You're in my seat."

The man across from Emlyn looks up, perhaps discomfited by the fact that he is sitting and the woman towers over him. He hefts himself toward the window. "There's room."

"No," the woman says, crossing her arms. "There isn't. So move."

Emlyn marvels at the woman's authority.

"Feisty," the man beside Emlyn says. He licks his lips.

"You know," the woman in the Carhartt says, "I grew up on a ranch in Idaho. There are bears and other nuisances. And my daddy always taught me to be prepared." She plucks a large black canister from the water-bottle sleeve of her backpack. "This," she continues, slamming it down on the table, the metal canister clanging on the Formica, "is bear spray. It's pepper spray, but thirty times more powerful. I hear if you get it in your eye, you'll go blind, permanently." With her thumb she clicks off the orange safety.

Emlyn sees the spark in the woman's eyes; the torn, baggy jeans; the

Carhartt jacket; and thinks: at last, a friend. She can barely allow herself to wish for such a thing. It's her third semester, and she loves her classes but hates the rest of it. The sorority sisters, with their raspy voices and tan midriffs. The fancy cars. The talks of spring and winter break plans— *I'm going to the Dominican Republic, I'm flying to Barcelona, I'm skiing in Vail.* So much of it like a foreign language to her, a discourse she cannot grasp. Her plans: going home to Shingletown and working at the Savvy Shopper to earn enough money to buy food for the rest of the semester. The highlight will be swapping a handful of paperbacks with Grandpa.

But this is not a sorority sister standing at the end of the table. And maybe Emlyn's loneliness has come to an end.

Later, she will learn that all that business about a ranch in Idaho is not untrue, but also not exactly what it implied. The "ranch" is a sprawling mansion on fourteen acres in a small sea of other mansions, and Janessa's father is more the skeet-shooting-at-the-gun-club type than a sidearm-toting cowboy.

But here, in Bumpy's Diner, Emlyn is convinced that the woman might press the black button and douse the place with pepper spray, that she sort of wants to, and apparently the men are uneasy, too, because the one next to her says, "C'mon, Davey. Let's go." And they do.

With a wary eye Emlyn watches as they push through the glass door and saunter out to their Ford truck. They spin one doughnut in the parking lot, tires squealing, smoke rising from the asphalt, and then tear onto the empty street.

"I'M Janessa," the woman says, sliding into the booth across from her. "We're in Western Civ together."

"We are?"

"You raise your hand a lot," Janessa says. "And I sit in the back."

Emlyn gives a sheepish smile. It's her favorite class. "I'm Emlyn," she says. "Thanks for rescuing me."

"I have a strong propulsion toward justice," Janessa says, rolling her eyes and flashing a bright smile. "That's what all the personality quizzes tell me." Then she adds with a wink, "Plus I've always had a sick desire to bear-spray a dirtbag. I mean, who hasn't, right?"

Emlyn does not say aloud that the thought has never occurred to her.

She stuffs her books into her backpack, and the two of them rise from the booth. Outside, Janessa scans the empty parking lot. "Where are you parked?"

Emlyn points to her bike.

"You can't ride that back."

"I can't leave it." The bike is her only means of transportation.

"Grab it," Janessa says, pulling keys from her pocket.

For a moment Emlyn stands there, debating, but then she obeys, grabbing the bike by the handlebar and walking it to an old Volvo station wagon. Her helmet, strung onto the handle, sways as they walk. Janessa climbs into the back of the car and the two of them work together to heft Emlyn's bike through the hatch. "Done," she says. "Hop in."

Emlyn walks to the front of the vehicle and gets in. "Do you really live on a ranch?"

Janessa turns the ignition. In the parking lot she spins a doughnut, just like the two jerks in the truck, the old Volvo long and slow, Emlyn's stomach lurching, and throws her head back in laughter.

THE next morning, in Western Civ, Emlyn sits in her usual seat in the front row of her lecture hall in the Vaughan Building, two minutes before class begins. Dr. Rodkey pours himself a cup of coffee from a tall green Stanley thermos and then drags the metal stool from behind the podium. He has glasses and abundant white hair and a fluffy white beard, and Emlyn adores him.

"Hey," a voice says, and Janessa slides into the seat next to her.

"Miss Thomas," Dr. Rodkey says with a grin, raising his steaming cup of coffee. "Good to see you branching out from the nosebleed section."

"Hi, Dr. Rodkey."

"You're in good company," he says, tipping his head to Emlyn.

She can feel her cheeks flushing. Nearly every week she is in Dr. Rodkey's office, sorting through a reading or an assignment. But also—and she is barely able to admit this to herself—seeking conversation, connection.

"That's why I'm here," Janessa says.

Janessa is different, though. Gone are the Carhartt jacket and ball cap. Today her eyelashes are thick with mascara, and her lips are a shimmery pink. Today her hair, which was tucked beneath her trucker hat the night before, brushes her shoulders, blond and pin straight. Stylish glasses frame her face and give her an air of studiousness. She wears a V-neck T-shirt and a pair of short denim cutoffs. The transformation is somewhat mystifying. If Janessa hadn't plopped down next to her, Emlyn's not sure she would've recognized her.

After class Janessa asks what she's doing later.

Emlyn traces the zipper on her backpack. "I have a paper due Monday morning," she says, because she has no plans, as usual. And more importantly, she cannot afford to have plans.

Janessa stares at her for a moment, studying her face. "No," she says, and shakes her head. "Sorry, that is unacceptable. A girl like you, sitting in the library on a Friday night, is not acceptable. You're mine for the evening. We are going out."

"I don't go out. I don't . . . like that scene," Emlyn says.

Janessa rolls her eyes. "Yes, the library is so much more riveting. Tell you what. You come out with me tonight, and I'll go to the library with you tomorrow. Deal?" She nudges Emlyn's side with her elbow. "Deal?"

Emlyn shrugs. What's she going to do, refuse? "I guess."

"Shower, then come to my place. I'm in Fry C3. Do not touch your hair."

LATER, Janessa dots foundation across Emlyn's forehead and cheeks. She takes a brush and swirls it in. She sweeps blush up her cheeks, glides eyeliner across her lids. She twists her hair around a curling iron, tousles the waves, shakes an aerosol can and tells Emlyn to hold her breath. When Janessa spins her to look in the mirror, Emlyn stares at herself. The change is startling. Unnerving. And also exhilarating.

"Listen," Janessa says, squinting as she dabs gloss on Emlyn's lips. "Here's the game. Think of it like dress-up, or being in a play. Tonight you are not Emlyn the quiet girl who sits in the library on a Friday night. Tonight you don't spend a penny of your own money. Tonight you are someone else. You are fun and flirty. No—" She frowns, leans back, assessing Emlyn's face. "That won't work, will it? You are cool and mysterious. Now, watch." She dips her chin, looks down, then up, right into Emlyn's eyes. "'Buy me a drink?' That's what you do. Easy peasy. Practice, okay?"

Emlyn dips her chin, looks down, then bats her eyes dramatically and says, in a pitiful Southern accent, "Buy me a drink?"

The two of them burst into laughter.

"No! Please no. Try again."

"Buy me a drink, bro," Emlyn says, imitating the fraternity brothers she loathes.

Janessa giggles. "Do another one."

Emlyn is pleased with herself. In her best Pennsylvania drawl, she says, "Any of yinz wanna buy me a drink?"

"Like that," Janessa says, snorting. She dabs a tissue beneath her eyes, dotting tears. "Just like that."

When they get to the campus parking lot, Emlyn searches for the Volvo, but they stop at a Maserati. "Whose car is this?" she asks.

"Mine."

"What about the station wagon?"

"That's my roommate's. I borrowed it."

"Why?"

"Would you drive this car to Bumpy's Diner?"

Would she drive this car anywhere? Emlyn's dad was a mechanic. And, though he was a loser and a leaver, all those early years in his shop wore off on her, she can't help it. She still peruses *Car and Driver* in the checkout line, she still clicks on headlines about new releases. "GranTurismo. V-eight, six-speed?"

Janessa takes a deep breath and closes her green eyes, dramatically. "I could kiss you right now, for knowing that. Not even joking. Four point seven liter." She tosses her blond hair (wavy now, messy, with an air of effortlessness that Emlyn knows for a fact took forty minutes to style). It is in this moment, Janessa in her miniskirt and black leather jacket, the autumn air crisp and smooth, that Emlyn assigns her a word. *Alluring*: "mystifyingly glamorous and attractive; enigmatic; seductive."

"All right," Janessa says, unlocking the doors. "Here we go."

THREE

AT the fly shop, Emlyn shuffles through memories of Janessa.

Since yesterday at the Sunny Creek Lodge, Emlyn has called and left multiple voicemails, all with increasing degrees of urgency. *Janessa, you were on the news. I hope there's been a mistake. I hope you're okay. Janessa, I'm worried. Janessa, call me as soon as you get this, please.*

Emlyn tries to focus, be present. But this is harder than it sounds, especially in the shop, where Oliver has her fielding customer questions and tying flies to restock the shelves. Her mind keeps looping between a past she has worked hard to put behind her and the bewildering but unavoidable new terrain of *what happened?* What was it that Janessa had needed to tell her? And why hadn't Emlyn been more diligent about returning the call? Of course she feels guilty about this. She should've called back sooner. She should've turned around and backtracked to a place where she had reception. She should've sensed some sort of urgency in her friend's voice.

She is perched on a metal stool, her back to the shop door, leaning over the little fly-tying desk with its bright light and magnifying glass. Behind her, Lindsey, the college student from Michigan who's joined them for the summer, scans price tags and slides credit cards. (Her word is *flighty,* which is unkind, perhaps, but fitting.) Emlyn begins tying another Royal Coachman. She plucks a size 16 long shank hook from its magnet, puts the hook into the vise, and pushes the lever down to hold it in place. Next, she cuts a piece of brown hackle, about four inches in length, and places it to the side.

Someone approaches and stands close by. Customers like to watch. Sometimes, they ask to buy the very one she is making, so they can say they saw the guide tie it, as though that somehow makes it more authentic, or luckier, maybe.

"Hello," she says, threading the bobbin with dark brown waxed thread. She does not look up. She wraps the thread around the shank of the hook and then begins to spin the bobbin, round and round and round. Soon the customer will ask a question or two, soon they will compliment her. They will marvel at how she works so quickly, the steps and movements memorized. She knows the conversation.

But—

A presence, a scent. A tingle rolls up her spine.

"Hello, Em."

That voice.

Tyler.

She raises her eyes. Her heart seems to leap from its usual place and crash into her throat. She pushes herself back from the table, nearly knocking over the metal stool.

"I'm sorry. I realize this is unexpected."

A spool of thread clatters to the floor and rolls across the pine boards.

Still she doesn't speak. She doesn't look away.

"But it's Janessa."

Emlyn tilts at the mention of her friend's name. The room beyond Tyler begins to spin and blur, and she feels herself reaching for the table to hold herself steady.

"Look, it's a long story, but I think she's in trouble, and I need your help."

All of the pain. All of the lies. He had destroyed her and left her in a heap, and she's spent the last three years working so very hard to stagger back to her feet. And now, Tyler is here, dropped right in front of her in her new life, erupting everything into chaos, and the only thing she can think of is his word. *Captivating.*

"HOW did you find me?" Emlyn asks, when at last she finds her voice. This is a strange question.

She isn't hiding, after all. For a long time, a part of her wanted him to find her. Look for her, at least. She didn't want him back. She didn't want to reconcile. But if he'd come, if he'd tried, there would be some reassurance that he hadn't forgotten her. That she was not forgettable, that she was worth pursuing. She admitted this desire to no one, not to Rev, and barely to herself, but for a long time, when a vehicle trundled up the road, or the door of the shop jangled, she would raise her eyes, and she would feel it: the tiny bird of hope, fluttering in her chest.

But Tyler never came. And after a while she stopped wanting him to.

With a deep breath she eases herself back onto the stool to resume the Royal Coachman. Hands shaking, she picks a golden pheasant neck feather, orange with a black tip, and trims it to a quarter inch in length.

Tyler pulls his orange trucker hat from his head and runs his fingers through his thick blond hair. "A guy I know. You took him fishing. He posted all about it online with this photo of the two of you along a river, and I was like, Ohmygod, it's her. You were gorgeous, it was like"—he gestures, holding his hand over his chest—"the breath was just sucked from my lungs when I saw you. Which is how it's always been, I guess." He forms an O with his lips and exhales. "Still is, apparently." He looks down, shuffling his feet. "He said some lovely things about your guiding skills, by the way."

She tries not to cling to Tyler's words, not to let that sweet openheartedness of his bore its way into her. She focuses on the Royal Coachman, holding the golden feather right at the bend of the hook and wrapping it to attach it. "You shouldn't be here."

Tyler takes a deep breath and closes his eyes. "I know. I know there are so many things I should say to you. So many things I've wanted to say. Trust me, I've played through them a thousand times."

You left me.

"I can only imagine how it must feel to have me show up like this. But please, I need you to know—I wouldn't be here if I had any other choice. I promise you that."

Outside, Oliver pulls up in his pickup. He and a client climb out.

She picks up a strand of peacock herl.

The door clangs, and Oliver walks in. He looks at her before greeting a customer, and she knows he's probably processing a multitude of observations in that glance—*This doesn't seem like a professional interaction; You're on the clock, Emlyn;* but also, *Everything's okay over there, right?* (Oliver's word: *fastidious.*)

"Listen," she says to Tyler, lowering her voice. "I can't talk right now." Her mind veers toward Janessa. What does Tyler know? Should she tell him about the dropped phone call? She ties a whip finish and another and another and then raises her eyes to look at him. "I'm sorry. I can't help you."

Tyler's shoulders slump, weighted with defeat. He opens his mouth and then closes it, and when he looks away, she sees that his blue eyes are brimmed with tears. "Okay," he says, and she is surprised. The Tyler she knew would've pushed. He would've coaxed and begged and promised until she broke and gave in. Instead, he nods and takes a deep breath. "If you change your mind, I'll be at the lake house. Until I'm not."

He looks at her then, and her heart feels a thousand pinpricks. All these years, she'd convinced herself she wanted nothing to do with him. That he had ruined her and she hated him for it. But now, she watches him turn and walk across the planked floor, watches as the sunlight catches the glass in the front door and shoots a blinding flash of light across the shop, watches him pause at his truck and look at her for a moment, and then climb in and drive off. There is no denying it: she wants to follow him.

Tyler had leaned into his addiction. She had seen him succumb. She'd believed she was not that kind of person, that things could not grab hold of her the way they could him. But the truth is that right now, every inch of her wants to run after him. She can feel herself being drawn, tugged. Like a boat she saw once, being towed behind a larger and more powerful ship, up the St. Johns River. And with all that she's been working toward now on the brink of being untethered, she can't help but wonder if the two of them, they are not so different after all.

FOUR

REV is in the garden, kneeling and tugging weeds from a patch of beets. She rises when Emlyn's truck pulls into the parking area, holds her hand at her brow to shield the sun, and waves. Rev is a tall woman, slender and strong. Her white hair falls in waves well below her shoulders, and a wide-brimmed sun hat sits atop her head. *Radiant* is Rev's word—"giving off light; glowing"—and every time Emlyn steps into her presence, she is reminded of this. There is something about Rev that seems to push back the darkness of the world, that exudes warmth and acceptance and wisdom, which is probably why, over the years, the locals had turned to her for advice and help, and eventually come to think of her as a spiritual guide. Rev wraps her arms around Emlyn's waist and squeezes, and as always Emlyn is surprised at the woman's strength. She is old. Not ancient, but pushing eighty, and she's lived in this valley for decades.

"Young lady," Rev says, leaning back to look at Emlyn's face. "I am so glad to see you." She squeezes again. "You here for tea? I'm just about done with these weeds."

"Let me help."

"All right then," Rev says, releasing her. "I won't turn down the extra hands." She turns and wobbles back to the garden.

"How's the hip?" Emlyn asks.

"Tight and pinched and a pain in the rear, like always," Rev says, grinning. Years ago, her doctor recommended surgery, but she refused.

"You shouldn't be doing this. Kneeling, working like this. Call me. I'm always happy to come and help."

Rev waves her off. "What brings you this way? Varden chase you down?"

Emlyn smiles. "Well, yes. He did pay me a visit. But—that's not why I'm here."

"No, I guess it's not."

Emlyn kneels and tugs a weed from between two beets and pitches it into Rev's bucket. "You know?"

"Oliver called last night, said you had a visitor."

After three years here in the valley, Emlyn should've predicted this. Every summer, half a million people float through, renting houses and bikes and kayaks for a week or two at a time. They crowd the two restaurants and buy coffee and alcohol in abundance. They besiege the gas station and clear the shelves of the tiny grocery store attached to it. But the seventy-eight locals who live here year-round, snowbound in the winter and overrun by tourists in the summer, form a tight community, and within it, news travels fast.

"Tyler," Emlyn says.

"I figured as much. Oliver said you seemed a bit shaken."

"Janessa might be missing."

Rev stops weeding and closes her eyes. "Lord," she breathes, and Emlyn understands: the word itself is a prayer.

"He wants me to help . . . I don't know, look for her, I guess." Emlyn has known, of course, that Tyler and Janessa had reconnected, after what happened—they'd been close friends since childhood, so it made sense— but for obvious reasons, it was not a thing she and Janessa ever talked about. "He thinks she's in trouble."

"Well, what're you gonna do?" Rev asks.

Emlyn shakes her head. "What *should* I do?"

"That's up to you, young lady."

"I've done everything in my power to put him behind me."

Rev nods, shaking dirt from a weed. "Yes ma'am. You sure have."

"But I told you about how last week, Janessa and I were talking and the call dropped. She was about to tell me something, or ask me something, and what if she needed my help, and now it's too late? What do I do with that?" She can feel the distress rising in her throat.

Rev is silent. With her thumb she brushes a clump of dirt off a beet leaf.

"Don't be shy, Rev. I know you have an answer. One of your feelings." (She knows Rev does not call them feelings. They are "stirrings," and they are from the Holy Spirit.)

Rev leans closer and grabs Emlyn's hand. Her blue eyes are waxing white with cataracts. "Well, first off, this ain't about him. You owe that man nothing. You understand that, don't you, honey?"

They'd been over this, years ago, when Emlyn told Rev everything about her relationship with Tyler, all the good, bad, and ugly details. Rev knows, of course, that Tyler abandoned her. She knows about Janessa, too: the way their friendship splintered that summer, five years ago now, how things between the two of them have never been the same. In those early days of grief and confusion, Rev spent long hours listening as Emlyn processed all she'd gone through. Sometimes Rev would sit in her rocking chair, knitting. Sometimes she'd bake. And sometimes, she'd simply sit across from Emlyn at the wooden table in her cabin while the two of them sipped tea. That first winter in the valley, the snow piling up and up, Emlyn nearly succumbed to the gloom. She found herself wishing Varden had never found her. On particularly bad days, she dreamed of wandering off into the waist-deep white. But she didn't, she couldn't. Rev's light held her close. And Varden—well, there was something warm and steady about him that wielded its own sort of power.

Now, Emlyn nods. "I know."

"Good," Rev says. "So long as you know that, then I'll say this next part." She squeezes Emlyn's hand and then lets go, leaning back against the raised bed behind her. "I guess I have trouble imagining you can just let this lie. I mean, I know you and your friend had a falling-out, but still, you two were awful close for a long time before that, and you know her better than anyone else, don't you?"

Emlyn shrugs. There was a time when this may have been true.

"Well, maybe you could help." She pauses, taking a deep breath. "Maybe this is an opportunity. Maybe, strange as it sounds, you owe this to yourself." Rev shrugs. "I can't say what it is you need to reckon with. What it is you need to clear up for yourself, what needs to happen in there." She points a gnarled finger at Emlyn's chest. "But there's something. I do feel that."

Emlyn frowns. "What if I'm not ready?" she whispers.

Rev shakes her head. "Naw. Like I've told you a hundred times, you are strong, young lady. So strong. And smart. And resilient. You are absolutely chock-full of mettle."

Emlyn has never thought of herself as any of those things, and she certainly isn't convinced right now. If anything, her interaction with Tyler— that undeniable desire to drop what she was doing and follow him out the door, toward whatever wild pursuit he had in mind—served as an unpleasant reminder that he has not lost his power over her, and that she hasn't gained any power of her own. "I'm not so sure about that," she says quietly, pushing her thumb into the dirt.

Rev takes a deep breath. She closes her eyes and tilts her chin to the great blue sky and then raises both hands high into the air.

"Abba," she begins, and Emlyn, realizing that Rev is about to begin one of her prayers, also shuts her eyes. "Abba, we know that Emlyn is your child. That we are all your children. And yet we know that this world is not without its trials. Yessir, we do." Rev does not continue, but instead murmurs and then falls silent. Emlyn cracks open one eye for a glimpse. Is the prayer over? Rev's eyes remain closed. Her brow furrows and her lips purse, and she is nodding her head. Then, suddenly, one of Rev's hands drops to Emlyn's forehead. After a moment—or two? how much time has passed?—Rev lifts her hand, the warmth of her palm lingering. "Yes, thank you, Father, amen." Emlyn's eyes flutter open, and she squints in the sunlight.

Rev plucks another weed from the patch and shakes it. "'Trust,' young lady. That's the word the Lord gave me, just now."

"Trust? Trust what? Trust who?" Emlyn shakes her head. "I have no idea what that's supposed to mean."

Rev tilts her head to the side and smiles. "Oh, sugar. I reckon that's for you to figure out."

SIX YEARS AGO

THE second time Janessa saves Emlyn is toward the end of their junior year.

The two of them go out dancing. They've met a pair of guys from a nearby school, Jonah and Todd, and, by this point in the evening, the four of them have sort of paired up in what has become their usual arrangement: Janessa with the better-looking one, and Emlyn with the other. Todd, with his brown hair and killer dimples, is beautiful, and Janessa claimed him early in the evening.

Jonah, his roommate, is cute. He seems sweet and polite, and he has an earnest look to him. They dance and dance, but Emlyn grows tired. Late in the evening, Jonah leans close. "Let me grab you a drink," he says. "I'll meet you by the door."

Emlyn nods. She presses her way through the crowd, shimmying between dancers. She's lost track of Janessa, but she scans, now, hoping to find her. A flash of fear ripples through her: that Janessa has left with Todd and abandoned her, though Janessa has never done such a thing, and swears she never would.

Jonah has snagged a booth near the door, and he raises a hand. "Here you go," he says, sliding a drink her way.

She's hot and thirsty, and she takes a big gulp and then another. "Thanks."

Jonah leans back in his seat.

Emlyn again searches the crowd for Janessa. She takes another sip. "What time is it?" she asks Jonah.

He looks at his watch. "One."

The music thumps. She grows dizzy. In the crowd, she finally catches Janessa's eye and tries to signal that she's ready to go home. She waves, raises her eyebrows, tilts her head toward the door. Janessa waves back and blows a kiss.

Emlyn takes another drink. The room tilts. What time did they get here? Is this the first place they came to? "What's your name again?" she asks aloud.

He grins. "Jonah."

It's so hot and loud.

"Hey," Jonah says, grabbing her hand, "let's get some air."

She feels herself rising, feels her feet moving toward the door. Is there smoke in the room? What's this guy's name? Does she know him? She follows him outside.

He flashes his keys. "You want to get out of here?"

"My friend—"

He takes her by the elbow. "Don't worry about her. She's with Todd."

Emlyn walks with him across the parking lot. "I don't think I should leave her. Where are we going?" Somewhere deep in her mind she recognizes something is wrong, but her legs keep moving away from the building.

"Hey!" Someone yanks on Emlyn's arm and tugs her free. "What's going on here?"

Then Janessa is there: a bright, wavy presence in the dark. "Where are you going?" She puts her face close to Emlyn's, holds both hands to her cheeks. "Emmie? Emmie, do you hear me?" Janessa spins toward Jonah, hands on her hips. "What did you give her? Where were you taking her?"

She spews a constellation of insults in Jonah's direction. Todd's, too. She holds tight to Emlyn's hand. "Let's go. I'm calling the police."

And she does. She reports the boys to the bartender, dials 911. The two of them sit on the curb and wait. Emlyn slumps against Janessa, barely able to stay awake. By the time the police arrive, Jonah and Todd are long gone.

"LISTEN," Janessa says the next morning, "what happened last night—that was scary. That could've ended in catastrophe." They are in Janessa's dorm, and the sun falls in patches on her desk. She slides a coffee from the campus café toward Emlyn.

"I tried to get your attention," Emlyn explains.

"I thought you were just saying hi," Janessa says. She shakes her head. "You have to be more careful. *We* have to be more careful, together." Her voice grows shaky. "Emmie, if something happened to you, I'd never forgive myself."

"It's not your fault," she says, wanting to reassure Janessa that she isn't upset; she doesn't blame her.

"It *is,* sort of. I took you there. I introduced you to that whole scene. You never went to places like that before you met me."

"Well, it's not your job to protect me." This is what Emlyn says out loud, but deep down, she likes this side of Janessa, and always has. That nerve, that boldness. She's never had a friend who cared so much, who'd do anything for her. And it feels good, knowing she matters.

Janessa waves her off. "We need a signal. A sign that says, 'I need to get out of this situation; help me.' And when someone does it, the other person never, ever ignores it. Something only you and I know, something subtle."

Emlyn takes a sip of the coffee, thinking. She sweeps her long, tangled hair across her neck and twists it over her left shoulder.

"Yes! That's perfect," Janessa says. "It's brilliant."

"What's brilliant?"

"That thing you just did with your hair." She imitates the move, pulling her hair to the side. "You take it, twist it around your hand, and pull it over your left shoulder. Okay, do it again."

Emlyn obeys.

"That's our sign. Our distress signal, our SOS." She leans her head against Emlyn's shoulder. "Because you're wrong, about it being my job to protect you. That's what friends do. We look out for each other, no matter what. We keep each other safe."

FIVE

AS Emlyn pulls out of Rev's place and heads back to her spot in the national forest, she can't stop thinking about that morning, years ago, when Janessa devised their signal. And, bolstered by Rev's assurance, Emlyn makes a decision: she will go to the cabin at Patten Lake. She'll tell Tyler what she knows; she'll find out what he knows; she'll do what she can. Maybe if they put their heads together they can piece together enough information to help their friend. After all, this is what Janessa would do. Track her down, do whatever it took. In fact, she'd already done this for Emlyn, once.

She calls Janessa again, and again the phone goes straight to voicemail. Emlyn fights off panic as she slides the phone into her pocket and begins hooking up the Airstream to the truck. With her drill she drives up the leveling jacks. She backs up the truck, door open, left leg hanging out as she stretches to see behind her. She attaches the hitch, slides the pins in, and clicks down the lock. Sorry to leave the place, she takes one last glance in her rearview mirror.

Airstream attached, she trundles down the long dirt national forest road, turns on the paved Route 75, and eventually pulls into the large turnaround spot at Rev's. Heart pounding, she scans for Varden's white Jeep. She hopes she won't run into him. It was Varden who found her, three years ago, seven miles up that dirt road. Hypothermic and dehydrated. There are many things Emlyn can bear, and has, but disappointing Varden, having to see the look on his face when she explains that she is going back into the woods with the very person who'd once left her there is not something she can handle at the moment.

She can't take the Airstream to Patten Lake—it would never survive the potholes with its low ground clearance—so she parks it in her usual spot behind Rev's barn and unhooks the truck.

HER pack is already loaded with emergency supplies, but she grabs a cooler and begins shoving in additional items. Peanut butter, two sleeves of crackers. She opens the refrigerator and grabs yogurt, a carton of eggs, and what remains of a block of cheddar. Now, clothing. She walks to the bedroom, pulls her backpack from the hook, and opens the small wardrobe. Two pairs of hiking pants. A fleece, beanie, gloves. The packable warm jacket that she splurged on last fall. Merino long johns, two tank tops. Layers. Always layers in the mountains, where the temperature, even in the summer, could range a good fifty degrees in a day. She shoves three shirts into her pack. Then, she shimmies into the Airstream's tiny bathroom and flips on the light. She isn't really a makeup person, but she reaches into the small bag of supplies she keeps under the sink. She dots concealer under her eyes, fluffs her eyebrows. She sweeps a two-in-one tint on her cheeks and lips, and then rolls her eyes at herself in the little mirror. "Pathetic," she mutters, scowling at herself. Her word. She returns the cosmetic bag to the compartment below the sink and turns off the light.

"Tell Varden I'll be in touch," she says to Rev, who knocks at the door of the Airstream and hands over a loaf of banana bread that is still warm.

"I will."

"And tell him—" Emlyn searches for the words. "Tell him I had to do this. For Janessa. And that I hope it doesn't change things." Her heart quickens its pace. "With us."

Rev gives her a knowing glance. "I'll make sure he understands."

THE road to the cabin at Patten Lake where Tyler is staying is long and badly rutted. Were it not for the twenty-one buildings that dot the lake's perimeter, all of which are valued in the millions, the road might be forsaken altogether. The "cabins" are cabins only in the sense that they are all made of log, they aren't terribly big, and they are spaced far enough from one another that they offer their owners a sense of privacy. But, there is a landscaping crew, there are staff. There is an unspoken pact among the owners to maintain the original feel of the place, and for decades nobody has dared to violate this expectation. So, for instance, when Tyler's mother wanted to make "updates" to their cabin, an interior designer had been hired. The décor had been carefully curated, with items gathered and ordered from antique shops across the country. Though the cabins could feature fancy appliances, hot tubs, and smart TVs, the expectation is that these features must be tastefully incorporated.

Now, as Emlyn turns the truck onto the short lane, a memory swims to her. Fourth of July, years ago. The house and patio overrun with people, the caterers ferrying food, Tyler whisking her down to the lake to swim in the dark. This was early on in their relationship, before Tyler's accident, before her life had tilted in an entirely different direction. Tyler's hand in hers, the rough pebbles of the lake pressing into her toes, her cover-up slipping over her head. The water cold, blasting through the drinks she'd had. Had she ever felt so awake?

She pulls in and parks next to a gray Mercedes camper van. For a moment she sits and stares at the cabin. The dark logs and chinking, the cheery red door. Her eyes travel upward, to the window of the room where she used to sleep when she visited. This is a terrible idea, isn't it? Coming here. She grips the shifter and considers clicking the truck into reverse.

Rev would pray. She'd know what to say, and God would be listening because Rev is good and holy and radiant. But Emlyn isn't any of those things, not even close, and, though Rev has told her more than once that the Lord doesn't just listen to the pious, that He is always waiting with arms open, Emlyn isn't so sure. Nor does she even know what to say or how to say it.

She turns off the ignition. She takes a deep breath, grabs her water bottle and the banana bread, and climbs out. She walks the wide flagstone path to the door and knocks lightly. She hears footsteps coming closer, and then Tyler is there, standing in the doorway, wearing a striped apron. At the sight of her, his face lights up, and his eyes grow moist. "You came," he says. "I'm making pizza." On his cheek, a streak of white dust. "You know how I am. When I need to think, I cook." He steps toward her and then seems to think better of it. "Come on in," he says instead, turning away and waving for her to follow.

She stands at the threshold, looking in. She bends down, unlaces her hiking boots, and steps inside. Immediately she is ferried backward: five years ago, four. The same entryway table, a gorgeous piece of walnut atop a tangle of branches at its base, stands to her left. The same red and blue Persian rug leads to the kitchen, straight ahead. To her right, the same moose head (purchased, not hunted by anyone the family knew) looms above the large fireplace in the living room. That fireplace, she knows, is see-through, and can also be enjoyed from the room beyond, which has a pool table and a large television.

She walks down the hallway in her wool socks, stopping at the entrance to the kitchen. It's still there: a basket full of slippers for guests. She slips into a pair, tugging them over her heels.

Tyler stands at the island, spooning sauce and spreading it over the crust.

"Well," she says, her heart pounding, "here I am." She places Rev's banana bread on the counter. Same white marble countertops, same industrial refrigerator, same huge pendant lights hanging over the island. Emlyn reels at the place's impact on her. Its familiarity, all the happiness it once held. She isn't prepared for the barrage of emotions, and she clears her throat. "The first thing you need to know," she says, steadying herself, "is that last week, Janessa called me. She said she had something to tell me, but the call dropped before she got to say what it was."

Tyler frowns, the spoon in his hand suspended, midair. "Any idea what it might've been?"

Emlyn shrugs. "I thought maybe you might know."

"Did she say something before that, like a clue or anything?"

She shakes her head. "I don't know, I don't think so. Not that I could tell. I was hoping maybe it would make sense to you. Maybe it would be helpful." Now that she has shared her information out loud, she sees that it is not particularly useful. She grabs a lock of hair and weaves it through two fingers.

"Did you call her back?"

"Of course."

"She told me you guys were in touch again," Tyler says, spreading sauce across the pizza. "I was glad to hear it. I always felt bad about how things went sideways between the two of you, once I came into the picture. I never meant for that to happen."

Emlyn swallows hard, an old thought tiptoeing in, flashing its teeth. Despite Tyler's many reassurances that it wasn't "like that" between him and Janessa, Emlyn had always felt insecure about it, never quite believed it. After all, who wouldn't choose Janessa over her? Emlyn is nervous to ask, but she needs to know. She tries to sound nonchalant, indifferent. "Are the two of you . . . together?"

Tyler coughs. "Janessa and me? God, no. I mean, I love her, but no. Never." He looks up and holds Emlyn's eyes, a smile playing at his lips. "Still hung up on that, huh?"

"What? No. I was just wondering." Emlyn is sure her cheeks are burning pink, giving her away. She hates the relief she feels at Tyler's response, some hidden weight lifted. Emlyn turns away, walking toward the table. Two laptops lie open. A stack of newspapers, a blue folder, a heap of printed pages. Used paper plates, splotched with grease. Three glass kombucha bottles, four cans of seltzer. A saucepan crusted with what appears to have been cheese sauce.

"It's a mess, sorry," Tyler says, shaking cheese from his palm. "Give me a sec." He grabs a handful of mushrooms and places them on the pizza.

She always loved to watch him cook.

He grabs the handle of a pizza peel, pivots to the stove, and slides the pizza in. He sets a timer and then wipes his hands on his apron and comes to stand next to her at the table. "Thanks for coming. I can't tell you how much it means. That you would do this." He is so close she can smell him, and the scent grabs hold of her. "Listen, Em, I know this probably isn't the time, I know I should've done it years ago, but there are so many things I've wanted to say to you—"

She steps away from him. A part of her wants to hear it, those things. Hasn't she spent a thousand hours imagining this moment? The apology, the explanation, the I-love-you. But she also spent years trying to convince herself that she didn't need those words to move on, to be okay. It wasn't about what Tyler said or didn't say. It wasn't about him at all. And she's just started to believe that to be true. Although she's not cold, her ring finger tingles.

"Whatever you want to say about us, Tyler, the time for saying it is long gone," she tells him, the firmness in her voice surprising her. "Let's be clear about this. I'm here for Janessa and Janessa only. She's all that matters anymore."

Tyler closes his eyes, the tiny scar on his cheek edging deeper. He presses his lips tight and nods. "Okay. That's fair. Okay."

Emlyn clears her throat. "I'm assuming you called the police?"

"Of course. The Forest Service, too. But nobody seems to be taking me seriously because you know, all I have to go on is, 'Hey, my friend isn't posting on social media, and she hasn't returned my calls.' And apparently that's not enough to warrant a whole lot of law-enforcement attention."

"What do her parents say? I would think her dad would have the governor himself out there looking for her."

"I called them. Right away." Tyler taps a finger on the table. "She got in touch with them every Sunday, her parents. Apparently she texted them and said she had poor reception, but that she was fine, and she loved them."

"When?"

"Sunday, five days ago." He shakes his head. "And they just received some sort of package from her yesterday. A birthday gift for her mom."

"So they're not concerned?"

"I guess not? I think, from their point of view, nothing seems out of the ordinary." He runs his thumb over his jawline. "You know what? The truth is, it's a little more complicated than that. They haven't spoken to me in years. They've never forgiven me, for what I did to you. And honestly, I don't blame them." He takes a deep breath, then turns to the table. "Anyway, here's a quick recap," he says, pulling out one of the chairs. "Janessa hit the road a week ago. She missed a post on Monday. I wasn't too worried at that point. It wasn't common, but it happened on occasion. Spotty cell service, no cell service. It's the nature of the beast, being out there. But she'd always post the next day. They'd drive somewhere if they had to. Tuesday, though, no word. At that point, I texted her. Called her. Wednesday, she missed another post, and still nothing. By then I was starting to get concerned."

Emlyn slips into the chair next to Tyler, sliding it farther away. Discreetly, she hopes. "Okay, rewind. What do you mean 'she missed a post'?"

"YouTube, Instagram." Tyler shuffles through the stack of papers on the table and hands her a blue folder.

She opens the file and begins leafing through the pages. An Excel sheet, a typed list of dates, driving distances, and places, color coded, with company names and notes about photo ops.

Tyler points to a page in the itinerary, traces his fingers down the column of dates. "Pinedale, Wyoming. That's where she's supposed to be right now." He looks at his watch. "They were coming in from the north, through the Bridger-Teton forest." He plucks an atlas from his right and shuffles through the pages, opening to Wyoming. "Which, you might remember, is huge and remote. No cell reception through most of it." He points, tracing their route. "There's a lake there. Or a couple of lakes. She had a rod and reel from a sponsor. I lined up a lesson. We always had a schedule. Date, content, all of it."

"'We'?"

Tyler takes his orange hat from his head and places it on the table. "She works for me. For the company I started. After—" He runs his hand through his hair, glancing away. "Two years ago, I launched it. We do vans. Camper vans."

"Like we used to talk about." The words slip from her mouth before she has time to stop them, and immediately she wishes she could yank them back. She has no right to feel hurt by this, technically. There were no contracts, no plans. Just dreams. But the news that Tyler has taken hold of those dreams and built something, and that he's built it without her—it nips and burns, fanning to life some feeling inside her that she cannot name and does not like.

"Yes," he says. He reaches for her hand and then pulls back suddenly, standing up and walking to the refrigerator. "Only better. All the bells and whistles, but designed for overlanding. I mean, you can really get off the beaten path. Increased ground clearance, better shocks and struts. I was just really lucky as far as the timing. I put together my first prototype right when people were really wanting to hit the road. Janessa stepped in and suggested taking the van out and documenting her travels, and once that got some momentum, it all just kind of blew up. This past year has been insane. So many orders, we can't keep up." He pulls two kombuchas from the fridge and hands her one.

"No Recoil?" she asks, remembering Tyler's favorite beer, an India pale ale brewed in the state.

He raises the bottle and shakes his head. "Nope, not anymore. I'm clean. Haven't touched any of it since—" He clears his throat. "—since we broke up. I'm completely, one hundred percent addiction-free." He raises his eyebrows. "Which, for a guy like me, means I don't do any of it. Not even a beer. Not even coffee."

Does her heart quiver when he says that?

Is that hope spinning in her gut?

But—she makes herself remember—she has heard this before. *I'm clean, I'm done.* Sometimes it was a lie. Sometimes he really was clean, for a while. And then, a month, two, six, he was back at it. Still, she forces a smile. "That's great, Tyler. I'm happy for you."

"Well, I still have sugar sometimes," he adds with a grin. He sits back down and pulls up an Instagram page on one of the laptops. "Okay. Like I said, we had an itinerary. It was complicated, because she would never post where she really was. That's how it was set up, with a two-day delay." He frowns. "The two of them had an issue, maybe six months ago. Some wacko used Instagram to track them down, I guess. Approached them at a state park. Janessa was shaken, understandably. But Bush, that's her partner, he was much worse off. He can be a little, I don't know . . . paranoid? Protective. He wanted to call it quits, but Janessa persuaded him to keep going." Tyler scrolls quickly through the photos. Janessa in a bikini and a bright red beanie, standing on top of a boulder, a turquoise lake shimmering behind her.

"'Partner' as in business partner?"

Janessa lying on a beach in the same bikini. Same red hat. Janessa in the outdoor shower. Janessa again with her trademark red beanie, tangled up in the sheets of the camper van bed.

"Oh, partner as in *that* kind of partner," she says.

"I know, I know," Tyler says, shaking his head. "It's a little salacious. I wasn't expecting it, necessarily, back when we were setting it all up. But that's the direction the two of them went."

"Well, they're both . . ." What's the word? Gorgeous? Sexy? *Alluring.* "Attractive."

He takes a swig of his drink. "I gotta say—it works. Janessa, she's just a natural. I mean, you know how she is—people flock to her. Both of them, really. And in turn, the vans. The company's called WonderLust, so I guess it's part of the branding. Little bit of wonder, little bit of lust."

She turns and sees that Tyler is studying her face. She blinks, self-conscious. "She looks different." The word "better" comes to mind, and Emlyn cringes just a little when she recognizes the thought. Janessa had always been pretty, but the Janessa in these photographs is more than that. She glows, she is perfect. "I'm just surprised, that's all," Emlyn says, looking back at the screen. Although maybe she shouldn't be. Study groups, lunch with classmates, drinks with friends, parties—no matter where they were or what they were doing, Janessa had always found a way to be the center of attention.

"So . . . how did you get the authorities to start looking for her?" she asks.

Tyler takes another drink. "Well, the authorities aren't looking, not really. I mean, I've tried. So she's on a list somewhere, she's on their radar. Supposedly. But you know how it goes with these government agencies. Park Service, Forest Service, Bureau of Land Management. In theory they're supposed to work together, but it's not that simple. One has to sign off, another doesn't want to step on anyone's toes. Plus, there's just so much land. Millions of acres in each division, sometimes, and it's not like I can give them a starting point to start looking anyway. To top it all off, with this year's forest fires, well, let's just say a social media starlet who's taken a few days off is not exactly a top priority—for anyone."

"What about the FBI?"

Tyler shakes his head. "Same thing. Not a priority."

Emlyn frowns, trying to make sense of this. "But it was on the news."

"I've got a friend at CNN."

She nods. It has always felt strange to her, the way certain people were so connected, and how, in the end, it made everything in life easier. Tyler wasn't even rich, not like Janessa, anyway, but still—he knew the right people. A quick phone call, a message. How many times had she watched either of them fix a problem that would've taken Emlyn days to resolve, with the smallest gesture of effort, like waving a wand. Tyler getting arrested at a concert—erased. Janessa writing a scathing exposé about the deplorable wages her father paid his employees at the resort—never published, even though it had been under contract with a magazine. Janessa's mother and a scandalous affair with the gardener—nothing. It never happened. All of them skated through life making choices that could be swept away and tidied up with incomprehensible ease, simply because of who they were.

"Okay, her parents aren't concerned. The authorities aren't concerned . . ." Emlyn pauses, hoping that when she says this aloud, Tyler will fill in the blanks, but he just stares, waiting. "Maybe you don't need to be concerned, either?"

Tyler shakes his head. "I *am* concerned, I can't help it. Things don't add up."

Emlyn nods. That mysterious call from Janessa, the ensuing social media silence, the timing. She can't really disagree with him on this. "So, what are you thinking? They're lost?"

Tyler humphs. "No."

"Well, you can't be sure."

"No, but I'm pretty sure. Bush—his real name is Roderick Medina. He fishes, hunts. Runs a YouTube channel on survival skills and bush-craft." He looks at her, his eyes dancing. "You might be the most skilled tracker in Idaho, but Bush is the most skilled tracker in the West." He finishes his kombucha. "No offense."

Emlyn feels her cheeks burning pink. She raises her eyes and meets his. A year ago, she was featured in *Afield* magazine. One of their contributors had scored an elk tag, and he'd convinced his editor to send a photographer along and let him write about it. They'd reached out to Oliver, and when they met the team, they'd selected Emlyn as the guide. The whole thing had been dramatized, of course; not contrived, but almost, strung as a series of challenging, unlikely events. They'd trekked up a steep ravine, studied her movements, snapped photographs of her kneeling next to a patch of blood. "You read that?" she asks.

"Of course I read it," he says, grinning. "But only like four or five times." The timer begins to buzz, and Tyler stands and walks to the oven. "So, uh, yeah. I fibbed, earlier. It wasn't Tony Myers who led me to you. I've always known where you were."

To be upset over this, or thrilled. She's a little bit of both.

"The photos in the article were nice," Tyler says. "You looked happy."

She *was* happy, that day. Well, "happy" was a slippery word. She'd asked Varden to tag along, telling him (and herself) that it seemed unwise to trek into the woods with four men she didn't know, regardless of their reputation and credentials. Varden had rearranged his work schedule to join them, because she'd asked, and because he was simply not the type of person to say no to a friend.

Tyler removes the pizza and places it on the counter. The smell wafts toward her. "Anyway," he says, turning off the oven, "Bush—he's not some weekend warrior from Boise. He's legit. Lost is not impossible, but let's say it's unlikely."

She looks back at the laptop screen and scrolls through the Instagram again. "So, what are you thinking?"

He leans against the oven and crosses his arms. "Lately they've been sort of upping the ante, so to speak. Going a little farther, a little higher, pushing their limits." He rolls his eyes. "Seeing if they can get the next amazing shot or video, mostly. This whole social media thing, I think it's gone to her head."

"So . . . injury?"

Tyler holds her gaze. "Maybe."

The possibility pricks and throbs. Because it could happen, of course. Because it *had*. Like a moth to light, her mind trembles toward that terrible memory. Four and a half years ago, deep in the Gila Wilderness: Tyler badly injured and the two of them far, far from the rest of the world. Darkness slinking in, miles to cover to get help. She pulls herself back to the present.

Tyler tilts his head toward the patio door. "Let's eat outside."

She grabs her drink, rises, and follows him. Outside the glass doors, there is a flagstone patio, large enough that a long teak dining table sits on one end, and a fire pit surrounded by cheery red Adirondack chairs is laid out on the other. Two chaise lounges face the rocky beach. The sinking sun glistens on the water, turning the lake orange. "That's a work of art," she says, pulling out a chair and sitting across from him at the teak table.

"The pizza, or the view?"

"Both."

He cuts slices and tells her to help herself.

She carefully tugs out a piece of pizza and places it on her plate. She realizes she hasn't eaten anything except the banana and oatmeal she had for breakfast, and all at once she is ravenous. She leans forward, blows on the steaming slice, and takes a cautious bite. In a long-lost chapter of her life, Tyler made pizza on Sunday nights. They'd sit on their rooftop patio, cocooned in blankets, the mountain air cool.

"Can't you locate her with her phone?" she asks, forcing herself to focus on the now, the present, the real reason she is here.

"Not if she has her location settings turned off. I keep checking."

"And the boyfriend?"

Tyler shakes his head. "Same thing."

"Well, let's not get ahead of ourselves. What if this is a publicity stunt?" She feels a little guilty suggesting this, but she can't help but wonder: Is Tyler being paranoid? Is she?

Tyler frowns. "We work together. If it was a publicity stunt, she would've primed me."

She takes a drink. "Okay, what about the opposite? What if she just . . . wanted out? Maybe she needed a break."

"If she needed a break, she would've just said so."

Emlyn wrinkles her nose. "Maybe. Maybe she didn't want to disappoint you." She traces the seam on her sleeve. "Think about it. If she wanted out, don't you think she might have a hard time telling you?"

"She could tell me anything," Tyler says. "She knew that. And she always did. She knew she could trust me, no matter what." He turns and looks at Emlyn. "Something happened out there. Something's wrong. I can feel it. And I have to find her."

SEVENTEEN YEARS AGO

IN the early weeks after Emlyn's father slings his duffel bag over his shoulder, kisses her forehead, and saunters down the sidewalk before roaring off in his Camaro, her mother, Marlene, rarely leaves her bedroom. This has happened before, her mother's sudden and startling tumble into a darkness that Emlyn cannot seem to penetrate: once when Marlene lost a baby, fourteen weeks into a pregnancy, and once after learning that her own mother had passed. But those times, Emlyn's dad was around. He ordered pizza and brought home frozen dinners. They watched the Discovery Channel together, and Emlyn didn't worry. Years later, in a college psychology class, she will learn terms for this kind of descent, as well as for Marlene's equally confusing periods of euphoria, but now, at age twelve, Emlyn lacks the words.

After school Emlyn pencils tidy columns of long division, fills out science worksheets, studies her list of twenty vocabulary words. When she's done with her homework, she scrambles up the lone tree in her backyard, rests her back on a branch, and opens her dictionary. Every night in the living room, she watches a DVD of *Napoleon Dynamite,* which her father gave her for Christmas the year before. She whispers the lines with the actors, she laughs at Kip's song at the end. Some nights when she is particularly lonely, she watches the scene where Uncle Rico brags about his football accomplishments on the patio with Kip. Every time her dad watched that part, he laughed and laughed.

Someone—she assumes it's her father—slips an envelope of cash through the mail slot once a week while she's at school. This Emlyn takes in forty-dollar increments to the IGA two blocks away, where she buys margarine, milk, eggs, bread, cheese, bananas, peanut butter, oatmeal, and as many cans of soup as she can afford. From these ingredients, her mother had taught her long before her most recent retreat to her bedroom, various meals can be made. She cycles through them all, ferrying meals to Marlene's bedroom. "You have to eat, Mom," she insists, and Marlene does. Each evening as they eat together on her parents' bed, Marlene forces a smile, asks about Emlyn's day. Still, she has lost weight, and Emlyn worries about the dark circles blooming beneath her mom's eyes, the gaunt cheekbones.

When Mrs. Boyer, the nosy woman next door, comments that she hasn't seen either of Emlyn's parents for quite some time, Emlyn lies and says her dad is out of town for work and her mother is ill. A week later, Mrs. Boyer inquires again after Marlene. By this point Emlyn has discovered the word *meddlesome* in her dictionary and assigned it to Mrs. Boyer, whom she has observed floating through the neighborhood, gathering and spreading community news.

Maybe it's malicious, maybe not; Emlyn isn't sure why she decides to do it, but that second time when Mrs. Boyer asks, Emlyn tucks her chin to her chest and mutters, "It's terminal." Immediately she wishes she could sweep back the lie. Mrs. Boyer's wide eyes, the veined and withered hand that flies to her mouth, and then, worst of all, the way she reaches for Emlyn and pulls her close, holding her tight for just a few moments; surely there is nothing the woman could've done to spark such a deep and cavernous remorse in Emlyn as that unbearable moment of real, heartfelt empathy. Emlyn cringes in her arms, burning with self-loathing.

"I'm so sorry, dear," Mrs. Boyer says, and Emlyn nods against her chest.

LATER, as Emlyn cranks open a can of chicken noodle soup and pours it into two bowls, the noodles plopping out in one great clump, she attempts to reason her way out of the odious predicament she's fabricated from two small words. *She* is *terminal,* Emlyn reasons. *She's dying back there, with no sign of pulling out of it, and I don't know how to help her.*

The next day, when Mrs. Boyer shows up with a piping-hot lasagna that smells so good Emlyn nearly weeps, the insufferable guilt resumes, and she almost comes clean. Two days later, a different neighbor, Mrs. Ralston, appears with a bubbling chicken alfredo casserole and salad, and then two days after that, someone Emlyn recognizes but doesn't even know arrives with a pot roast. Emlyn realizes there can be no confessing, now; there can be no taking this back. The suppers keep coming, the neighborhood wrapping around her like an unwanted hug from an overperfumed aunt. She gobbles up the food but at the same time feels a new burning sensation at the top of her gut. Is it guilt? Shame? An ulcer? Maybe all three. Emlyn is certain she will face some horrible consequence for her deception—in this life or the next. And, based on the fire seething in her abdomen, it seems like it's this one.

In the V of the tree in the backyard, Emlyn thumbs through her dictionary and finds the word *pathetic.* "Pitiful, particularly through tragedy or weakness." She knows this word. The definition fits her, she realizes. It's no doubt how her neighbors see her right now; it explains the meals and sorry looks. But there is more to the definition—"miserably frail; feeble; useless"—and Emlyn leans back in the tree and stares at the wide leaves that flicker overhead and acknowledges with dismay that this definition fits her, too. She thinks of her dad, waltzing away from her with a wave. Twenty-dollar bills slipped through the mail slot, promises, lies. People don't do that to someone who is lovely and vibrant and strong and fun. They do it to someone who is miserably frail, feeble, and useless. There, in the maple tree with the dictionary in her lap, Emlyn accepts with reluctance that this is her word, her essence: pathetic.

To avoid facing the neighbors, Emlyn runs full-tilt from the school bus each afternoon. She ducks behind trees, clambers into a row of boxwoods. (This, too, is pathetic.) It's only a matter of time before the neighbors find out she lied, or her mother finds out she lied. She isn't sure which will be worse, although, she eventually realizes, it won't be just one or the other. It'll be both.

BUT then, one day, when Emlyn comes home from school, Marlene greets her at the door. She has cleaned the kitchen and showered. She smells fresh and lovely, she smells like the mom Emlyn knows and loves, and just like that, the sad, sunken-eyed woman in the bedroom has disappeared. A plate of fresh-baked cookies sits on a clean kitchen table, where a glass of milk and a mug of coffee await. "Come on," Marlene says. "I made cookies."

The chocolate in the cookies is gooey and warm, and Emlyn burns her tongue on the first bite. Of course she's relieved to see her mother back to her old self, to see the kitchen tidied and to have cookies on the table. "Is Dad home?" she asks, scuffling back the hallway, sure that he's returned.

A cloud of disgust flashes across Marlene's face. She presses a piece of hair between her fingers and wrings a droplet of water onto the table. "No. Sweetie, your father's not coming home. He's gone."

"But he said—"

"He lied," Marlene interrupts. "He's always lied." She leans back in the captain's chair and crosses her arms. "For instance, he said he would love me forever. Rich or poor, sickness or health. He said we would move here and I would be happy. But then he met someone else. Someone younger, someone new. And poof, gone."

Surely this isn't true. Surely her dad wouldn't meet someone else—what did that even mean, anyway? And where would he meet someone? He was always at the shop. Wasn't he? "He didn't," Emlyn hisses.

Marlene seems to soften, reaching for Emlyn's hand. "I realize this is upsetting."

"He wouldn't—he said he was coming back."

"I'm sorry to be the one to tell you." She pulls off a piece of Emlyn's cookie and eats it. "But I'm not gonna lie for him, either."

For a long time Emlyn sits in silence. The cookie is too sweet, the milk is warm. "Why?"

Marlene shakes her head. "I don't know, sugar. Some people are just leavers, that's the bottom line. The going gets tough and they can't handle it. But you and I—we'll stick together. We will get through this."

It's then that Emlyn notices the boxes stacked in the living room, the cleared shelves.

"What's all that?"

"We're moving."

Emlyn's heart lurches into her throat. "Moving?" A new knot, a thing she does not quite recognize just yet, has begun in her belly. A fear. Fear that her mother can't be left alone, fear that Marlene, too, will leave. Right now, this fear is a small thing, recently formed. But over time it will grow, it will wind its way through every inch of her. It will cripple her and shape every conversation in every relationship.

"Yes."

"When?"

"Soon," Marlene says.

Another part of Emlyn is relieved. The castle of lies she's built around her mother's "illness" is feeling tenuous, and now she can swish out the door without having to witness its collapse. "Where are we going?"

Marlene tilts her head back and finishes off her coffee. "We," she says, grabbing a cookie and rising to her feet, "are going home."

WITHIN a week Marlene has emptied the little house. They've hauled three loads of stuff to the Salvation Army. They've stacked other junk at the curb, a FREE sign leaning against the heap. A lamp from the living room, a bicycle Emlyn's outgrown, a pile of cassette tapes from Marlene's youth. When she thinks Emlyn has left the house for good and won't see, Marlene tapes a note to the mail slot, where Emlyn's dad slides the cash. Two words, one with four letters that Emlyn has been forbidden to utter. When they climb into the car, she asks, "What did you leave on the door?"

Marlene pulls her sunglasses over eyes. "Just a note for your father," she says as she starts the Subaru.

"Will he know where we are?"

"Of course," Marlene says.

Emlyn isn't sure this is true.

They've packed the Subaru to the roof, and in the front seat Emlyn's legs are squished between a bag of her mother's cosmetics and a cooler of sandwiches and leftover chili from Mrs. Tompkins, a neighbor three houses down. Marlene rolls down the window and waves as they drive past Mrs. Boyer, who stands in her driveway with a broom in her hand and a bewildered look on her face. The guilt resumes its burn in Emlyn's chest, and she raises a hand and waves out the window. At least she's leaving that, too.

IT'S a fifteen-hour drive from South Carolina to the town in Pennsylvania where Emlyn's mom grew up. Emlyn has never met the grandfather who had a heart attack two days after her mother left home at eighteen and supposedly blamed Marlene and the stress she'd caused him. He does send Emlyn a Christmas card each year, one crisp hundred-dollar bill inside, as well as a birthday card with the same, and he signs the cards in tidy cursive: *Grandpa.* But Marlene has painted a rather dire portrait of the man—"grumpy," "unforgiving," and "callous" are among the words she's used to describe him—and Emlyn can't help but feel anxious about her mother's decision to surprise him with their arrival.

Outside the car window, the palmettos and swamps of Emlyn's youth begin to shift into massive rolling hills of yellow-green grass, and then again into endless rows of tall corn, and then into thick stretches of tall hardwoods so lush with leaves she is sure they have entered some new world. At her feet is a book she grabbed at the Salvation Army for a quarter during one of their drop-offs, but she hasn't touched it. Marlene stops for ice cream in every state, mostly at little mom-and-pop shops just off the road, and once at a McDonald's. She finds radio stations with songs from the eighties and nineties and sings, windows down, hair lifting and whipping across her face. When an old Foo Fighters song comes on, Marlene freezes, and then violently slams her palm against the knob to turn off the stereo. Emlyn doesn't have to ask why. She knows the song. Her dad always loved the Foo Fighters.

WHEN, at last, they pull off the highway and drift into a sleepy town with one stoplight, Emlyn peers out the window, reading the signs of the storefronts that float past. Bob's Hardware, Savvy Shopper, Ritchey's Pharmacy. Soon Marlene swings the car into a dirt driveway, the road deeply rutted and so skinny the Subaru barely fits. The trees arching overhead scrape the roof and windows. The canopy ends, and they enter an opening in the woods, where a tidy cabin sits at its center. A man stands at the edge of a little pond, tossing handfuls of something into the water, and he turns.

"Stay here," Marlene says, and she climbs out of the car.

Emlyn leans out the window, listening. Marlene shoves her hands into the deep pockets of her old jeans. She talks and talks and purses her lips. So far as Emlyn can tell, Grandpa hasn't said a word. But then at last he plucks a cigarette from the chest pocket of his flannel. "It's like I told you, first time I met that boy," he says, looking toward the Subaru and catching Emlyn's eye. "Never trust a Rebel."

GRANDPA, it turns out, has a workshop, tucked in the woods a hundred yards beyond the main house on his property, and this is what Marlene has her sights set on. It has windows and electricity and running water, along with abundant rodents that have left abundant waste. With a little TLC, it will be perfect, Marlene assures Emlyn, when she asks why they can't just live in the house with Grandpa. And, Marlene explains, Grandpa is a smoker, and the secondhand smoke will clog her lungs and mess with her neural development.

Emlyn sees the concrete floor, which is so burdened with feces it looks like someone took a gallon of chocolate sprinkles and tossed it everywhere. She sees the corners crammed white with cobwebs. She sees the vises and table saw and sander. And she nearly gags with the stench of mold and must and animal excrement. Grandpa grumbles about hantavirus and other illnesses and eventually convinces Marlene to stay in the main house until the workshop has been properly converted.

The first night, they haul their duffel bags to Marlene's old bedroom. Grandpa opens a can of tomato soup and makes grilled cheese on his wide, white stove. He eyes Emlyn's novel with a disparaging glance, and, later, hands her a worn paperback of *Brave New World*. "If you want to read something scary," he says, "try this."

MARLENE throws herself into the "renovation" of the workshop. She orders a dumpster and fills it. She hires a neighbor kid, a huge lumberjack of a fellow who winks at Emlyn every time he sees her, to help move Grandpa's equipment to the nearby shed. Sporting a mask and respirator that look like the ones Emlyn has seen medical professionals wearing, Marlene runs a shop vac and clears decades of dirt and crap from the floor.

Emlyn, banished temporarily from entering her new home, begins exploring the land behind her grandfather's place. All summer she wanders the woods, pressing deeper each time. She looks for her dad, following trails. She organizes imaginary search parties. She persuades Grandpa to take her to the library, where she borrows books about animal sign and tracking. She hauls them into the woods and sifts through them, leaving brown fingerprints on the pages. Deep down, she knows her dad isn't in those woods. She knows her mother wouldn't lie about her dad finding someone else; she knows he really has left them of his own volition. But looking for him offers a bandage, and, even though she is eleven and maybe ought to be beyond pretending, she pretends.

She catches newts under fallen logs and cradles them in her palms, stroking their soft orange backs. She watches gray squirrels zip and sail through the treetops overhead. She scales the tall face of rocks, too, where the land falls deeply and suddenly into a dark river that meanders its way toward the Atlantic. She steals a little box of matches from Grandpa's shelf and, using one of her library books as a guide, clears a huge circle and teaches herself to start a fire. In the wild, she isn't quiet, fearful, forgettable Emlyn, who never raises her hand in class and sits alone in the lunchroom, who fabricates lies to cover family troubles. In the woods, she becomes someone else. She is brave, self-assured, intrepid.

Well, not quite. That knot in her belly that began shortly after her father walked down the sidewalk—it's no longer just a knot, and it no longer remains in her gut. It stretches itself out; it grows and grows. She fears that Grandpa will die. She insists on joining Marlene for every little trip to the store, every little errand. She begs to be homeschooled, attempts to persuade her mother against applying for jobs. (Marlene does not agree to either.) On the first day of school that fall, Emlyn looks in the mirror and tells herself to trust no one. She likes Ms. Gardner, whose classroom walls are covered in interesting artwork, and whose smile is as sweet as a bowl of cherries, but she politely declines joining the after-school poetry club, even when Ms. Gardner pulls her aside after class and personally invites her. She will not allow herself to get close. Not to Ms. Gardner, not to anyone.

BY the time she gets to college Emlyn will have gotten over the whole "tracking a father who is long gone and who'd never been lost to begin with" thing, but the wild will still hold its lure. She'll join the outdoors club and sign up for every workshop they host—basic land navigation, advanced land navigation, wilderness survival, wilderness first aid. Though she'll make no real friends in the club, she'll soak up the information, and she'll be good at all of it. The fall of her sophomore year, in Psychology 101 with Dr. Hartnett, she will come to a page in her textbook about "abandonment issues" and feel like she is reading her own autobiography. At first this discovery feels like a death sentence: that she will never have the capacity to form healthy relationships, that she will never be happy. In one sentence, though, the textbook says that therapy can help. And, in a brave and desperate move, Emlyn will sign up for a session at the student health center and start seeing Rhonda. Rhonda will tell her that developing her outdoor skills has been a constructive way to build confidence outside of personal relationships. That it's good to check in at home, but maybe not quite as frequently as she does. That yes, her father's departure may have triggered all of this. That it doesn't have to be a death sentence. That baby steps toward forging a new friendship could be healthy. That Emlyn must try to be open to that.

A week later, Emlyn will be studying at Bumpy's Diner. Two men will slide into her booth, and a gorgeous, confident Janessa will march up in her Carhartt jacket and ball cap, slam a can of bear spray onto the Formica, and tell them to get lost. Janessa will sit beside her in Western Civ the next morning, she'll invite her out. And Emlyn will think of Rhonda's advice, and she will remind herself that she does indeed want to move toward health and happiness, and she'll say yes.

SIX

AFTER supper, Tyler starts a fire in the fire pit and brews two cups of tea. Emlyn carries one of the laptops out to the patio, and Tyler sets the mugs on the table. The night has cooled.

"I want to read through her posts," she says. "Maybe something's there."

"Trust me, I've done that, but sure, have a look." He slides his chair closer.

She opens the laptop, the bright screen illuminating their faces. Tyler leans over, pecking out a password. She scrolls through the account, starting all the way back, the spring before. The very first photo: Janessa and Bush huddled close together, with a black Lab looking up at them, standing in front of the gray camper van.

Hey, everyone! We're Janessa and Bush, and this is our trusty pal, Clyde. We're about to embark on a grand adventure in this incredible campervan, designed and hand-built by my amazing

BFF, @tylerthestone. Hopefully, we'll see new places and try new things. We'll challenge ourselves and grow in unexpected ways. There will be ups and downs; we're sure of that. But, highs, lows, and everything in between, we'll bring you all along for the ride. #WonderLust #vanlife #campervan #adventure #nature #travel #wilderness

Four posts from this initial trip. Sweeping views of the Grand Canyon: the red rock speckled with green, the notes describing an easy one-mile hike to the spot. Next, the camper van is shown parked just outside of the national park boundary, in Kaibab National Forest. Pines tower overhead. The third post includes a quick reel of the view from the camper van, not a vehicle in sight. In the final photograph, Clyde leans against Janessa, head resting on her shoulder, as she stares into the red abyss of the Grand Canyon.

"That's the thing that drew everyone in, I think," Tyler says. "That initial promise. Highs and lows. People felt she was authentic. They didn't just want the shiny, beautiful, everything-is-amazing stuff. They wanted the real Janessa."

Emlyn nods as she continues reading, but Tyler's words give her pause. She thinks back to the first time she met her friend: Janessa dressed like a Pennsylvania local in the ball cap and the Carhartt jacket. The very next day, she'd come to class transformed, a sexy but studious college student. She could chameleon herself, she could metamorphose. And she was fickle, capricious. In college she'd drifted quickly from crush to crush. Then, after one dreadful fight, she'd shocked everyone and taken a job back East, leaving the Idaho she'd lured Emlyn to. As Emlyn stares at picture after picture of her old friend, she can't help but return to a question she'd first thought of a long time ago—who was the real Janessa, anyway?

A flat tire, deep in the woods. Janessa with a pouty face, lip curled, as Bush works to fix it and Clyde licks his cheek. A ROAD CLOSED sign. National park notices, canceled tours, masks. These the promised "lows."

"She told me about Clyde," Emlyn says.

"Yeah," Tyler says with a smile. "He's the real love of her life."

More stops, more photos.

Tyler heads inside to clean up the kitchen, and Emlyn steals glimpses of him through the window. Dish towel slung over his shoulder, trucker hat turned backward. He stands at the giant farmhouse sink, bobbing his head to music she cannot hear. All this time she'd convinced herself that she'd put this life behind her, that she had no desire for it, that she didn't miss it. Miss him. But here on the patio at Patten Lake, in this place where she'd known such happiness, she cannot deny the sense of longing that lies just beneath the surface of her skin, tingling and charged.

Tyler is Tyler again. That's the problem. Fresh-faced, clear-eyed, attentive and charming. The Tyler who left her in the woods? That wasn't the real Tyler. That was the Tyler held captive by the claws of addiction. That Tyler lied and stole and did who knows what else. That Tyler nearly killed her. But this Tyler—the one making pizza and looking at her with those mesmerizing blue eyes—this is the Tyler she fell for so many years ago. And if this Tyler really is free of his addiction . . .

She opens the laptop, forcing her mind away from him.

She clicks on the Messages tab. Sycophants, scammers. *You are so beautiful, I love you. Marry me, Janessa? OMG you are gorgeous.* And also: *Gain 50K Followers! DM us @hikerparadise.* A backpack company offering a free pack. Another company asking if Janessa and Bush would be willing to endorse their new line of recycled fleece. A third offering free water bottles. One thread toward the bottom catches her eye, from an account titled @hikefishrepeat. The top message, dated six months ago:

I realize I went too far, sorry. I just really wanted to meet you. I promise I won't bother you again.

Emlyn's heart lurches. This must be what Tyler was referring to.

She scrolls to the initial message.

Hi, I've been following your account since it started, and I love being part of your adventure! Janessa replied with a like, but there are many more messages from the same person. *We chatted in the laundromat at Koda-chrome.* Janessa hasn't responded to this. *Me again. I have a confession to make. It wasn't a coincidence, running into you at Kodachrome! I knew you guys were at Bryce Canyon just before that, and I sorta guessed where you might go next. Is that weird?*

Emlyn shivers in the dark. She keeps on reading. A message from @ozkerwild, last month: *I thought we had an understanding.* No response from Janessa. Another from two weeks ago: *You can't keep me guessing like this.* And finally, from eight days ago. *Are we done?* Janessa has responded to this final message from @ozkerwild, but her reply makes no sense: *44%N*679,1/114.W?42>17.* It could have been a mistake, Emlyn thinks, a phone tossed in a handbag, keys pressed by accident.

She clicks on the person's profile. No posts, no followers. Could this be the same person from Kodachrome, using a different name, or is it someone else? Did Janessa have some sort of relationship with this person? Was she cheating on Bush? Creepy as the thread from the Koda-chrome person is, these three messages somehow feel worse.

Emlyn goes back to the profile, looking for posts from Kodachrome. Years ago, she and Tyler were there, and she feels certain she'll recognize the towering red spires and fins that jut up from the earth like the back-bone of some giant, sleeping monster. The white, tan, orange, rust, red striped rocks. Yes, there. She notes the date. Earlier this year, in the spring, six months ago. Emlyn taps on the post. A horseback ride through the rock formations, Janessa sporting jeans and a cowboy hat. A mountain-bike trek up a rock face. Bush and Janessa huddled close together, Grosvenor Arch looming in the background. Big smiles, blue skies. Even a photo of the park laundromat, a sweet little log building just outside the campground.

Emlyn bites her lip. She closes Instagram and does an internet search for Bush. A newspaper article: PHILANTHROPIST FUNDS NEW WILDLIFE REFUGE. A photo, Bush cutting a ceremonial ribbon, dressed in suit and tie—and, somehow, she can't help but notice, looking just as at ease as he is in his camo hunting gear and face paint. Janessa stands in the background in a conservative blue midi dress, hands folded at her waist. Next, an article in *Afield*, two years before Emlyn trekked into the wilderness with their crew. "Lord of the Flies," it's titled, Bush telling a journalist how he wanted to see if he could tie flies solely from materials he had sourced himself. Elk hair, mule deer hair, even grizzly hackle plucked from a neighbor's rooster.

She searches for Bush's video channel and finds it quickly. Bush bow-fishing from a canoe in Arkansas, Bush killing a white-tailed deer in West Virginia with a blowgun. There are dozens of videos, but she chooses one of Bush hunting an elk with his longbow. The bow is handmade from black locust, the arrows crafted of reeds and fletched with turkey feathers. He shoots the elk, a massive, drooling six-by-six, at forty yards. He capes it out, dropping huge quarters of meat into cheesecloth bags before hauling it back to his truck in four trips. An hours-long process, Emlyn knows, but in the video it's fast-forwarded and compressed to a few minutes. On one trip, he stops to pluck a few handfuls of gooseberries and drops them into the pocket of his jacket.

Toward the end of the video, Bush washes a portion of the tenderloin in a stream. "I'm beat," he admits to the camera, splashing water on his face with his opposite hand. A streak of blood stains his cheek. "Absolutely wrecked." He wipes his face with his sleeve. "Like, I might not be able to drag myself out of bed tomorrow. And I'll probably need a chiropractic adjustment, stat." He grins. "But," he says, holding up the meat, "this right here, is what it's all about." He gets a fire going, slices the meat into thin rounds. He chats easily to the camera, explaining each step as he cooks. He holds up a baggie filled with flour, garlic salt, and pepper. "Sure, it's a little extra weight to pack this in, but believe me: it's well worth it," he says with a smile. His voice is deep, and he speaks with ease and confidence. She knows hunters; she's a hunter herself. She understands immediately the appeal of a guy like this, trekking deep into the backcountry, harvesting an elk with his own hand-hewn instruments, and then hauling it out alone. It's not just the skill, though that in and of itself is impressive. It's *him*. He's likable, relatable. *Charismatic.* ("Demonstrating a magnetic appeal which sparks devotion in others.") No wonder he and Janessa have accrued such a following.

In the video, Bush adds slices of meat to the baggie, tosses it gently, places the medallions on a skillet. He sprinkles in the gooseberries from earlier, then eats his beautiful meal with his pocketknife.

It's strange, she realizes as she closes Tyler's laptop, how you can read two articles, browse someone's social media pages, watch a video, and, in less than an hour's time, feel like you know a person. What they stand for, what they love, how their relationship works. Who they are.

She leaves the computer on the table and stretches out on a chaise lounge by the fire. According to Tyler, Janessa and Bush had originally hit popular spots. National parks, monuments. But in the past few months, they'd started to seek out the lesser-known locales. National forests, national recreation areas, big swaths of BLM land, wilderness areas. These are not places where you drive your car on a well-marked road to a well-marked parking lot where you embark on a well-marked trail. They're a whole different story. That's part of the draw. The roads are not maintained to the same degree, deterring the majority of people from even attempting to get there. You can go a day, two, three, more, without seeing another soul. The hiking trails can blend seamlessly into game trails. In fact, they are sometimes one and the same, the animals using the path of least resistance. If you don't have a good map, or strong navigational skills, you can easily lose your way. The problem is, by the time you figure out you're lost, your clock has already begun ticking. You can run out of food and water before you really even know you've gotten off-track.

But also: a misstep, a falling rock. The terrain in many of these places is sheer and unforgiving. The trails are often thin tracks that cut along the steep hillsides and drop precipitously into formidable ravines. From the looks of Janessa's photos, she and Bush are fit and competent, but the trouble is that even a rather minor injury can become serious, depending on how far from help you are. And, God forbid, something major—well, that can be a game changer. Emlyn knows that better than anyone.

What else? Maybe Janessa and Bush wandered onto private land and ran into some hermit deep in the woods? Idahoans have little tolerance for trespassers. A memory of Rev swims to her. Springtime, the river full and white and loud, the two of them in Rev's kitchen, getting ready for a walk. Emlyn watched her friend load a bullet into the chamber of a Beretta Pico, click the magazine in with her palm. Rev tucked the pistol into the pocket of her pants and pulled a hat over her ears.

"What's that for?" Emlyn asked, plucking a beanie from the coatrack. It was her first spring in the valley. "Bears?"

Rev tugged on a glove. "Oh, young lady. You live out here in this wild long enough, you just learn you're best off prepared for whatever comes your way." She pulled the other glove over her gnarled hand. "Bears, cougars. I guess. But, truth is, I always found the most dangerous animal of all—"

She paused here, holding Emlyn's eye. "—that's got to be the two-legged kind."

Now, on the chaise lounge, Emlyn rolls Rev's words around her mind. She thinks of the Instagram messages: What kind of weirdo stalks a person into a state park laundromat? Then again, does a stalker who admits they were stalking really warrant that much concern? And who is this @ozkerwild?

It's possible that whatever is going on has nothing to do with either of those threads, Emlyn tells herself. Janessa is vivacious, gregarious, *alluring.* Maybe she struck up a conversation with some wacko at a trailhead and gave him or her the wrong idea. Emlyn thinks back to a party, junior year, a jerk sidling up and slipping a hand up Janessa's dress. She punched the guy in the face, hard, blood everywhere, and then kneed him in the groin for good measure, the party halting to a standstill.

In the dark, Emlyn smiles at the memory. Her beautiful friend, full of guts and spirit and life.

Janessa, she thinks, staring into the night sky, *where are you?*

FIVE YEARS AGO

A few weeks before graduation, Janessa stretches beside Emlyn after mountain biking on a trail north of campus. She stands on one leg, crossing her foot over her knee, and says, "You should come home with me to Idaho."

Emlyn stretches her left quad. "I don't know."

"Come on," Janessa pleads. "We have more adventures ahead." She grabs Emlyn by the shoulders. "Diana Barry and Anne Shirley aren't done yet."

One Monday back in February, when the ice had piled up and coated the cars and sidewalks and classes were canceled, Janessa trudged through the snow to Emlyn's dorm. She brought a basket with Drambuie, fancy hot-chocolate mixes from Christmas, and her collection of DVDs for the old Canadian miniseries of *Anne of Green Gables*. "It's a tradition," she explained. "When I was a kid, I always made my best friend, Tyler, come over on snow days. We watched this every time." And she added, with a laugh, "I'm sure you'll enjoy it more than he ever did." She made Cocoa Buie, and they watched television in their pajamas until midnight. At the end of the day, Janessa pronounced the two of them Anne Shirley and Diana Barry. It wasn't an apt designation—Janessa was smart, spunky, and pretty, really the best of both Anne and Diana, and Emlyn seemed only to have Anne's smarts. But she loves that ever since then, Janessa has referred to her as her "bosom friend," and she loves the idea that Janessa sees their friendship extending beyond their college years.

Emlyn has a job offer, in the district where she attended school as a teenager, which somehow feels like a victory—it's her first real job, after all—as well as a giant step backward. Does she really want to go home? Grandpa still putters around, grumpy as ever. Marlene now runs an after-school art program for the community center. They'd both welcome Emlyn with open arms, she knows that. But does she really want to live in the converted workshop with her mom? (At the same time, does she want to pay for some crummy apartment when she could live for free with Marlene?) "I have that offer," she reminds Janessa.

"I know, I know. Of course you do. They would be crazy not to hire you. But—" Here she pauses, clearing her throat. Emlyn knows this means a song is about to be sung.

"No, how am I supposed to slow it down
So I can figure out who I am?"

Emlyn bursts into laughter. Janessa is a terrible singer. But that doesn't keep her from belting it out with shameless abandon, though her voice seems particularly ill-suited for Judah & the Lion. "You know that your singing is maybe my favorite thing about you, right?"

"Um, I'm pretty sure it's everybody's favorite thing about me," Janessa says, squinting and wrinkling her nose. She reaches for Emlyn's hand. "So . . . promise you'll at least think about it, okay?"

"I'll think about it," Emlyn tells her, trying to sound noncommittal, but even then she knows she won't say no to Janessa; she *can't,* and most of the time, she doesn't want to. The prospect of holding on to her friend, of delaying adulthood and all its accoutrements, has never been more appealing than it is right now, three weeks before the university president will shake her hand and send her on her way.

The morning after graduation, Emlyn crams what she can into the Maserati, drops everything else at the local Goodwill, and she and Janessa hop on I-80 and head west.

"Summer," she tells Janessa as they trundle across Ohio. "I'll stay for the summer and after that, we'll see." When she says this, she means it. She asks the school district for more time to make her decision, telling herself that if she wants to return to Pennsylvania to take that teaching job, she can do it in August.

WITHIN weeks, though, Emlyn is already in love with her new life. If there's one thing Janessa is particularly good at, it's making something wonderfully irresistible, and this is exactly what she does with Idaho. With Janessa's guidance, Emlyn quickly eases into a cheery and predictable rhythm. Tuesday evenings, they have dinner with Jack and Linda, Janessa's parents. Thursday nights, a movie at the one-dollar theater, even when the movie's bad or they've already seen it. Fridays, they go out. Saturdays typically involve adventures in the mountains, hiking, or biking. Sundays center around brunch with Janessa's intrepid grandmother, Betts, who wears red lipstick and kitten heels. If there's a party Janessa's invited to, she takes Emlyn. If her parents host a cookout, Emlyn attends. Janessa plans everything, and Emlyn is happy to go along.

Janessa scores Emlyn a job at one of her father's resorts, working as a summer camp teacher. It's a good place to put her elementary education degree to work, Janessa insists, so, even though she'd probably make more money waiting tables, Emlyn chooses the camp.

In one regard, Emlyn does not adhere to Janessa's design. She politely declines the repeated offers from Janessa and her parents to stay with them, and instead gets her own apartment. Even though this decision leaves her with roughly eighty dollars a month to cover food and any unexpected expenses, she knows that if there's one thing she does not want to be as she steps into adulthood, it's a charity case. Besides, crummy as it is, with its dingy walls and yellow appliances, Emlyn likes it there. It's home.

IT'S a Friday night, and Emlyn and Janessa are out dancing when Emlyn starts to feel sick. Not nausea, but pain. It isn't severe, but she's certainly not up for more hours on the dance floor, even though it's early. She slips through the crowd and slides into a booth. Janessa finds her quickly, a new guy in tow, already smitten, under Janessa's spell. Emlyn knows the game, by now. She knows Janessa's moves: the dazzling smile, the eyes that seem to offer something. Emlyn hates to be a killjoy—she has tried so hard to free herself from that quiet, reluctant girl she was before meeting Janessa—but she worries she won't be able to walk herself out of the building if she doesn't go soon.

Now, with the music thumping and the smell of sweat permeating the air, Emlyn catches Janessa's eye. She reaches for her hair and swings it over her left shoulder: their signal.

Janessa gives the slightest nod. Without a moment's hesitation, she turns to the boy. "Listen, we're gonna call it a night. Sorry." She gives him her number, and within minutes Emlyn and Janessa are outside, crossing the lot.

"Sorry about this," Emlyn mutters as they walk to the car, her arm looped through Janessa's. It hurts to walk. "He was cute."

"Don't worry about it," Janessa says, squeezing her arm. "You know you're always my number one. Are you okay?"

"I don't know."

Janessa stops. "Did something happen?"

"No, nothing like that." Emlyn knows Janessa is thinking about that close call their junior year. "I just don't feel well."

They keep walking. "Are you sure? Did anyone bring you a drink? Do you feel out of it?" Janessa unlocks the Maserati.

"No, no."

Janessa helps Emlyn climb into the car. "We'll get you to bed. I'll stay and keep an eye on you."

IN the morning Janessa makes toast and drizzles it with honey. Emlyn can barely eat it. For lunch Janessa brings chicken noodle soup. Emlyn tells her she shouldn't be here. She's probably contagious. Janessa waves her off. The pain migrates to Emlyn's right side. She vomits, spikes a fever, huddles on the couch, chills racking her body. Janessa brings a cool towel for her forehead. It hurts to walk.

"I don't think this is the flu," Janessa says, holding the back of her hand to Emlyn's cheeks. "I think you need to go to the hospital."

Emlyn resists, fights her off. Four hours, five. The day turns to another night. By morning she is delirious and no longer able to refuse. Janessa calls someone, an old childhood friend, who comes to the apartment and carries Emlyn to the Maserati. She slings her arms around the man's neck, delirious and weak. In some foggy corner of her brain, she registers that he smells good.

At the hospital, the doctors determine she has a burst appendix, and they wheel her off to surgery.

When Emlyn slowly emerges from the anesthesia, she sees the white clock, the television mounted in the corner of the room, an empty chair against the wall. Her throat aches, her limbs are heavy. She is confused. She cannot quite remember, the fever and anesthesia blurring the order of events. But there, by her left hand, Janessa is bent over, fast asleep, head resting on the edge of the hospital bed. By this point they've been friends for years, but all along Emlyn has struggled to trust that this is real, that Janessa won't move on to greener pastures, that she won't realize that Emlyn is dull and messy and that there are a million better people to be around. She knows all too well that even the people who seem to love you the most can leave you and move on as though you never existed.

But here, in the hospital bed, Emlyn stretches her fingers and pats Janessa's head and a tear slips from her eye because she believes that for the first time in her life, she has found a real friend.

LATER, Janessa drives Emlyn back to her apartment. She helps her up the four flights of stairs. By the time they reach her room, Emlyn is sweating and panting from the pain.

"Come stay with my parents," Janessa says. "This is ridiculous." The elevator is broken again. "It's like, probably illegal." She taps her red fingernails on the Emlyn's desk. "Let me make a call."

"No," Emlyn shakes her head. "Please don't." She doesn't want to feel more deeply indebted to Janessa than she already does. "I'll be fine. I just need to rest."

Janessa settles Emlyn into bed, tucks the blanket beneath her chin. She holds the back of her hand to Emlyn's cheek, leans close to press her cheek against her friend's forehead. "Rest," she whispers. She glances at her watch. "I have to run," she says, "but I'll be back soon. I'll bring soup."

Emlyn listens as the door closes quietly behind Janessa. The pain in her abdomen boils into her back. She slowly tries to roll onto her side. Worse. Other side. Even more painful. She resumes her position on her back. She stares at the dropped ceiling, the mottled white rectangles held up by metal frames. A water stain browns the far corner. She takes a deep breath. If women can breathe their way through childbirth, surely she can tolerate this? She conjures memories of women in labor from movies and shows. One, two, three. She shapes her mouth: round, round, wide, just like she's seen. But the pain is a burning coal whose heat seems to grow in size and intensity.

She remembers the brown bottle of pills the doctor prescribed. Where are they? Her backpack lies at the foot of her bed, six feet away. She sits up, inches her feet to the floor. Slow, careful. She bends down and lifts the backpack, and the pain that blasts through her gut is nearly unbearable. Her shoulder hurts, too. A sharp pain like someone has plunged a knife into her shoulder blade and continues to twist it back and forth. She slumps against the pillow, out of breath. Hands shaking, she rifles through the backpack and finds a white paper bag. Inside is the bottle of pills. She fishes one out and pops it onto her tongue, desperate now. She takes a swig of water and washes the pill down her throat.

Emlyn eases back onto her pillow. The pain burrows deeper. The minutes slog by. Fifteen, sixteen. Twenty-three.

At thirty minutes a heat surges through her. Happiness, more than happiness. A deep, body-rattling joy that circles around her, head to toe. The pain lifts, *woosh,* gone. With relief she sits up, swings her legs to the side of the bed. She takes a shower, dries her hair. She gets dressed. Her jeans won't button—her abdomen is still swollen—so she pulls a pair of sweatpants from her drawer. She finds yogurt and blueberries in her fridge and makes herself a snack. She puts on some music. She doesn't even hear the door unlock.

Janessa stands in the doorway, holding soup. "What's going on?"

Emlyn thinks maybe she looks angry, but she isn't sure. She runs to her friend, throws her arms around her neck, kisses her cheek. "You saved me," she gasps. "You always save me."

"Careful!" Janessa hisses. She shrugs out from under Emlyn's embrace. "You're gonna hurt yourself. What are you doing? Why aren't you in bed?"

"I'm fine! I feel great." "Euphoric" is the word that comes to mind, but it slips from her fingers like a fish. "Euphemism," she says, grinning.

"What?"

All at once Emlyn notices the ridges on the paneled wall. "Look at it," she whispers. She steps closer, runs her hand left, right. "Two different textures." She traces the seam with her pointer finger and then—she cannot help herself—she leans her face in close and licks the wall. Smooth, rough. The panel is smooth, the seam is rough.

"Okay," Janessa says. She puts the soup on the dresser and walks Emlyn to the bed. Emlyn leans against her. "I love you, J."

"I love you, too," Janessa says. "But you need to rest." She eases Emlyn onto the bed.

"I'm not tired," Emlyn insists.

Janessa grabs the bottle from the nightstand and holds it up. "Oxy!" She gives the bottle a shake. "They gave you oxy?"

"The doctor—"

"I don't care. That doctor is nuts." Janessa leans close. "You are not allowed to have any more of this. Do you understand me? You can muscle through this. You are strong, I know it."

"You," Emlyn says, pointing a finger, "are not my boss."

"Don't be ridiculous. Let's get you to bed before we end up back in the hospital."

The high lasts for hours. Janessa sits vigil at the base of the bed, phone in hand. Emlyn drifts in and out of sleep. Janessa runs her hands through Emlyn's hair. "I have to run home. Stay right here in this bed. I'll bring Chinese food, and we'll watch *Anne of Green Gables,* okay?"

Emlyn nods, happy at the thought. "Bosom friends," she whispers to Janessa.

Janessa squeezes her foot beneath a heap of blankets. "Always."

SEVEN

SOMEONE is next to her, a hand gently shaking her shoulder, a voice saying her name. She bolts upright, heart pounding, the blood rushing from her head.

"Em, sorry. Sorry to wake you." Tyler is there, kneeling, close.

She is still on the chaise lounge on the patio at Patten Lake. The sun has inched its way above the horizon, and she squints. A pillow is beneath her head. A heavy blanket has been draped over her, and she grips it in her palms. The lake shimmers in the morning light. "What is it? Is something wrong?"

"She's back."

"Here?"

"No, no. Online. She just posted."

"I made coffee," Tyler says, sliding a French press across the island. He takes a mug from the cabinet and hands it to her.

She pours herself coffee and wraps her hands around the mug. "Thanks."

For himself, Tyler pours hot water over a tea bag. He walks to the table, pointing to the laptop.

Emlyn takes a sip of her drink, hot and smooth, and turns her attention to the image on the screen. Janessa, tan and gorgeous, leaning into the chest of the equally beautiful Bush. In the background, deep, blue waters, and beyond the lake, a tall face of rock.

Sorry for the radio silence, friends. We decided to take a few days to re-center and just be together. For us that means lakeside yoga, fishing, and some much-needed downtime. Just the two of us. On to our next adventure soon. Xoxo. #vanlife #bliss #WonderLust #fishing #love #roadtrip #lifeontheroad

"She still hasn't called," Tyler says, "but what a relief. I mean, it turns out she's right where she's supposed to be, after all. At that lake in Wyoming. But, you were right: she needed a break. I get it. I should've listened to you." He takes a deep breath and closes his eyes. "I'm just glad she's okay."

"Yeah," Emlyn says, and she's glad, too. Relieved. Janessa and Bush are happy, they're good. She stares at the image on the screen. That lake. The old cypress just beyond Janessa's left shoulder, bent and gnarly. Something feels familiar about this place.

"Of course, that's what they told me all along," Tyler says. "The authorities. I guess people do this more often than you think. Disappear, then reappear. Stress their friends and family out, make everyone panic. That's exactly why nobody wanted to send out a search party." Tyler takes a drink of tea. "Which, you know, I'm glad about, now."

Emlyn drinks more coffee, willing herself to wake up. She continues studying the image on the screen. "Tyler, where did you say this was?"

"Wyoming." He shuffles through the itinerary. "Fremont Lake." He traces his finger along the spreadsheet. "Near the Bridger-Teton National Forest."

The tan restroom facilities in the right corner of the photo, blurred but definitely there. The gawdy and unexpected red metal roof. Emlyn has been here before. And she has never been to Fremont Lake.

"I was pushing too hard," he continues. "I see that now. But I can fix this. We can regroup, adjust the schedule. And I mean, if they want to be done, that's okay, too. The business is fine, we don't need that kind of publicity anymore."

Still Emlyn stares at the screen. That odd formation, almost like a face carved into the side of the rock: brow, nose, mouth. Now she is sure.

Tyler dunks the tea bag up and down. "Sorry to make you come out here," he says. "I know it probably seems like it was some ploy to be near you or something. But I really was worried."

"Tyler," she says softly. "This isn't right. This photo isn't in Wyoming."

"What?"

"This photograph. It's not in Wyoming. That's Martin Reservoir." Her heart pounds.

Tyler frowns and takes a sip of his tea. "I don't know where that is."

"North, off the Magellan Corridor." The Magellan Corridor Road is a rough, undeveloped 101-mile road that cuts between two adjacent wilderness areas, which, together, total more than 3.5 million acres.

"No, they're in Wyoming, at a lake, right where they're supposed to be." On his second laptop, Tyler begins pecking at keys, and soon a website for an outfitter in Wyoming pops up. A herd of elk grazing in a high meadow, a team of horses trekking through rough terrain, a lake with a granite face on the far side. "There," he says, pointing. "That's the place. See?" The lake in Janessa's post doesn't look all that different from the one on the outfitter's website.

Emlyn shakes her head. "That's not the same place."

He leans closer, frowning. "You sure?"

"Yes." She points to the first screen: the face in the rock, the restrooms, the tree.

Janessa is okay, Emlyn tells herself, trying to remain calm. She looks at the photograph on the screen: her friend, smiling, leaning into Bush. Janessa isn't injured; she isn't lost. This is strange, this post, but it's not bad news, per se. It isn't dire.

But it also doesn't add up. Why would Janessa post a picture saying they're in Wyoming, when they're in Idaho? Emlyn returns to her early thought: Maybe Janessa and Bush are reevaluating their arrangement with Tyler and WonderLust, forging other plans. Ready to move beyond the #vanlife that has consumed them for over a year. Maybe they believe this is the only way to slip away from Tyler. Misdirect, tell the whole world you're somewhere else. But that doesn't fit, not really. Tyler's right: Janessa never had trouble standing up to him, or anyone else, for that matter, and if she wanted out, she would just say so. So why lie? Why post anything at all?

Unless—

A dreadful, horrifying thought cuts loose and tears through her mind.

"I don't get it," Tyler says. "It doesn't make sense."

Emlyn swallows hard, taking a deep breath. The thought lingers; it spins and flicks and she cannot make it go away. She can barely bring herself to say it, but after a moment, she does: "Unless it's not her."

The stalker who'd managed to guess their locale at Kodachrome, @hikefishrepeat. Or the mysterious @ozkerwild. She looks at Tyler.

"I know it's a stretch, but what if someone else logged into their account and posted that? Someone who doesn't want anyone to know where they really are."

EIGHT

EMLYN'S theory launches them into action, and in a whirlwind, they pack. Emlyn transfers her belongings from her truck to the back of Tyler's van. She grabs a stack of worn white national forest maps, folded and creased, and shoves them into the pocket in the front door. Tyler grabs food from a well-stocked pantry, throws it in a plastic bin, and places it in the back.

In the rush of packing, she doesn't remember to message Varden until they're in the van and on their way. *I'm okay. Heading to Martin Reservoir,* she writes. The "delivered" notification does not appear.

They head north, crossing the wide valley between the Obsidians and the Borahs. Eventually the road veers east, narrowing, holding the course of the river. The mountains press in, the water glimmers to her right. Thirty miles with no cell reception. Tyler swings left onto a rutted dirt road, the van rocking over the dips, the road rumbling beneath them, a cloud of dust in their wake. He grips the steering wheel, white-knuckled and agitated, his lips tight with focus.

"You want me to drive?" she offers, feeling nervous about their speed. "Why don't I drive?"

"Sorry, am I making you nervous?"

"A little."

"I'll slow down."

She looks at her phone. No bars. "Do you have a booster on this thing?" she asks.

"Of course."

"I don't have service."

"Yeah, sorry. It can't boost where there's no signal to boost."

She slumps into her seat.

Tyler slams on the brakes. Shifts into reverse, then swings left. "Almost missed the turn," he mutters.

Now he drives slowly, though all at once the road becomes paved. They come to a locked metal gate, blocking the entrance to a parking lot. Tyler stops the van, turns off the ignition, and climbs out. She tucks her phone into her pocket and scrambles after him.

They fold themselves through the metal gate and Tyler pauses. Emlyn turns to him and sees the worry in his eyes, the fatigue. "This way," she says, reaching for his hand: an instinct. Too late, she realizes what she's done. She releases his fingers but he does not let go. They cross the parking lot and then a dry, neglected patch of lawn so parched it crunches beneath their feet. A Styrofoam cup tumbles over the grass.

Martin Reservoir is enormous, nearly four thousand acres in size and spanning two counties. Under normal conditions, it is filled with water from the massive snowmelt that bloats two rivers north of it each spring. The Idaho Department of Fish and Game stocks it heavily, and in the summers it's a popular recreation spot for anglers, though, oddly, no one is here today. The lake is nearly sixty feet deep in some places, with cold, blue water that holds bass, brook trout, sturgeon, and even a handful of tiger muskie. She fished here, the summer before, with Varden, and she thinks of him now.

That had been an *almost* day. They'd laughed and fished and, later, fried up their catch over a fire. They'd almost kissed, the two of them sitting side by side at the fire ring, knees touching, the night sky speckled with stars. She'd wanted it. That kiss, him. But, in that way of hers that seemed inescapable, she'd pulled away. Now, she wonders: Did her message even make it to Varden? Does anyone know where they are? Is she making the same exact mistake she made three years ago, following Tyler into the wilderness?

Shaking off the memory, Emlyn walks with Tyler toward the reservoir, but, as they get closer, she gasps. Where there had once been a shoreline that sloped gradually into the water, now it drops off suddenly and unforgivingly. She grips Tyler's hand tighter. Gone are the blue waters. Instead, as far as the eye can see stretches a wide, tan canyon, peppered with patches of short, green grass. Cattle wander far below. Deep in the gorge, a tiny, feeble stream meanders through the valley, brown and dismal.

"You were wrong," Tyler says. "This place doesn't look anything like their photo."

Emlyn takes a moment to get her bearings, then points. "See that? The face in the rocks?" She takes a step back, assessing. "And this tree. And the restrooms, over there. This is where that photo was taken. Maybe not recently, but this is the place."

Tyler steps back and takes it all in.

"Careful," a voice says behind them. "That's a sixty-foot drop there."

They both spin around to face a conservation officer who stands a few feet away, arms folded.

"Hope you two weren't planning on fishing," the man says with a grin.

"What's going on here? Where's the lake?" Tyler asks.

"Drained it on account of the drought."

"When?" Emlyn asks. "When did they drain it?"

The officer looks toward the sky, seeming to count. "Three weeks ago."

Tyler swears under his breath.

The officer adjusts his hat. "You two are really pushing your luck, aren't you? First driving down into the gorge, right past the no-entrance signs, then camping up in the wilderness in a spot that's not designated for camping. You can't just camp anywhere, you know. It's not a free-for-all. You have to use the motor vehicle use maps. You gotta find the triangles along the roads." He frowns and adjusts his hat again. "Now, here you are, blocking the gate. I know you camper van people like to march to your own drum, but the thing is, there's rules."

Tyler scowls. "No idea what you're talking about, man."

"Your van, you had it parked up in the wilderness area for the past few days. I left a note on the window twice."

Now Emlyn speaks. "Sir, we just got here."

The man tilts his head to the side. "Here, yes. But you been *here*"—he gestures widely—"for a while." He folds his arms. "Look, you're not in trouble. Any other summer, I'd run you off. But this place is a ghost town, so I won't. I'm just saying, glad you're all right. I was starting to get concerned."

Tyler releases Emlyn's hand, and it's only when he lets go that she registers he was still holding on to it. He steps closer to the officer. "Are you saying there's been a van, parked somewhere close by? For days? A van just like this one?"

He tilts his head as though thinking it over. "Pretty close, I'd say."

"Where is it?" Tyler demands. "The van."

The officer points up the valley. "Like I said, up that direction, eight, nine miles. Right past the entrance to the wilderness—"

Tyler spins on his heel and heads for the van.

Emlyn, unsure what to do, takes a step toward the van and then turns back. "We're signing in. Consider this our application for a backcountry permit. Emlyn Anthony and Tyler Stone."

"IT could be someone else," Tyler says, wiping his brow and turning the key. "Right? I mean, there are thousands of these things. They're everywhere. And there are plenty of other companies building vans." He drums his fingers along the steering wheel.

Tyler pulls out of the parking lot and heads up the road. Buzzing with nervous energy, he continues tapping his fingers on the steering wheel.

Emlyn pulls Rev's banana bread from the top of her backpack. She tugs off a chunk and hands it to Tyler. "Here."

"I'm not hungry," he mutters, but, when she continues to hold the piece in front of him, he takes it. "Mmm, wow. This is good."

"My friend made it. Rev."

"I mean, my whole life, I always thought banana bread was banana bread, but I now see that I was wrong."

Emlyn yanks off another hunk and hands it to him. "Rev has a way of helping you see things in a completely different light," she says with a smile. "She's pretty incredible."

"I'm glad you've been able to make friends," Tyler says, popping it in his mouth. "That came out wrong. I mean I'm glad you've settled, forged connections. After all that happened. Friends, relationships—they're everything."

They drive in silence, the dirt road roaring beneath them.

"I'm really glad you're here," Tyler says. "You were the first person I wanted to call." He swerves to avoid a pothole, and then, turning to look at her, adds, "You're always the first person I want to call."

FIVE YEARS AGO

EMLYN needs air.

The party Janessa has brought her to, held at a neighbor's house, is overrun with rich people, who, three hours into their drinks, are growing louder and less refined by the minute. But more importantly, Janessa's cousin, Jimmy, has been sidling close all evening, and at this point Emlyn has had one too many drinks to trust that she won't say or do something she'll regret. Jimmy is currently living in Los Angeles and pursuing his hip-hop career as J-Love, and, although Emlyn has insisted that he is not her type, Janessa seems convinced that the two of them could be great together. She just needs to give the guy a chance. J-Love has just excused himself for a trip to the restroom. Now is Emlyn's moment for escape.

She has her eye on the sliding glass doors that run the entire length of the house, opening onto a wooden deck. She feels certain there must be stairs out there, somewhere, and maybe she can slip away from the party undetected. She glides her way through the crowd, slides open one of the doors, and steals into the night. Her dress, borrowed from Janessa, is a smidge on the small side, and she's felt self-conscious all night. Her toes pinch in her high heels, also Janessa's. Emlyn tugs them off and walks toward the deck's edge. Her hair, long and tangled, is hot against her neck. It's longer than she likes it, but when she scheduled a haircut, Janessa told her it was "very sexy and very Idaho" as-is, so Emlyn canceled her appointment at the last minute. She tugs an elastic from her clutch and twists her hair into a bun, stealing a glimpse over her shoulder. Inside, she spies Jimmy in his bright white jumpsuit, searching the crowd.

"Hiding?" A voice in the darkness.

Emlyn startles.

"Oh, no—I didn't mean to scare you. That's totally creepy, sorry. Like, weird guy skulking in the shadows asking you if you're hiding. I don't know what's wrong with me."

A man steps into the light. He's young, her age, roughly, and in a green T-shirt and jeans he is sorely underdressed for the occasion. He smiles, his blue eyes twinkling, his teeth bright and perfect, and in an instant Emlyn doesn't feel like herself. The world around her seems to tilt. Later, she will notice the gold flecks of stubble on his chin. The light freckles that spatter his cheekbones. The star-shaped scar an inch below his right eye. But here, in these first moments, she notices only that he is beautiful, and that she is suddenly short of breath.

"It's okay," Emlyn says, looking away from him. "And yes, I am hiding, sort of."

"Me, too."

"Who are you hiding from?"

"Oh, everyone." He takes a swig of his beer. "You?"

She hesitates. "A guy."

"Jimmy?"

"Yeah, how did you know?"

"It's always Jimmy," he says with a laugh.

"I think he goes by J-Love now," Emlyn says, stifling a smile.

He coughs. "I was not aware of that. Thanks for bringing me up to speed. Here, step this way," he adds, gesturing. "You'll be out of sight from the window."

"I was hoping there might be stairs?" Emlyn moves toward him.

"Okay," the man says, "and then what?"

Her eyes are adjusting to the darkness. "And then I'm gonna walk to my friend's house." She peers into the dark, trying to orient herself. "It's close."

"I see."

"So, are there stairs?"

"Sure. You might want to use the road, just a thought. It's not really worth it to cut through the lawns, trust me."

"What, you've done this before?" she asks in a teasing voice.

"Oh, only about a thousand times." He smiles.

Emlyn pieces things together. "You're Tyler." Janessa's been talking about her childhood friend for years. Tyler: her partner in childhood antics, ally, neighbor. "And this is your house."

"My parents'. I have my own place, on the other side of town now." He finishes off his beer. "And you're Emlyn."

"How did you know?"

"We met, actually. A few weeks ago. You were really sick. I helped you to Janessa's car."

She can feel herself flushing. She remembers only that someone strong carried her to the Maserati, and that she was in very bad shape when it happened. (Also, she now recalls: he smelled good.) "I'm sorry," she says. "I don't remember you at all."

"I get that a lot." He laughs. "I'm extraordinarily ordinary. And very forgettable."

"Oh, I didn't mean that! I mean I don't remember anything from that day. It's all a blur."

Tyler extends a hand, his fingers cool and damp from the bottle. "Well, it's nice to meet you *again*."

She wishes she were not wearing Janessa's too-tight dress. She wishes she had not knotted her hair into a bun. "Yes, it's nice to meet you," she says. "I'm not counting the first time. I'm pretty sure that when your appendix bursts and you're on the brink of death, you get a free pass as far as remembering stuff."

"Fair enough." He sets his beer on the railing. Emlyn reads the label: RECOIL. He tilts his head. "Okay, follow me."

Barefoot, she follows him across the deck, with one last glance at the party inside. Tyler trots down the stairs. Motion-sensor lights flick on.

"You know where you're going?" he asks.

"Of course." She squints, searching for Janessa's house. "Okay, maybe I need a little hint," she admits.

"Come on, I'll show you."

"You don't have to—"

But Tyler is off, tramping through the lawn. She scampers after him in the dark.

Click. Whoosh, whoosh. All at once water showers them from every direction, left, right, above. Before Emlyn even realizes what's happening, she is drenched. Sprinklers! She gasps at the cold water pelting her. In the dark she feels Tyler grab hold of her hand and tug her, and she lets herself be pulled, running, her high heels dangling at her side.

At last they come to a dry spot, beyond the reach of all the sprinklers.

"I tried to warn you," Tyler says, laughing. He's drenched, too, his green T-shirt clinging to his chest.

"You could've been more—" She waves her hands and hunches her shoulders. "—specific."

"You seemed to have your mind made up." He grins. "Hey, I'm fine in these old clothes. You and that fancy dress, though: good luck." He stops and turns and looks at her. Those teasing blue eyes. "I mean, I'm not complaining. It's not a bad look."

He has not let go of her hand, and she does not let go of his. They walk the rest of the way to Janessa's parents' house. The grass is soaked and cold and pokes between her toes.

"Well, here you are," Tyler says.

"Thanks."

"Sure." A plane takes off from the nearby airport, guttering overhead. It lifts and lifts and then tilts east. He lets go of her hand. "I guess I'll see you around?"

She feels the night's happiness scuttling away from her, and her shyness returns. "Yeah."

He turns to go, cutting through the lawn again, but then stops. "Hey, Emlyn," he says, spinning back toward her. "Next time, don't break my heart and forget about me, okay?"

Her heart flutters, and she shivers in the dark. "Promise."

He grins, and Emlyn swears she will never forget the look of him there in his green T-shirt, sheepish and coy and beautiful.

The sprinklers hiss on again. She stands and watches as Tyler trots back to the party, the house lit up, all those voices drifting through the open windows. Just before the steps that lead to the deck, the motion lights flick on again and illuminate him. He turns and raises a hand, and she waves back. She taps in the entry code and slips into the empty house.

She tugs the wet dress over her shoulders and changes back into her cutoffs and T-shirt. She places Janessa's heels in the enormous closet and shoves the dress into her backpack to wash at home. She grabs her helmet and leaves the house and climbs on her bike. In the dark, she pedals hard, her lights blinking bright. By the time she gets home, she's already come up with a word for Tyler. "Enchantingly charming and hypnotizing": *captivating*.

NINE

THE van rumbles on and on, the sagebrush rolling past the window. Dust drifts in through the opened windows. Foothills, dotted in pine, rise to the right. Beyond them, the Borahs stretch tall, their peaks holding the last of the previous winter's snow. In the distance, a small herd of antelope graze, and one raises its head to watch as they sail past. To the left, the reservoir stretches on, empty and brown.

Here, the road veers right, toward the woods. The road grows suddenly worse, riddled with potholes. Tyler slows to a crawl, and they rock their way forward. Emlyn thinks of "shocks" and "struts," terms from her childhood. Afternoons at the garage, her dad beneath a hood. She would do her homework at his metal desk, slowly munching her way through a Snickers bar.

She reaches for the stereo and turns it on. Tyler's phone lights up, and a song begins to flit its way through the speakers. "Stay with Me," by Sam Smith. The music shuttling her backward: the two of them dancing at his college friend's wedding. Next, "Georgia" by Vance Joy, which they'd played on repeat while camping at Zion. Then "Believe" by Mumford & Sons. A weekend at Bear Lake, Tyler tearing across the blue water on a Jet Ski, Emlyn sitting behind him and holding tight to his waist, the sun on her back. These songs—they're an unwelcome blast from the past, and it is too much.

"What's with the music, Tyler?" she mutters, reaching for the phone, but Tyler grabs it, snatching it from her hand.

"Don't," he snaps. "Sorry. It's just—I'll get it." With his thumb he scrolls, slowing the van even more.

She rolls the words of that Mumford song through her mind: *"I had the strangest feeling / Your world's not all it seems . . ."* She looks at Tyler. Eyes darting, left shoulder hunched. She knows that posture all too well. He's lying.

"Stop the van."

He presses the brake but doesn't stop. "Why?"

"Now. Do it."

The van screeches to a halt, her body lurching forward against the seat belt. He clicks the shifter into park and looks at her.

"Let me see your phone," she says.

Reluctantly, Tyler hands it over.

She scrolls through his messages, opens his email. She's not sure what she's looking for, but she knows it's there—something untrue, something he wants to hide.

A message from his mother, emails from prospective camper van buyers, a bill from a tile company. Nothing suspicious.

Tyler pulls a piece of banana bread from the loaf, and, after a few minutes, says, "Happy?"

"Not really." She places the phone on the dash.

He sighs, gripping the steering wheel. Then he picks up the phone and presses buttons, hands it back. "Here."

She stares at the phone.

"Here, take it. This is what I didn't want you to see."

She takes the phone and looks at the white screen. A playlist. The ti-tle: "Emlyn." She reads through the songs. An anthology of their time together, a memory book. The songs she'd heard and connected, but oth-ers, too. St. Vincent's "Digital Witness": New Year's Eve on the roof. Wiz Khalifa and Charlie Puth: a picnic lunch at Natural Bridges. Her heart pitches, her mind roils. She doesn't know what to say.

Tyler rests his forehead on the steering wheel. "So now you know."

She clears her throat and looks out the window. They sit in silence. Tyler grabs another hunk of banana bread. "You all right if we keep moving?"

"Yes."

MORE miles, but not many, the road so bad now that for a while she climbs out and walks alongside the van, directing Tyler where to drive to avoid bottoming out. She is having trouble knowing what to hope for. If, at the end of this road, they come to Janessa's van, and she isn't there, what does that mean? What do they do next? But, if they come to the lot and it's not her van, where does that leave them?

At last they pass a brown sign announcing they've arrived at the wil-derness area.

"These boundaries," Tyler says, "never made sense to me. Seems like we've been in the wilderness for a long time now, doesn't it?"

"Do you mean that metaphorically?" she asks.

Tyler chuckles. "If I did, then the answer is yes, at least for me." He raps his thumb on the steering wheel. "You know that better than any-one."

She remembers one of Rev's church services, back when Emlyn first arrived in the valley. Verses from the book of Numbers. A searing realization, that snowy morning: she was in her own sort of wilderness, then.

Ahead, the trees open up, but just before that, tucked down to the left, a flash in the trees. Solar panels on top of a van. "There," Emlyn gasps, pointing.

Tyler slams on the brakes and yanks the van left. He pulls in behind an identical van. Another vehicle beside it. A white Isuzu truck, lifted, also prepped for off-road driving, mud dancing up its door panels.

"Is it theirs?" Emlyn asks, staring at the van.

Tyler gestures toward all the bumper stickers and nods. He puts the vehicle in park, reaches into the glove compartment, and pulls out a handgun.

"Tyler, what—?"

"Listen," he says, "You stay here." He holds her gaze. "I don't know what we might find."

"Where did you get that thing? Do you even know how to use it?"

"I don't plan to use it," he says, closing the door.

She grabs the bear spray from her backpack before scrambling out of the van. She has no intention of staying put.

Tyler holds a finger to his lips. She slides the lock off the spray, and thinks, of course, of Janessa, all those years ago, slamming the canister onto the tabletop at Bumpy's Diner. The world grows still. They walk closer, the pine needles crunching beneath their feet. Her mind begins to flood with fear. What lies inside that van? Maybe clues, maybe nothing. But also, maybe: answers. Death. Is she really ready to see something like that? She takes a deep breath and swallows, trying to calm her nerves.

Tyler approaches his side of the van. Both of them catch the scent— rot. Something foul. He turns to look at her, then presses his face to the tinted window, cupping his left palm over his forehead, gun in his right hand. Emlyn holds her breath. She tucks the bear spray beneath her arm, wiping her sweaty hands on her pants.

Tyler steps back, dropping the gun to his side. "Nothing," he says, and he lifts his head to the sky and exhales, shoulders falling. He doesn't have to explain his relief—Emlyn had been feeling the same thing. She steps closer, peering into the van. Then she circles it, walking slowly, looking for clues. The tires are solid, no flats. But maybe they'd run out of gas. Maybe the engine had blown, maybe the transmission had gone.

"Can you get inside?" she asks. She thinks of her flashlight from Rev. On its head there is a sharp metal point, designed for breaking glass, should she ever get stranded in her car. It seemed like maybe the most useless item she owned. After all, what were the odds that a person would get stranded in her car and need to shatter her way out? Plus it's a nuisance, the sharp point pressing into her chest when she has it in the waders pocket. She's always kept it close, though, since Rev gave it to her. She'd tucked it into her backpack, back at the cabin, and now—well, maybe she'll have a chance to use it.

Tyler reaches into his pocket and fishes out a set of keys.

He walks around to the side and then unlocks the door, sliding it open. A putrid scent wafts out. Sleeve over his face, he climbs in. Without looking, he reaches in and flicks on a light.

"See if it starts?" she suggests. Maybe the van broke down. Maybe another hiker or camper had come by, and Janessa and Bush had seen their one opportunity to hitch a ride out. This is not an impossible scenario. If such a thing happened to Emlyn, that's probably what she would do. Hikers, campers, especially, were a friendly, helpful band of people. Well, mostly.

Tyler slides into the driver's seat and turns the ignition. The van rumbles to life. He turns off the key, stands, shakes his head. Emlyn climbs into the van. Directly in front of her is a tiny shower with a retractable plastic door, and beside that, a small cabinet topped with a sink and counter space. On the counter, the source of the stench: a package of organic chicken breasts, thawing in a casserole dish with water. At least that's what it had been doing a day ago, or three, or five. Dread churns in her stomach. Janessa and Bush—wherever they are, they were planning to come back, long before this. Tyler picks up the chicken and chucks it out the door.

Emlyn turns. Another cabinet, with two burners on top. A hook with a mesh bag of bananas so black and soggy that a pool of glossy yellow liquid collects on the counter beneath it. A small fridge with a grocery list taped to its black front: *milk, honey, eggs, cheddar.* A skinny aisle leads to the back, where the bed is. Emlyn sees that it can be torn down and re-assembled to make two bench seats, and, she assumes, a dinette. She and Tyler talked about that, back when they were together, sketching the ideal layout. She walks back and kneels to have a look.

This is no cheaply assembled, haphazard build. It's homey, tasteful, functional. It is beautiful and impressive. "I like the way you did it," she says, standing up. A flash of jealousy, then. A spark of resentment. "All of it." She runs her hand along the white and black tile behind the sink, the rough-hewn wood above the bed. "It's really something, Tyler. What you've built here."

She recognizes the blanket that's draped neatly over the corner of the bed from one of Janessa's Instagram photos, and she sits down next to it, carefully. To her right is a small nightstand with a set of drawers. On top is a piece of paper. Janessa's curly, wide-lettered handwriting. Emlyn picks it up. A to-do list. *Mail gift for Mom, call Emlyn.* She stops reading, her heart thumping. More than a week has passed since that dropped call. The birthday gift had been delivered sometime between then and now.

The first two items, Janessa had completed—well, kind of. That call wasn't actually complete at all, was it? Neither item is crossed out.

What about the rest of the list?

Do laundry, get new Kindle books, cancel Netflix.

Emlyn traces a black thread, zigzagging across the blanket on the bed. She looks at the piece of paper one last time before placing it back on the nightstand.

The final item on Janessa's list: *Run.*

TEN

EMLYN climbs out of Janessa's abandoned van. Tucked beneath the windshield wipers, two pieces of paper flap in the breeze. She tugs them out: hand-scrawled notes from that ranger. She walks toward the white Isuzu, bends to assess the tire tracks. She reaches out and runs her fingertips along the ridges in the dirt, caked hard. Fox performance shocks, a Warn winch on the front. She rises. Two metal jerry cans of fuel on the back, a LifeSaver jerry can for water. Whoever this is, they're prepared for their overland treks. She cups a palm over her brows and peers through the tinted windows. Tidy, not a single piece of trash, no cup in the cupholder. She heads toward the truck cap, but every window is covered from within, solar shield taped to each one. Could this vehicle belong to @hikefishrepeat, from Kodachrome? She pulls her phone from her pocket to search the account for clues. Not surprisingly, no service.

She steps back, squinting in the sunlight. Beyond the trees, she hears the rush of water, and she walks toward the sound. The alders here grow tall and thick, towering overhead. Moose territory, or bear. She still holds the bear spray in her left hand. She stops and surveys the land, watching for any rustle of branches, any leaning of saplings. She steps forward, the ground growing soft, her feet sinking in. She looks down. Everywhere else the drought has parched the land, but here the earth is thick and rich and mottled with green.

The stream is close now, she can smell it. She pushes through the alders, branches scraping her arms, and then she is there. A small piece of water, but rushing and powerful, frothing white over the rocks. She finds a patch of gravel and plops down, placing the bear spray at her side. She unlaces her hiking boots and slips off her socks and rolls up her pant legs. Then, she stands and steps into the water. Toes, ankles, calves. The cold pitching a jolt through her that blasts right to her chest. Heart racing again now, and pain. This is a high Tyler never chased, she thinks, but should have. She takes a careful step, the round rocks slimy and slippery beneath her feet. A magpie flutters down and lands close by. It looks at her, tilts its head. Her ring finger tingles.

Ahead, a flash of color. Tucked in the alders on the other side. She bends down for a better look, adjusts her height. She takes a cautious step toward it, then another. Her legs are growing numb, but the pain remains.

A red beanie, snagged in a branch.

Fear lodges in Emlyn's throat as she shuffles through all those images of her friend in that same hat: Janessa beneath the arch at Moab, Janessa and Bush at the Tetons, Janessa in her bikini. Emlyn works the beanie loose, holding it by one thick thread. She crosses the stream, faster now, nearly losing her balance. She slips her wet feet into her boots, grabs her socks, and scrambles back to the vehicles.

"Tyler," she calls.

He is sitting on a boulder near the Isuzu.

She holds out the beanie.

Tyler takes it, and for a long time he holds it in his hands, turning it over, quiet. Then he stands up and heads to his van. He opens the back and pulls out a backpack.

"What are you doing?"

"We have a starting point. It's as close as we've been, and maybe as close as we'll ever be. We can follow their trail."

"No," she says, shaking her head. "We need help."

"You're a tracker. You follow animals, you can do this. Em, you can."

"No. We should go back and find that ranger from the parking lot. We can use his landline. Call the police, the Forest Service. Gather a search party." She takes a deep breath, sorting through the reasons. "They have dogs for these types of things. And with a team, we can cover so much more ground."

Tyler shakes his head. "No time. It took us over two hours to get from that parking lot to here."

In her mind she counts out the hours that would be lost to pursuing this plan. Two hours to the ranger station. Two or three more to gather information and confirm that this piece of news warrants launching a search. If the investigators do deem it worthy, at least an hour to alert a crew, but realistically, in this location, longer. Two more hours to get back. And this is if everything goes smoothly, if there are no hiccups or delays. By the time they return, it will be nearly dark, which means that the search would be delayed until the next morning. Even if they started at dawn, it's a lot of time lost. Seventeen, eighteen hours. Hours that could be the difference between life and death. Still.

"I can go get help," she says. "We'll catch up. We'll move fast."

Tyler face falls. He scuffs at the dirt, hesitating. "Listen," he says, at last, "think about what happened to me in the Gila. Things can go south, fast. One second you're fine, and then you're not. You and I know this better than anyone. If they need our help, they need it now. We might already be too late."

The mention of Gila sends a chill down Emlyn's spine.

So much could hinge on a day, on a series of small decisions, on one seemingly small choice. Its consequences could ripple out, shaking and shaping a life for months, years to come.

Tyler is right. In their case, if someone had known, if someone had come—everything might've turned out differently. Everything.

She thinks of Janessa's phone call from last week. The Instagram messages from @hikefishrepeat. The other, more cryptic thread from @ozkerwild. The chicken and bananas, rotting in the van. And now, most troubling of all, the red beanie. Emlyn doesn't know what has transpired, but she does know this: something isn't right.

Tyler holds up his pointer finger, signaling her to hold that thought, and darts to his van. "Look," he says, coming back with a small gray GPS unit. "I have a contact at the Forest Service. I'll send him our coordinates right now and tell him what we've found, say we're pushing after them." He begins pressing buttons on the unit, the small carabiner swinging as he types. "That way, someone knows where we are and what we're doing. And if we find Janessa and Bush, and it turns out they need immediate help, beyond what we can do for them, we press the SOS button. Then the folks out there send in the cavalry. Seriously, medics, chopper, whatever we need."

She can't afford one herself, not the unit or the monthly subscription fee, but she knows how they work. You hit the SOS button, the monitoring channels receive your distress call with your coordinates. The process is a little convoluted, but the bottom line is that it's a surefire way to know that if you do get into trouble out in the wild, you *will* get help.

Which means that it's not so dangerous or even foolish to press on—

not with that safety net in place, not with her skills, not if it means saving her friend. Leaning against a tree, watching Tyler push buttons on the GPS unit, Emlyn grasps that what's really holding her back is her own baggage, her desire to keep that wall of stones around herself. The way those old feelings for Tyler are fanning to life, the risk of what allowing them to catch fire might mean—she doesn't like it.

But is this really what she wants for herself? Is this who she wants to be?

Janessa would be brave. She'd already be on her way; she wouldn't even need to think about it. And right now, Janessa needs her to set aside her inhibitions and be all the things she is not: fearless, confident, heroic.

"Fine," Emlyn says. "I'll go with you. But this is on my terms. I call the shots. I say when and where we go. No going rogue. No whipping out the handgun and telling me to stay put. Are we clear?"

A look of relief washes over Tyler's face. He nods and shoves a tightly rolled sleeping bag into his pack, then he crosses his heart. "Promise."

FIVE YEARS AGO

EMLYN sets out for a bike ride. She's only been in Idaho for two months now, but she's already mapped out various routes from her apartment: some on the main road, some on back roads, some on the paved trail that winds all through town and out to one of the ski resorts. Today, she heads north. Up the small hill that connects to the main road, then along the berm until she hits the cindered trail a mile outside of town. It's early, so the air is cool, but the summer sun is already high in the sky. It's the perfect time for a ride.

Far ahead, a pickup is pulled over along the side of the road, hood propped open. Emlyn keeps pedaling. Before she gets there, she'll cross the road to avoid it. A man with an orange trucker hat appears from beneath the hood. He shields his brow and squints in her direction.

Emlyn recognizes him at once from the party, last week. Janessa's friend, Tyler. Her heart begins to pound. She's replayed that night over and over: the clingy dress, the sprinklers, Tyler's last words to her. "Hey," she says, slowing.

He's bent at the waist, leaning under the hood again. He raises his head and turns toward her, his face breaking into a smile. "Hey!"

She stops, straddling her bike, and he steps toward her, extending a hand.

"I don't know if you remember me, but I'm Tyler."

She tilts her head, playing along, and shakes his hand. "Emlyn Anthony. I'm sorry, have we met?"

"You know, actually, I think we have. Twice now." He gestures toward the bike. "So, what are you doing out here?"

She stifles a smile. "Um, riding my bike."

He takes his hat off and runs his hand through his hair. "Yeah, I guess I should've gathered that. What with the bike and the helmet and all. Stupid question, sorry. I'm a little frazzled at the moment."

"Anything I can do to help?"

He folds his arms across his chest and leans against the fender. "I've got my roller skates in the back. 'It'd be nice if you could pull me into town.'"

It's been years since those days when she watched the movie night after night, back when her dad left, but she recognizes the line from *Napoleon Dynamite* at once. Napoleon on the bike, towing his brother, Kip, on the roller skates. "Only if you bring me my ChapStick," she quips. "'My lips hurt real bad!'" she adds, in her best Jon Heder voice.

She's immediately embarrassed, but Tyler grins. "That's pretty good. The imitation. You sound like him." He adjusts his hat. "Best movie ever. It's my go-to, anytime I need a good laugh."

"Best movie ever might be a stretch, but it *is* funny." She steps closer to the truck, peeking under the hood. "So, what happened?"

"I don't know," Tyler says, shaking his head. "There was a herd of elk in that field," he says, pointing, "and I pulled over to watch for a few minutes. I went to turn the truck back on, and nothing. Won't even start."

"Mind if I take a look?"

"Be my guest." He steps aside.

Emlyn unclips her bike helmet and hangs it onto the handlebar. "Does it turn over?"

"No, nothing."

She peers inside. "Could be the starter solenoid."

"Yeah, that's what I was thinking." He laughs. "Just kidding. I have no idea what that is."

"You got a screwdriver?"

"I have a little tool kit in the truck somewhere. Let me check." Tyler disappears for a moment, rifling through the space behind the seat, then returns with the screwdriver.

"Perfect. I don't know if this will work, but it's worth a try." She nods toward the truck. "Try turning the ignition again."

Tyler climbs into the driver's seat, left leg hanging out the door.

The starter solenoid is mounted right inside the fender. Emlyn looks at the two small terminals where the wires attach. She takes the screwdriver and bridges the gap. The truck turns over and roars to life.

"Brilliant!" Tyler says. He leaps out of the truck. "Absolutely brilliant." He raises his fists into the air and begins to trot in place. "Victory!"

Emlyn grins. "For now. You do need to replace that starter solenoid. Unless you want to use a screwdriver every time you need to start your truck."

"How do I do that?"

"Just go to the auto parts store and tell them what you need. I can help you replace it, if you want."

"Seriously?"

"Sure." She blushes, thrilled that he seems impressed.

"Can I give you something for your help? I owe you. I was just about to call a tow truck. I mean, that alone warrants a sandwich."

She laughs. "You don't have to do that. I'm happy to help. I mean, I was literally right here."

"Come on," Tyler says. "Let me buy you lunch." He flashes a smile.

"Right now?"

"Yeah, right now. We'll throw the bike in the back."

A furtive glance at her reflection in the passenger window reveals that the helmet has not been kind. Her hair is matted to her forehead, and the inevitable wisp at her right temple is curling its way skyward like a small horn. And why, oh why, did she not brush her teeth before she left for her bike ride? Her word flickers. *Pathetic.* She slides her helmet from the handlebar. "You don't owe me anything, Tyler."

"Okay, fine." He looks at the field and then turns back to her. "Can I take you to lunch, anyway? Just because?" He rubs his palm up and down his neck. "Because maybe I wish I would've gotten your number the other night, and maybe when I asked Janessa for it, she refused, and maybe the universe is throwing me a bone here, with a second chance?"

Emlyn takes this in. "Wait, are you serious? Janessa wouldn't give you my number?" Her real question, which she does not say aloud, is *You wanted my number?* Her heart hammers.

"Nope, she refused."

"That's weird. Why would she do that?"

"Oh, she was very clear. You are hallowed ground to her. Untainted, pure. I think 'wholesome' was the word she used." His eyes twinkle, teasing.

Emlyn hates that Janessa has given Tyler some impression of her as chaste, or innocent—even if it's true. It isn't the first time Janessa has stepped in, steering Emlyn away from what she liked to call "Regrettables."

A wide receiver, junior year. An English major who moaned old Radio-head songs at the campus coffeehouse on Friday nights. The football player was beneath her (hot, but not even close to being smart enough, in Janessa's words). And the singer was a dirtbag Emlyn absolutely needed to avoid. She hadn't begrudged it, back then—well, maybe she had, a little—but she'd gone along.

Now, though, with the sun on her shoulders and the sky beyond Tyler a magnificent blue, a flicker of resentment twists in Emlyn's gut. She holds Tyler's gaze. "Janessa oversteps sometimes."

He laughs. "Isn't that the truth." He scuffs his boots in the gravel. A minivan rockets past. "It just means she cares about you. She loves you, and that's how she loves. She's . . ." He struggles for the word.

"Overbearing?" She doesn't mean for it to slip out, and she immediately twinges with guilt.

"I was gonna say, she likes to micromanage, but yeah, 'overbearing' also works." He shrugs. "She's just trying to protect you."

"Protect me from what?"

"Me, I guess."

"You?"

A smile plays at his lips. "She thinks I'll corrupt you."

"And what do you think?" she asks, dipping her head, teasing.

He seems to choose his words carefully. "I think, when it comes to Janessa, you're gonna have to stand your ground, sooner or later. You see, I've known her since we were toddlers. We've had lots of time to work that out. But you're kind of new to this Janessa thing. You've got to let her know she can't call all the shots, all the time. Once you do that, you two will be fine. Probably."

"I don't let her call all the shots," Emlyn insists, though even as she says this, she's not sure it's true. As if to prove it, though, to Tyler and to herself, she walks her bike to the back of the truck. "Lunch would be great," she says. "And if you still want it, I'll give you my number, too."

She climbs into the passenger seat and straps in. *This is not a date,* she tells herself. *It is not a date! It's a mere thank-you, a courtesy. It doesn't mean anything, don't read into it.* She leans to her right and takes one more wary glance in the mirror.

They do a U-turn and head back toward town, miles south. At the drive-through of Ptarmigan's, Tyler buys three sandwiches, and hands her one. "Best in town," he says.

In the corner of the lot, an old man with a thick, tawny beard sits on the ground, knees tucked, leaning against the base of a metal shopping cart laden with stuff.

"Be right back," Tyler says, putting the truck in park and hopping out.

The old man struggles to rise. Tyler lends a hand and then gives him the sandwich. He places a palm on the man's shoulder, both toss their heads in laughter. Curious, Emlyn cracks the window. The two are chatting. Weather, a wildfire in California, which flies are biting on the Big Wood River. Emlyn notes the fly rod sticking out of the shopping cart. After a couple of minutes, Tyler shakes the man's hand and heads back to the truck. Emlyn presses the button to close the window.

"Who's that?" she asks.

"That's Jorge."

"How do you know him?"

"I met him a couple years ago when he was camped out near my apartment building."

"And . . . ?"

Tyler shrugs. "We're friends."

"You buy him sandwiches."

As they pull out of the lot, Tyler opens his window and waves. Jorge, deep in the business of eating his sandwich, raises a hand. "Yep."

"Every day?" Emlyn asks.

"Just Saturdays."

"Why?"

Tyler grips the steering wheel with his left hand, holds his sandwich in his right. "Why not?"

WHEN Tyler pulls up in front of her rented apartment and asks if she wants to go swimming later, she says yes. Because now she's deeply enamored. "I'll be back in three hours," he tells her. And in a trance, she walks up the metal stairs to her apartment.

She stands in her tiny bedroom, staring at herself in the mirror that hangs on the back of the door. Here, her insecurities launch their usual assault. The mousy brown hair, the freckles dotting her nose. The small breasts and lack of hips. She's fit but not skinny. Surely a guy like Tyler would never be interested in a girl like her. Surely agreeing to join him for "a swim" will end in heartache, or worse.

But Jorge, the sandwich.

"Not every cute guy is a dirtbag," she says to the mirror, frowning, not sure she believes herself, because her experience, limited as it might be, would suggest otherwise. But why not give the guy a chance? And besides—a bold, Janessa-like thought—maybe she doesn't need pure intentions, or want them.

The truth is, she is tired of being afraid, of being unnoticed. She takes a shower. Again she assesses herself, this time in the bathroom mirror.

Her cheeks have gone pink from the morning in the sun, which, she decides, is maybe cute.

Which swimsuit? Which clothes? She has very few possessions, none of which are nice. Emlyn picks one of her two swimsuits, grabs a pair of jeans, a plain white tee, a fleece. She gets dressed and shoves the suit and a towel in her backpack. Whatever this evening holds, she is stepping into it.

ELEVEN

FROM their parking spot next to Janessa's van, Emlyn and Tyler head back
to the stream where she discovered the hat. They push through the alders, the branches scraping their arms. When they come to a log that crosses
the water, Tyler goes first, balancing, arms wide. Emlyn follows, step step
step, left foot, right. She feels wobbly, the weight of the pack throwing her
off-balance. At last she is across, the solid ground a comfort beneath her.
Game trails everywhere, paths cutting through the alders. She crouches
down, searching for footprints. Moose, coyote, mule deer. She stands and
assesses, scanning the possibilities. Tyler veers to her left, and she tells him
to look for prints, too.

"Here," he calls.

She presses toward him and kneels. Yes. Boot prints. The word DANNER
barely visible. She places her foot next to it. Almost the same size. Then
a larger print: longer, wider. Kenetrek. Hunting boots, high end. Two
people. This is good. Are there more? Emlyn shrugs the heavy pack from
her back and, leaning down, continues to follow the tracks. But—she

leans even closer, face near the ground—a third track. Merrells. A spot where someone lost their footing, a smear in the mud. Slipped. No, maybe not. Dragged?

She stands up and circles back for her pack. "This way," she says to Tyler, deciding not to mention the third print.

They walk in silence, north, until at last they are on the far side of the alders and at the base of a skinny valley, the mountains on either side rising sharp and steep. Emlyn pauses to take stock of what lies ahead. Here there is no sign of grass bent over by a recent traveler, human or animal. There is only one trail, and they follow it. Animals, humans included, will almost always take the path of least resistance. They cross the valley, circle around, climb. The pines begin. The terrain grows steeper still.

"You all right?" Tyler asks.

"Sure," she says, though her legs burn and her back is killing her and beads of sweat slide down her hairline. "You?"

"I started triathlons. Just sprints, so far. After, you know. It became my new addiction." He stops and takes a drink from his Platypus. "I like to think I'm in shape." He smiles. "But—sometimes the world provides me with a friendly reminder that I'm not as in shape as I like to think I am."

"You're tired," she says, pulling her own Platypus nozzle loose from its clip. "You probably haven't been sleeping."

He looks down, brushes a hitchhiker from his pant leg. "Not much. Not enough."

EMLYN sees it first.

Movement. Far ahead, a person heading toward them, trundling down the hillside off trail, moving quickly. Dust rising, a line indicating their path. Too far to tell size or gender, but her heart lurches. "Tyler," she says, pointing. She isn't sure whether to feel hope or dread. They're look-ing for two people, after all. And if only one of them is rattling in their direction, it's not good.

They close the distance, though the figure remains off trail, twenty yards away. Tyler raises an arm in a wave. "Hi there!" he hollers.

Large. Tall, sure in his footing. A man. Bush?

Tyler and Emlyn stop. This is what you do, if you happen to run into someone way back in the woods. Stop, say hello, chat. Where are you from? How long have you been out here? But the man keeps moving. He slows his pace, but he doesn't stop. He raises an arm as he passes them.

Backpack, charcoal cargo pants, a long sleeve camo tee, baseball cap, sunglasses. A light blue Buff pulled up over his nose. A sidearm holstered at his right hip. Emlyn tries to take a mental snapshot, but already he is past them, already he is five yards away, ten. At last the man slows and spins toward them. "Just so you know, I ran into a sow and a cub up that way." He points in the direction they're heading. "I must've startled them because she charged. I think I scared them off, but maybe not."

"Thanks," Tyler says.

Now the man stops. He is twenty yards away, the sun at his back. "Just saying: you might want to rethink your path."

Is there a menacing tone in that statement?

"We're looking for someone," Tyler calls.

"A man and a woman," Emlyn adds. She wishes she could see the man's face, try to search for a reaction to her words.

The man holds both hands out wide and shrugs. "Haven't seen a soul. Other than the bears." He turns to go but then stops, looking at them. "Be careful out there," he adds, and then he leaves, swinging back to the trail.

Tyler watches him. "That was weird," he says.

"Yeah."

"Like, what's with the Buff?"

Emlyn shakes her head. She wears one herself sometimes, out on the water. "The sun's intense. It's easier than hauling sunscreen." Which is true. Or maybe he's sensitive to the smoke. Or nervous about getting sick. There's nothing abnormal, nothing strange about each component of the man's attire. And sometimes people deviate from the trail to make room for someone coming in the opposite direction.

But in her mind she is realizing: that man was perfectly disguised. With the sunglasses, hat, and Buff, there is absolutely nothing specific she could determine about him besides his height and build, and even that would be a rough estimate, assessed from twenty yards away and over the span of thirty seconds. Maybe he was a forty-five-year-old Black man with brown eyes and short silver hair. Maybe he was a twenty-five-year-old white man with blue eyes and long blond hair. Maybe he had distinguishing tattoos, maybe he had a scar. Other than his outfit, she couldn't identify a thing about him.

Of course she thinks of the Isuzu parked next to Bush and Janessa's van. That belonged to him, it had to. Was that @hikefishrepeat? Was it @ozkerwild? And the guy's words—*you might want to rethink your path; be careful*—were those a threat, or a friendly caution?

She watches the man trot out of sight, then walks toward the place where he passed through, the grass bent in the direction he was heading. She searches for a patch of dirt. There. A Merrell footprint.

"That wasn't him, was it?" Emlyn asks Tyler, who has squatted next to her. "Since we couldn't see his face, I'm just wondering—it wasn't Bush, right?"

Tyler shakes his head.

"You're sure?"

"I'm sure." Tyler rises to his feet. "Bush is bigger than that."

TWELVE

TOWARD the end of the day, Emlyn and Tyler scramble up to a ledge, a large rock, level and relatively flat. Before them spreads a view of four mountains and part of the valley below. Exactly what Emlyn was hoping for. She shrugs the pack from her shoulders and slumps to the ground, leaning back against the rock. "We need to stop," she says, scanning the sky. The sun has slipped below the tallest peaks, and soon it will be dark. She fishes her binoculars from the top compartment of her backpack and, starting to her far left, begins to glass. Up, down, a pattern. She looks for movement, unexpected color, smoke. The light wanes quickly.

Behind her, Tyler clears a campsite, kicking branches and stones. "No burn ban here, right?"

"Not yet," she says. She continues glassing. He sets up his tent, climbs out of sight, comes back with an armload of sticks. On a far hillside, movement, a flash of brown. She quickly adjusts to find it again. Pines, rock, sage. There. One elk, another. She thinks of her archery tag, back in a drawer of her Airstream. All the hours she's spent practicing, building her strength. For a moment she watches them. A line of three, four, trotting from the trees. All bulls. Any day their peace will be broken, and they'll be at war with each other due to the mating season. Gathering their harems. Bugling, drooling, rolling in their own urine. Fighting. The rut, it's called. It was hard not to consider the stupidity that sex could bring out in creatures with such a show. She sets the binoculars down and glances at Tyler, who is now on the ground, stacking wood and kindling in a tidy circle. He stops, raises his eyes to meet hers, and smiles.

She finishes glassing all that she can see and then begins setting up her own tent. Tyler has a double, but she brought hers anyway. Already she is tempting fate, being out here with him, half-heartedly fighting all the old feelings that are bubbling to the surface. There's no need to tumble over the edge by sleeping in the same tent. Her heart can't afford such a slip.

Tyler pulls the Jetboil from his pack and sets out an array of dehydrated meals. "Tonight, madam, for your dining pleasure, we have chicken with vegetables and risotto; beef tips with mushrooms; and three sisters stew." He fills the Jetboil with water from his pack and clicks on the flame.

"Surprise me," she says, taking out her pocketknife and shaving strips from a dry stick.

Her pile of kindling grows, and she slides it under Tyler's stack of larger sticks. She reaches for her strike igniter, but Tyler plucks a lighter from his pocket. He holds it to the kindling and flicks his thumb, the flame catching the shavings. She leans in close and blows lightly and the fire licks up and up.

The Jetboil is ready now. Tyler turns off the fuel and pours the water into one of the meal packets. Darkness pushes close; the air grows cool. She pulls a fleece from her pack and slides it over her head. The fire is growing and bright but not yet warm. Tyler stares at the flames, and she can't help it, she looks at him, studies his face.

"You're different," she says.

He nods. "I sure hope so. I'm trying, I really am. I've just got a few loose ends to tie up, and truly, all of it will be behind me."

"Loose ends?"

"Yeah," he says, poking the fire. "That whole world I lived in, I just want to make sure every single connection to it is—" He shrugs. "—gone, out of reach, so I can really, fully move on. Does that make sense?"

She nods, tugging her sleeves over her knuckles. She'd done the same thing, with him: cut off all connections, put it all behind her. "It makes sense."

He boils another serving of water and adds it to a second meal. "Funny—well, not funny. *Sad* that it took losing the one thing that mattered most to me to get my life cleaned up."

She does not respond to this, keeps staring into the fire.

They wait. The mountains are now silhouetted giants, black against an almost-black sky. "By the way, you're different, too," he says.

"How so?"

"I don't know. Stronger, more confident. It's almost like—well, I guess it's like all the things I saw in you, back when we first met, they've magnified, they've sprung to life. It's like this is what you were made for, this world. And it's good, it's just fantastic. I have no right to be proud of you, but I am." He hands her one of the meals. "Here you go."

She plucks her camping spoon from her pack and opens the food. Steam rolls out, and she scoops a bite. "Beef tips," she reads, holding the package in the light of the fire. "It's good. What did you pick?"

"The stew. Here, try." He scoops some, slides closer, and holds out the spoon. She leans and takes a bite. He doesn't move away, and she offers him some of hers. The fire begins to throw heat. Their knees touch.

For one brief, sparkling moment, she nearly forgets that it isn't four, five years ago. That they are not together, that Tyler left her, that he always loved something more than her. That he could not help that.

The trouble is that she likes the forgetting.

"This was it, wasn't it?" Tyler says. "You and me out here. Nothing better. Everything I've seen and done in life—it's these times that stand out." He seals the empty meal packet and pitches it into the fire. It catches and the flames grow bright, green, blue, and then it is gone. "Of course, you always make anything better."

Don't talk like that, she could say. She could slide away from him, crawl into her tent. But she doesn't, and when he joins her on the pad, even closer, she stays right where she is. "Thanks," she mutters, sliding her sleeping bag out and unrolling it.

"Em, I know you said what happened between us, you don't want to talk about that. But there are two things I've been needing to say. Two things I need you to know. If you're willing to hear them."

This is a bad idea, isn't it? Dangerous. Whatever Tyler wants to say—it could open up a path to forgiveness, and healing. A whole constellation of possibilities. And the route she is on is just fine. A rocky trail, a lonely one, stones stacked around her heart. Lonely, yes, but safe. Protected. There is nothing wrong with such a course.

But she thinks of the word Rev whispered to her after that strange prayer in the garden: "trust." And she feels herself nodding, saying, "Okay."

"First, I'm sorry. I never meant to hurt you. I hope you know that." Tyler wipes his sleeve across his eyes. "There are people who would say it was my addiction that almost killed you. But I don't buy that. It was me. I put you in that situation, I left you. I accept responsibility for it. And I am so, so sorry. Not a day goes by that I don't think about it. Not a single day."

A tear slips from her eye and ambles down her cheek. Another, another. This is exactly what she wanted to avoid. For years her anger has been anchoring her, holding her tight. There is security in this stance. Now she feels as though she is losing her footing.

He puts his arm around her and pulls her close. She refuses to look at him, but she leans into him. She has no idea how long the two of them sit there. At last Tyler pulls away to grab another piece of wood from the stack.

"The second thing?" she asks. If they are doing this now, best to get it all over with in one fell swoop.

Tyler places the wood on the fire but does not return to the spot beside her. Instead, he seats himself on a log across from her. He pulls on a beanie and then looks at her. Those blue eyes, that beautiful mouth. "The second thing is that I never stopped loving you."

"Tyler," she whispers.

Beyond him, a pair of eyes appear in the dark: glowing, yellow.

He reaches for a stick and pokes the coals. "I probably never will."

"Tyler," she says, louder.

"Yeah?"

"There's something in the woods. Behind you."

His eyes grow wide. "What is it?"

She shakes her head, unsure. "Mountain lion, maybe."

The eyes disappear, reappear.

He swears and bolts to his feet. "What do we do?"

"Try not to freak out," she hisses. Her pulse roars.

The eyes flicker. No body, no movement, no noise. Just a set of eyes that move right. Then they disappear for a moment. Now left. It is pacing, watching. Deciding.

"Grab a rock," she says. "Throw it in his direction. And get the gun, too, but don't fire it unless it comes closer." The gun has to be a last resort. Firing into the dark at something you *think* is a threat is a cardinal sin in the woods.

She reaches for more branches and adds them to the fire, building it up. Tyler pitches a rock toward the moving eyes. Never taking her eyes off the animal, she reaches for her backpack and feels around for a small metal cooking pot. At last her fingers wrap around its handle. She yanks it out and then begins to hit it with her spoon. Clang, clang, clang.

"Hey!" she yells into the darkness. "Go away!"

Tyler pitches another rock. This time he must come close, because the eyes dart quickly to the left, as though the cat is jumping aside. He launches another. Emlyn continues banging the pot and hollering nonsense: *Go away, mountain lion. You cannot eat us tonight. We don't want you here. Go, get now. No thank you, mountain lion!* Tyler comes close with a rock again. The eyes disappear, and the two of them hear a crashing through the brush.

Tyler screams a string of profanities into the dark, and then turns to look at her from across the campfire. She stops banging the pot and shouting, and then they both burst into laughter because what, just seconds earlier, felt terrifying and desperate is suddenly ridiculous. Emlyn playing her makeshift instrument and howling into the wilderness, Tyler pitching stones at yellow eyes in the dark. The vast and unthinkable swing of emotions.

They rehash it, laugh some more. She keeps an eye on the woods, worried that the mountain lion will come back for another look, but there's no sign of it. They keep the fire big and hot. They do not return to Tyler's earlier words. He has said them, and now she knows. She can play them again and again, she can roll them in her palm. She veers dangerously close to letting this thing between them unfurl. Late into the night, she is still not tired, but her trust in herself and in the stability of her walls is fading in the orange, lulling glow of the fire, so she rises, tells Tyler good night, and crawls into her tent.

FIVE YEARS AGO

TYLER pulls up in his truck in front of Emlyn's apartment. He is three minutes early but she is waiting for him on the metal stairs outside her building. He wears baggy jeans and a T-shirt with a Sasquatch hauling an axe through the woods. And, she realizes as she climbs into the truck, breathing him in, he has showered.

She tucks her backpack between her feet.

"Hope you like burgers?" He points to a brown paper bag on the floor. "I should've asked."

They drive and drive. Through downtown, then a neighborhood with huge, sprawling houses on huge, sprawling lots. The houses shrink, grow less predictable, less fancy, and, with a dip, the road turns to dirt. More miles. They pass a national forest sign, close their windows to keep out the dust. Mumford & Sons holler through the speakers. She doesn't tell him she owns the album, too.

Tyler slows and turns the truck in to a small pullout on the right. "Let's eat," he says. "It's a bit of a hike."

The burgers are cold now, but still good, and they peel the silver wrappers and eat them in the parking lot. He reaches out and wipes a speck of ketchup from her chin.

They trek all the way down a dirt path to a sparkling blue lake, Tyler grabbing her hand when she stumbles. She slips into some bushes to change, and then he does the same. From a huge boulder, he runs and dives in. He whoops as he surfaces. "Come on!" he calls, treading water, and she leaps.

The sun dips, darkness creeps in. Tyler builds a fire on a flat outcropping that overlooks the water. She doesn't want the date to end, but she doesn't like the possibility that certain expectations may fall on her as time stretches into the night. Where is he expecting this to go? She is not the type of person who hooks up on a first date. Is she?

"Are all of your dates overnight adventures?" she asks at last, her anxiety getting the better of her.

He laughs. "No," he says, poking the fire. "Are yours?"

Now it's her turn to laugh. "No!" She pulls her palms into the sleeves of her fleece. "But I'm not the one who brought us here."

"Fair enough." He pulls a sleeping bag from his pack. "Here," he says, unrolling it.

Her heart thumps. Thrill but also fear. She's relieved and maybe a tiny bit disappointed when he pulls a second bag from his pack for himself.

He leans back against a log. "Look at that sky," he says. He points out Cassiopeia, Cepheus. The Milky Way stretches above them, a stream of lavender and white.

"Tell me something about yourself that nobody knows," Tyler ventures, deep into the night. He still sits across from her, the fire shrinking low.

Later, she will come to understand that this is a typical Tyler question. Small groups, large groups, just the two of them—he gambols past small talk and dives into the heart of things.

But now, Emlyn squirms. There are so many things she holds tight to herself, wounds that tingle and corrode every relationship, and life is so much easier when you keep your pain hidden beneath a shiny veneer. "You first," she says.

He bites his lip, pokes the embers with a stick. "This scar," he says, pointing to the tiny star shape on his cheek, "my family thinks I got it wrecking my bike. That's what I told them. But really I got it climbing up into my dad's liquor cabinet when I was thirteen. Janessa knows. She was there, but she never said a word. Your turn."

Doe she really want to answer? She hesitates, but Tyler looks at her and grins, his eyes sparkling in the firelight. "When I was eleven, my dad got me a dictionary, and then, a few months later, he left." She reaches for the sleeping bag and pulls it over her legs. "For a long time, I read it. I memorized definitions. Not every word, of course, and just a few each day." She remembers those lonely hours after school, tucked in the tree. And later, the red cabinets of the converted workshop, the pleated cream lampshade, the stack of library books. "He called, for a while. Sent cards and postcards. I kept reading and memorizing definitions." She steals a glance at Tyler. Already there is an alarming chink in her armor with this reveal. But there is also a lightness, like a weight has been removed. "And I do this thing. I choose a word for people." She's never told anyone about this.

"A word?"

"Yeah, one word that can really summarize a person."

He tilts his head to the side. "Is there such a thing? Are people really so . . . simple?"

"You'd be surprised."

"What's my word?"

She looks at him from across the fire and lies. "You don't have one yet."

THEY don't kiss. He doesn't even touch her. She is sure this is not a sign of his restraint or gentlemanliness, but a mark of her staggering inadequacy, and the thought burns in her gut. Tyler was just being nice, inviting her out. And as usual, Emlyn was naïve and pathetic in saying yes. She should've declined, because already she feels connected to Tyler in a way she's never felt with anyone else before. Already she dreads pulling into the parking lot of her apartment building, the "see you later" that really means "so long."

In the morning they drive back to town for breakfast at a place she has never noticed, Tyler greeting the server, Gus, and the cook, Jada, both with a peck on the cheek. He introduces her, and she wonders whether he has done this before.

When Tyler drops her off, they stand together in front of his truck. He towers over her, and he leans close and presses his lips to her forehead. She grips the bumper, steadying herself. He adds her number to his phone and promises to call.

She walks up the steps to her apartment and turns around, and he is watching, he hasn't moved. She smiles and waves and steps into the building. She unlocks her apartment and collapses on her ugly plaid couch, exhausted but also buzzing. When she peers from behind the window curtain and watches Tyler leave (how is this possible?), she feels adrift. Like maybe a day like this will never happen again, like maybe she has blown it. She takes a shower and tries not to think of her word.

*　*　*

BUT Tyler texts her, later that day. And again the next day. Three days later, they go out for ice cream. The following weekend, they play tennis. When they're together, they avoid any mention of Janessa, a tacit agreement between the two of them. But, Emlyn wonders, at what point are she and Tyler *seeing* each other? And how long can this go on, both of them ignoring the fact that they are both deeply bonded to a person who doesn't know they're together? A person who, for whatever reason, never wanted them to connect. Emlyn doesn't want to think about it. She doesn't want to admit that there could be trouble ahead. For now, she wants to bask in this unexpected happiness. The joy of being with someone as fun and funny and exhilarating as Tyler, the thrill of new love.

THIRTEEN

IN the morning, Emlyn emerges from her tent to find Tyler awake, sitting by the campfire. When he sees her, he rises and hands her a small red camp cup full of steaming coffee as well as a silver bag of dehydrated eggs, already prepared.

"Made you breakfast."

"Fancy," she says, taking the cup. Their knuckles graze. "Thank you."

Tyler leans against a log.

The coffee is sharp and hot, steam rolling off.

"You know, when I was a kid, we didn't have this," he says, waving his hand, gesturing toward the smoke that has reappeared. "We'd have a fire or two, somewhere in the state, every summer. But nothing like this."

"Is it close?" she asks. Her mapping app will show fires: little flames marking places the Forest Service is aware of. But without cell service, would that update? A terrifying thought: if they shut down the forest, if they sent out alerts, if they announced on the news or Forest Service website that a new wildfire had started, the two of them would have no way of knowing—and possibly no way out.

Tyler shrugs. "No idea."

THEY pack up the tents and other equipment, and Emlyn heaves under the weight of the backpack, which somehow feels heavier than the day before. She checks her onX mapping app, the fine green line showing the ground they've covered. She drops a waypoint to indicate where they camped and checks the miles they've already come: four. The battery on the phone is waning, the mapping app zapping it quickly. Forty-one percent left.

They clamber down the rocky outcropping and pick up the trail where they left it the night before. Wind through a patch of pines, up and up. They stop for a break, munching on a packet of almonds. She holds up her Platypus, tipping it side to side, assessing. Soon, they'll need water.

Tyler stands and slides his pack on again. "Ready?" He reaches out a hand to help her up.

She takes it and he does not let go and the two of them stand face-to-face. He swipes a strand of hair from her eyes. She turns and picks up her pack.

The trees thin. The sun is high in the sky now and the air hot and dry. They are at maybe eight or nine thousand feet in elevation. At last the ground begins to level out. An alpine meadow, the field dotted yellow with patches of arrowleaf balsamroot. Tyler and Emlyn pick up their pace on the skinny trail, the wheatgrass scraping her pant legs. She reminds Tyler to keep drinking.

A shadow crosses the grass in front of her, then another. Emlyn looks up. Birds circle overhead. She stops, squints. Turkey vultures, the white belly of a ferruginous hawk. Round and round they go. Dozens of them.

She cranes her neck, stands on her tiptoes. Ahead, the valley grows thick with bitterbrush and sage. Her mind flashes to the mountain lion from the night before. They do not want to startle an animal eating its kill.

"Make some noise," she tells Tyler, pointing to the sky. "Just in case there's something up there. Let's let it know we're coming." She claps her hands, shouts. Tyler, walking in front of her, does the same.

"Whoa," he says, stopping suddenly. He takes a quick step back, nearly knocking her over.

"What is it?" She grips the bear spray strapped to her chest and clicks off the safety.

Tyler steps off the trail and points. A dead animal, pink, stripped of its skin, resting in the branches of a bitterbrush. Its limbs have been pecked, its face. A marmot? A white maggot wriggles from the flesh of its round belly.

"Disgusting," Tyler says, turning away. He has never had a stomach for such things. "What kind of animal does that?"

"You'd be surprised." Orcas that pitched dolphins from the water, breaking their spines. Grizzlies that ate their prey before it was dead. Those people who liked to believe nature was all beauty and dance—they were wrong. Anyone who spent enough time in the wild could tell you that.

She lifts her head to the sky and watches the birds. "Let's keep moving," she says.

They walk in silence, both troubled. And then another animal, a hare, hanging by its neck.

Goose bumps stipple her arms. Emlyn steps closer. The stench is overwhelming. She yanks a branch from the bush. She gags, pulls her left sleeve over her mouth and nose, leans closer, then uses the branch to lift the head of the animal. There. A small, gray wire circling the neck. "This was trapped," she says, circling back to check the marmot. Same thing.

They keep walking, and a hundred yards ahead, more animals. Some with wire at their necks, some with other materials: twine, a fine white string of animal sinew.

"Emlyn?" Tyler calls over his shoulder. He has walked ahead and stands frozen on the trail. All at once the sound of thrashing fills the air.

She runs to him. A deer, gaunt and wide-eyed and wild with fear, alive. Its head is in a snare, and it has struggled for who knows how long, the wire cutting into its neck, the fur worn off and the neck raw and red. On either side of the trail stand two trees, and across the trail, almost invisible, the wire. The doe reels in fear at their approach, staggers back and falls and rolls. The trees lurch with her weight and then bounce back up, yanking her forward with violence.

"Give me the gun, Tyler," she whispers, but she is too late. Tyler holds it in his hand, and before she can offer, he pulls the trigger. She starts. The sound reverberates off the mountains. The doe lies in a heap. Emlyn reaches out and takes hold of his arm, lowering it gently. She leans into him, arm wrapped at his back.

Emlyn struggles to make sense of this grisly scene. Trapping season is in the winter. Plus, too many traps, too close together. Any good trapper would space them out, and more importantly, wouldn't leave the animals to rot. Not to mention, this far in the woods, a trapper would never be able to haul all of this out. And that deer snare? That type of trap was never designed to *kill* an animal—the creature would always need to be finished off. Was this some novice, out here messing around? Someone who didn't know the seasons or the ethics?

What was the story here? What had gone wrong?

These are not mistakes, Emlyn realizes. These are not accidents or experiments. There is a fixed snare; there is a squirrel noose. And, almost unbelievably, the use of animal sinew. Whoever did this—they were no amateur. They were knowledgeable and skilled. An expert, a craftsman.

She is hot and dizzy, the sun brutal overhead. Tyler pulls away from her, wipes his eyes on the sleeve of his T-shirt. Flies, frenzied and abundant, descend upon the deer. A magpie lands in a nearby sapling. Emlyn circles back, running her finger over the soft ear of a rabbit. She thinks of her quick internet search of Janessa's partner, back at the cabin. The hunting and fishing videos. The handmade bow and arrows, the elk.

"Tyler," she says, walking back to him, "what can you tell me about Bush?"

FIVE YEARS AGO

"I met someone," Emlyn tells Janessa.

Her nerves seem to sizzle. Three weeks have passed since she met Tyler at the party, and they've already seen each other five times. Emlyn has never kept something like this from Janessa, and the secrecy is killing her, not only because she wants to tell her friend, but also because she knows it's only a matter of time before Janessa finds out. And if there's one thing Emlyn's certain of, it's that this news better come from her. It must be handled with delicacy, Emlyn knows, but—it must be handled, and soon.

Janessa's jaw drops. "What?" She waves her hands in that way of hers. "How do I not know this already?" She plops onto Emlyn's couch and scoots closer. "Tell me *everything.*"

Emlyn has recited this; she has practiced. A slow, cautious reveal. She cannot seem too excited, she cannot get ahead of herself. She absolutely cannot, under any circumstances, let the word "serious" slip from her mouth. She cannot admit that she is falling, tumbling, hard and fast, for Tyler. "Well," she begins, "I met him at a party."

"Which one? When?"

"The one at your neighbor's house." She tilts her head to the side, as though this part is a little fuzzy for her. As though she hasn't been back to that same house, twice now: once to play tennis and once for lunch with Tyler's parents.

"I thought you were with Jimmy that night."

"I was. I mean, I wasn't *with* him, but I tried to be nice. For a little while." She turns to Janessa. "He's really not my type, I'm sorry." She's not sure why she's apologizing.

Janessa waves her off. "I know, it's fine. I promised him I would try." She takes a sip of her latte. "So, go on. Tell me about this new guy."

"He's smart. Kind. Thoughtful. Funny. So funny. Cute . . ."

"He sounds perfect."

"Yeah," Emlyn says quietly. "I think maybe he is. I just felt this immediate connection, you know?" As soon as she says that, she wants to snap it back.

"Your face!" Janessa gasps. "I've never seen you like this."

Emlyn wishes she could do a better job of hiding her elation. Has she already revealed too much?

Janessa squeals. She bites her lip and flutters her feet, giddy with excitement. "So, who is it? Do I know him?"

"You do know him," Emlyn says carefully. Her pulse drums at her throat. "You know him well, actually. It's your neighbor. Your old friend. Tyler."

Janessa blinks. Once, twice. The silence bleeds between the two of them. "Tyler?" she sputters at last. "*My* Tyler?"

Emlyn winces, that pronoun like a punch to the gut. She shifts position on the couch, willing herself to remain calm. "I don't think he considers himself *yours,* but yes. The Tyler you knew growing up."

"No," Janessa says. She slams her latte on the coffee table and rises to her feet. "Absolutely not."

"*No?*"

"Pick someone else. Anyone else." Janessa spins on her heel. "I'm telling you. I'm asking you, please."

"What? Why?" Emlyn asks, and the edge in her voice surprises her.

Janessa purses her lips. "Let's just say he's off-limits."

Dread roils in Emlyn's gut. "Are you two . . . involved? Or were you, at some point?" (Even this could be a hang-up, Emlyn realizes. Some romantic history, good or bad.)

"No, never. It's just—anyone else, you do what you want to do. I'll stay out of it, cross my heart. But you need to stay away from him."

"Stay away from him? He's your best friend. I'm your best friend." She holds out her hands, palms up.

"Yeah, well, I didn't think—"

"You didn't think what?" Emlyn interrupts, and some feeling she cannot name—not quite fury, not quite indignation; something subtler, but not necessarily less hazardous—begins to twirl inside her. Her pulse roars, her head feels light. At last she says the thought aloud: "That a guy like Tyler would be interested in a girl like me?"

Emlyn is inferior to Janessa, in every way. She knows this and accepts it without qualms because it is foundational not only to their relationship, but to all friendships among women. At least as Emlyn understands them. In every friendship, there is always a prettier one, a flirtier one, a more likable one of the two. If they meet two guys at the bar, the better-looking one chooses Janessa, every time.

"No!" Janessa slumps into the sofa. "I didn't say that."

"But it's what you were thinking."

"No. It wasn't." She crosses her arms. "You know, I wish you would stop seeing yourself like that. At first, it was kind of endearing, but at this point it's exhausting, it really is." She raises her eyes to meet Emlyn's. She dips her chin, unfolding her arms. "Listen. I love you, I want what's best for you. And of course I love Tyler, too. But it's—complicated. I wish I could explain, and maybe someday I can, but for now, please: don't get involved."

"But why?"

"I've known Tyler forever. My whole life. And trust me, nobody knows his charm better than I do." She reaches for Emlyn's hand and tugs her onto the sofa next to her. "But believe me, that charm wears off. I'm telling you: Tyler is the ultimate Regrettable. Do you trust me?"

Emlyn bites her lip. "Yeah," she says. And she does. Janessa has never let her down, she has been nothing but good to her. "Of course."

"Good. Then I need you to trust me right now. Tyler is trouble." She leans in and kisses Emlyn's cheek, and Emlyn catches a whiff of her perfume. "You understand, right?"

"I guess."

"I love you, you know that." Janessa rises to her feet. "Listen, I have to run. I'll call you later. We'll hang out." At the door she turns and smiles. "We will find you another guy. Someone so much better, I promise."

EMLYN takes a shower. She brews herself a cup of tea. She picks up her library book and tries to read. She wanders back to the bathroom and combs her long hair, still wet.

What just happened? Did Janessa, in a matter of five minutes, completely convince Emlyn to stop seeing someone? A person she'd felt a real connection with. Who maybe liked her, too. And she'd barely pushed back; she'd hardly resisted. Her word swims to her. *Pathetic.* She stares at herself in the mirror and sees that she is frowning, eyes narrowed. She looks like her mother.

Tyler was right. Since that first meeting at Bumpy's Diner, Janessa has always called the shots. She decides where they go on a Friday night, what they eat, what they drink. She sets the tone. And Emlyn has gone along with it. But she thinks of her swim with Tyler, the stars glittering overhead, the feel of his lips to her forehead, and for the first time, she doesn't want to go along with Janessa's plans.

Here in the bathroom, a handful of memories sizzle and spit. Sophomore year: when Emlyn says she's heading home for spring break to work at the Savvy Shopper, Janessa buys her a plane ticket to Miami. (Her grandmother insisted, she explains with a grin.) Junior year: when Emlyn swears she doesn't want to go to the Spring Fling, Janessa assumes it's because she can't afford a dress (which is not untrue), and buys her one. A gorgeous midi, off-the-shoulder sleeves, a seafoam that matches Emlyn's eyes. Also junior year: a hundred lattes at Janessa's favorite off-campus café, an "anonymous" gift card to the school bookstore when she knew Emlyn was stressed about the price tag of a certain textbook, a warm winter coat that Janessa no longer needed and "was going to drop off at Goodwill" if Emlyn didn't take it. (It still had the tags on it.)

A small caterpillar of resentment begins to inch along Emlyn's skin. At the time, each and every one of those things had felt like a precious gift. Emlyn had marveled at her good fortune and her friend's generosity; she'd felt full of gratitude. But now, a different possibility appears, new and unnerving: What if those gifts hadn't just been acts of kindness? They were nice, sure, but each one had also ultimately been a tool for Janessa to get her way. Janessa had wanted company on the trip to Miami. She'd wanted Emlyn to go to the dance with her. Even the jacket had meant that Emlyn would ultimately be persuaded to join Janessa on a family ski trip, later that year.

But. This is an unpleasant and discomfiting, not to mention potentially incorrect, way of looking at the world, isn't it? Her therapist back in college, Rhonda, had challenged her to stop seeing the universe through that dark lens of distrust, and Emlyn has made great strides. After all, it's entirely possible that those gestures truly were a mark of Janessa's generosity. Janessa is her best friend. Her bosom friend, her person. She has always been there for her. She has helped her, she has torn Emlyn out of her shell, she has made her braver and stronger and better. Emlyn cannot imagine life without her. And Janessa really does always have her best interests at heart.

Right?

FOURTEEN

IN the valley of traps, Emlyn begins to panic. What signs has she walked past? Where should she have slowed down? What has she missed? She thinks back to Janessa's dropped call and begins filling in a different set of possibilities. *I'm in danger. Bush has gone off the deep end. Please call the police. Help.* Why hadn't she considered this sooner? How could she have been so naïve? Because Bush seemed like a good guy in his videos? Because all the images of Janessa and Bush showed two people who were head over heels in love with each other? A different type of fear begins to trail along Emlyn's skin.

Tyler hasn't answered her question about Bush. He hasn't moved from the dead deer, and he stands there, frozen, the pistol resting against his thigh. Flies sing, the deer's pink tongue hangs from its jaw. The magpie watches from the sapling, as though considering a descent, tilting its head, flicking its long tail, the branch bobbing with its movement. Overhead, the vultures continue to circle. Hungry, waiting.

"I've never killed anything," Tyler says. His eyes are fixed on the wound where the bullet entered the deer: tousled brown hair, splats of bright red flesh. The magpie ventures down. It lands on the doe's chest, plucks a hunk of meat in its beak, then flaps back to its branch.

She reaches for Tyler's hand, wrapping her fingers around the butt of the pistol. He does not let go. "You did the right thing, Tyler."

"Did I?"

He releases the gun, and she takes it and clicks on the safety. "Yes," she says. "You did." She doesn't say aloud that the animal had already suffered far too many hours tethered to those saplings, that she was probably almost dead from thirst or exhaustion, that it was only a matter of time before the wilderness would have turned on her. Bears, wolves, that mountain lion. Even the vultures spinning overhead. Everything hungry, resourceful, desperate. She thinks of handing the gun back to Tyler but instead tucks it into the deep external pocket, where, on shorter jaunts, she keeps a water bottle.

Her eyes scan their surroundings. The smoke has thickened, the valley now shrouded in white. Gone are the looming mountains from the night before. The pines, too, are smudged, barely visible, dark ghosts in a sea of white. She has gone back and forth, circled the trapline in search of answers, and in her searching, in the smoke, she has lost her bearings. Which way did they come in? Which way is north? Where are they?

This is how it happens, of course. You let your guard down, you get distracted, you pivot and pivot again. Soon you lose your bearings. Factor in people's general tendency to panic at the notion of being lost in the wilderness, and you have a problem. But, while Emlyn has indeed lost her bearings momentarily, that's not what's troubling her. She has her mapping app, and she has a compass. Back in Wilderness Navigation, at the end of a weekend retreat in college, they'd plopped her class down in the middle of nowhere with the backpacks they'd packed, and told them to find their way back to camp. She'd been the first one to return. Getting turned around in this valley is not what's really unsettling her. No.

It's that they're in the open, out here. And if someone set those traps and has been waiting—to scare them, send a message, do something more sinister—she and Tyler are completely exposed. She imagines herself hunting this valley, mule deer or elk lumbering through, browsing on the sagebrush and bitterbrush, sniffing out forbs. If she were hunting, she'd tuck herself in the trees, where she could hide, watch, and wait for a good shot.

"Come on," she says, forcing a calmness into her voice. If there is one thing her work as a guide has taught her, it's how to read the client. To know what it is they need or want from you. Sometimes, they need instruction. Sometimes, they want to have their ego stroked. And sometimes, they simply need you to be a calming, reassuring presence. Right now, she sees, that is what Tyler needs from her. Tyler can quickly topple into despair—she has witnessed it too many times—and she knows that she cannot allow him to sense any distress in her, not right now. She must seem unruffled, serene. Well, she can't just seem calm; she must *be* calm. Tyler will see right through any pretentions.

Lists of survival "rules" are abundant. There are various renditions and orders. But, on almost every list, in some wording or other: Don't get lost to begin with, always tell someone else where you are, and, if something goes awry, stay calm. She has violated the second rule by leaving the cabin at Patten Lake without confirming that Varden received her message, but Tyler has remedied this bungle with the GPS and his contact at the Forest Service. And they are not really lost, just a tiny bit turned around. Thus— stay calm.

She places a hand on Tyler's elbow. "Let's get to the trees."

He follows, quietly, still in a daze, and she pushes toward the fringe of dark shapes to their right. Once they've made it, she looks around again before sliding her pack from her shoulders, setting it down, and leaning against it. Tyler slumps next to her. She fiddles with the zipper and tugs her phone from a pocket. The battery has dropped to thirty-seven percent, the mapping app draining it more quickly than she'd anticipated. She has a solar charger, but it works slowly, and she assumes it'll work even less efficiently with the smoke. Still, she fishes it from her backpack and plugs in her phone. She opens her app, studies it. Zooms in, zooms out. There, yes. She looks carefully at the map, noting the waypoints. The vans, last night's camp. In her mind she pictures their trek: the terrain, the landmarks, the rock where they camped, the elk on a distant hillside, and after a moment she has a good grasp of where they are, even in the smoke. She drops yet another waypoint to mark the trapline, then zooms way out for a bigger picture. To the south, where they've come from, and to the east, they're buffered by abundant designated wilderness. To the west, and not too far off, forty thousand acres of BLM land. To the north, private land, RM Ranch. Still, they are decidedly on public land at the moment. Tyler stares into the white.

"We should drink," she says, and reaches for the mouthpiece of her Platypus. She tugs the bladder from her backpack, too, assessing what is left. Maybe half a liter. This isn't dire—at least, it doesn't have to be—but getting to water should be their number one priority, even if it means going out of the way. Stay hydrated, stay energized. Without meeting those two goals, they'll never make it to their other goals of finding Janessa, and, after that, making their way home.

"Water," she says aloud. "That's the next step. We get it, filter it while we rest and have some lunch. Then we reassess. If we're lucky, this smoke will clear." *And if the phone dies, we'll be able to see well enough to navigate without it,* she thinks. She looks at the app again, locating the stream she marked earlier. "Come on," she says. "We'll stay in the trees for a bit. More shade." Of course she cannot tell him what she's really thinking— that maybe they're being watched, that trouble might be looming nearby. "Let's get moving."

Tyler rolls a pinecone in his palm. He looks at her, as though contemplating whether to rise, but finally stands up.

They stay in the woods, skirting the valley for as long as they can, but at last they must cross it to get to the water. The smoke remains thick, like the fog that used to settle among the trees back in Pennsylvania on damp spring mornings. That fog was palpable, magical. She could feel the air's heaviness hitting her face, she could gulp it into her mouth. Emlyn stops, staring into the white, watching for movement, color. Nothing. A whiteness so impenetrable it's like darkness. Strangely, this smoke often holds little odor. It could distort and disorient; it could take a toll on your body, too—she imagines the air quality index is in the hundreds today—and yet not smell like much at all.

"You asked about Bush," Tyler says, finally. "What do you want to know?"

"Well, I looked him up, back at the cabin. I watched a couple videos while you did dishes."

"He's good, right?"

"He definitely knows what he's doing." She thinks back to the videos. Bush shooting the elk with his longbow, Bush spearing a carp. "Does he trap, too?"

"Yeah." Tyler lifts a branch and stops. "Wait, you don't think—you don't think he set those traps. Do you?"

She shrugs. "You tell me."

Tyler shakes his head. "I'd say it's much more likely that creep in the Buff did this."

The odds that two people with that level of skill would both be out here are slim, almost impossible. Unless they are together. *Were* together. A tinge of fear prickles across her back. Again the thought that Janessa and Bush had run into a third person—that Janessa had somehow gotten herself embroiled in a love triangle—flickers through Emlyn's mind. She shakes it off. "Okay, what else? How well do you know him? How did he and Janessa get together?"

Tyler quickens his pace to walk beside her. "I've known Bush a long time. Since high school."

"And Janessa? Were the three of you friends?"

He snorts. "No. Janessa wouldn't have given him the time of day back then."

"What do you mean?"

"He was a loser, he ran with the wrong crowd. She was the beautiful, straitlaced prom queen. She wouldn't have said it outright, but he was beneath her."

This isn't surprising. Emlyn thinks back to their many conversations in college. *Gross,* Janessa had declared, once, when Emlyn expressed interest in a guy in her outdoors club. *Perv,* she'd said of someone in their Western Civ class who said hi to Emlyn every day. Her never-ending list of Regrettables. "So, how did he and Janessa connect, more recently?"

"It was me, actually. Though even that was orchestrated by Janessa. One weekend, right after she came back to Idaho, she said she was throwing a party at one of her dad's restaurants and asked me to invite him." He shrugs. "So I did."

"You didn't think that was strange? Her sudden interest in him?" Emlyn tilts her head. Once Janessa had made up her mind about someone, she rarely had a change of heart.

Tyler shrugs. "He'd grown up. He'd sort of reinvented himself, the past couple years. They both had."

"Okay, so they met at the party, and then what?"

Tyler props his trucker hat higher on his head. "I don't know. I think maybe they left together that first night? Beyond that, um, I don't ask for the details of Janessa's romantic affairs. I never have."

Emlyn rolls her eyes. "That's not what I meant."

"Yeah, I know. I mean—I guess they hit it off, right? I didn't really ask. I think you and I both know what it's like to meet someone and fall hard, just when you least expect it." He pauses, scuffs his boot against the grass. "It's like your world tips. It doesn't make any sense, and yet it makes complete sense."

Emlyn steals a glance at him. "So they hit it off at the party . . . and then what?"

"They'd been seeing each other, I don't know, a few months, and then one day they show up at the shop, trying to convince me to loan them a van so they can ramble around and give this whole influencer thing a go."

"That's it? They asked for a van and you just gave it to them?"

"Well, they sort of pitched me. They had ideas for content. Janessa knew I wanted to get the ball rolling with social media—I just didn't have the time. Or the interest, for that matter. Bush already had a huge following online, and Janessa kind of convinced me that the two of them, working together, could get some attention." He shrugs. "And she was right."

Emlyn steps around a sagebrush on the trail. "So, she dates the guy for a few months, and then moves into a van with him?" Even as she says this aloud, she realizes it doesn't sound that unbelievable, that out-of-character for Janessa. In her head, she runs through the long list of her friend's questionable decisions. Janessa blowing off a final to go to a Judah & the Lion concert, Janessa ditching her parents in Miami to hook up with a bartender named Pablo. A scandalous spring break video that she "accidentally" sent to all her friends.

Tyler nudges her with his elbow. "Didn't you do the same thing?"

I did, she thinks. *And look where it landed me. I basically derailed my life for the better part of a decade.* "Yeah, and how well did that work out for me?"

"Oh, come on. It wasn't all bad, was it?" He takes off his hat and runs his hands through his hair, swearing under his breath. He steps closer, looking her in the eye. "I screwed it all up, but before that, we were happy. We were in love. At least I was."

She sees the tiny beads of sweat that have formed above his thick upper lip. The blond curls she used to love to run her fingers through. She takes a step backward, and she doesn't like the wave of unsteadiness she feels in her legs.

Tyler slides his hat back on and takes a sip of water.

She turns away from him and keeps walking. Soon she hears the rush of the stream, and the sound brings a sense of relief. The map showed water, and she hoped they'd find it, but with years of drought and a drier than usual winter, even a reliable stream could be a trickle this time of year. Just a few weeks ago, she and Varden had hiked three miles to a stream they'd fished the summer before, only to find it had mostly dried up.

They stop, sliding out of their packs. She steps toward the water and kneels, cupping her hands and bringing water to her face. It's cold, almost painful, but it's refreshing, too. She hasn't washed her face since yesterday.

Emlyn digs the water-filtration system out of her pack. She kneels and plunges the first bag into the water, filling it. "Tyler," she says, trying to piece together the best way to say what she needs to say, "I need to ask you something. I need you to be realistic. And honest."

He frowns. "Okay?"

"Those traps. They're specialized. As in, not just anyone could set them. I know how to set a snare. I know how to set up a deadfall. But that, what we saw in that valley, those things were a different level." She hangs the full bag and hooks up the second one. "We have to assume it was him. I mean—" She waves her hand around, indicating the remoteness of their location. "—who else would it be, right? At the same time, something was wrong, there." She shakes her head. "That's not how you set up a trapline. It was . . . it was something else."

"Something else?"

She nods. "A message, maybe. A warning? A means of showing off? So I guess what I need you to think about is why. Why would Bush have set them. And Tyler, I need you to level with me." She tries to think of the best way to word this. "I know the online version of Bush and Janessa is all fun and love and adventure. But it can't have been just that, all the time, it never is. So, I guess what I'm asking is, did they fight? Was there another side to their relationship? A side that maybe only people close to them might see? A dark side?" She reaches for the Platypus and presses water through.

A dimness passes over his face. "They fought, I guess. Everyone fights, right? And everyone has a dark side."

"I mean did Bush have a temper, or a tendency toward violence? I mean is there any way he might've hurt her?" She thinks back to that footprint by the van, a foot sliding. Or being dragged.

He swears under his breath. "I don't know." Tyler plunges his hat into the stream and swishes it back and forth. He takes a deep breath, and lifts his eyes. Pines sway overhead as a breeze sweeps through the valley. Pollen cones from the lodgepoles drift downward, showering both of them. Emlyn waits for an answer, but Tyler is silent.

"You know," he says at last, "I went through a religious phase, after we broke up."

"Really?" The thought surprises her. A tiny pollen cone lands on her knee.

He nods. "Sort of. There was a Bible in my room at rehab, and I picked it up. I would just open it and read it. Sometimes I wrote down the verses on the stationery they gave us. I even memorized a few. It's not for me, religion, but still: there's a lot of wisdom in that book."

Emlyn wonders where this is going.

"There's one verse that always stuck with me."

She looks at him, waiting.

"'The heart is deceitful above all things, and desperately wicked: who can know it?' That's Jeremiah 17:9."

The words unsettle her, churning along her skin. She frowns. "What are you saying?"

"I guess I'm saying if there's one thing I know for certain, it's that you can never really know a person." He wrings the water from his hat, gives it a shake. The droplets dance across the stream. "You know what they *want* you to know."

The truth of this prickles and burns. All those years of Tyler dipping in and out of addiction, all the massive lows: she never told a soul. Not the neighbors, not her mother. In fact, she did the opposite. She covered for him, she lied, just like she'd done for her parents when she was a kid. She fabricated health problems to defend the ambulances. She invented work trips to explain the long periods when Tyler was in rehab and wasn't around. Why? What was it that had made her do those things? Shame? Protectiveness? She certainly didn't know then, and, she realizes, she still doesn't know.

Tyler slides his hat back on his head and rises. "And even when you think you know someone, they can surprise you. In good and bad ways. They impress you, they delight you. And they can also betray you. Hurt you." He grabs his Platypus and plunges it into the water, filling it up. "Leave you."

Emlyn squeezes the last of the dirty water through the filtration system.

"So I guess I'm saying, yes." He closes his eyes. "There's a chance." Emlyn looks at him and sees that his lips are trembling. "There's a chance that maybe he would hurt her."

FIVE YEARS AGO

EMLYN does not keep her promise to Janessa to steer clear of Tyler.

When he calls and asks her out for ice cream, Emlyn says yes. And when he invites her to his family's cabin at Patten Lake for the weekend, she says yes again. She still hasn't had a chance to tell Janessa that she has decided to disregard her request—well, that's not true. It's not that she hasn't had a chance. She's avoided telling Janessa; she's largely avoided her altogether. She doesn't want to face her wrath, or disapproval, or whatever the confession might spark. For the first time in a long time, she lies, the old habit returning with a bewildering ease. She builds elaborate tales of her boss's unreasonable demands. She feigns a virus, she complains of a sprained ankle.

The whole time, she has a feeling Janessa knows the truth, anyway.

JANESSA posts a reel to Instagram. Two tweens, hunkered over a board game. Two teens, faces pressed close, knee-deep in crystal-blue water. Two young kids, red-cheeked and bundled in winter gear, stacking blocks of snow. And the last one, two young adults: the girl looking sloppy and kissing the boy not quite on the mouth, the boy grinning at the camera, obviously taking the photo.

The caption:

> Happy Birthday, @tylerthestone! From playing Boggle in the basement to snorkeling in Waimea Bay, from building snow forts in the yard to hiking in the Alps, we've done it all. Thick or thin, rain or shine, you've been there. You know you'll always be my one and only. Love you forever. xx, Janessa

Emlyn rolls through the photos again and again. She has no right to be mad about this. Or frustrated, or hurt, or confused. She and Tyler have been spending a lot of time together, but they haven't spoken a word about titles or expectations. He hasn't even kissed her. And this post from Janessa? What does it even mean, anyway? Is she being sweet and genuine, or is this some sort of weird ploy to mark her territory? Should Emlyn say something? Should she ask Janessa for clarification? How is she supposed to navigate the swamp of feelings she now finds herself stuck in? She doesn't even know where to begin.

But when Janessa invites Emlyn to go to the hot springs she's been talking about, Emlyn agrees. She can't stand living in limbo any longer. She can't lie to Janessa forever. She has to sort this out, before it's too late.

Janessa arrives in her father's Porsche Cayenne. They go through town with all its crosswalks and stoplights, then Janessa swings onto a national forest road, and they start to climb. The road is narrow, and when another car approaches, Janessa pulls over, hugging the hillside, to let it pass. She is chipper today, relentless with the small talk, and this makes Emlyn suspicious. Is Janessa buttering Emlyn up before she begins some sort of indictment? Or worse, should Emlyn brace herself for some type of confession? Janessa has always had feelings for Tyler; they've finally gotten together; she hopes Emlyn can understand?

Janessa veers into a small pullout. "Here we are!" she says. She grabs a towel from the back seat, and the two of them cross the road to where a small stream bubbles over the rocks. Janessa tugs off her shorts and T-shirt to a red bikini, and Emlyn strips to her high-necked navy suit.

"Okay," Janessa says, pointing toward the stream, "the trick here is to get the temperature just right. The cold water from the stream is too cold, and the hot water from the springs is too hot." She places her clothes on a large boulder and then gingerly steps into the stream and squeals. "Too cold!" She bends and wriggles her fingers in a small eddy to her right. "Too hot." She picks up a rock and stacks it behind her, then picks up another and another, letting the hot water mix with the cold. Rock by rock, she builds a small round pool, just big enough for the two of them. "But, with just a little bit of tweaking, it can be absolutely divine." She slips in her toe and closes her eyes and grins. "Perfect."

She slowly slides into the water, submerging herself to her shoulders, and Emlyn follows. The smell of sulfur rises from the water, pungent in her nose.

"So," Janessa says after a moment, "I hope this won't be awkward, but we need to talk about Tyler."

Emlyn pulls her legs to her chest. She clears her throat. "I saw your happy birthday message," she ventures, steadying herself. She can spin the narrative on this, she thinks. She can steer how things go. "That was sweet. If not a little confusing."

"Confusing?" Janessa leans back against a rock. "Tyler and I have always been close, you know that."

"Close *friends,* sure. But, 'you'll always be my one and only'? And 'love you forever'?" She doesn't mean for her voice to turn shrill, but it does, she hears it.

"I knew it!" Janessa snaps, smacking the water with her palm. "I knew you two were sneaking around behind my back, and I knew you'd be upset when you saw that. I knew you couldn't keep quiet about it."

Emlyn frowns, mystified. "You baited me?"

"I baited both of you," Janessa says with a smug smile. "And you both took it. Tyler called me and asked me to take it down. He said he didn't want anyone to get the wrong idea." She folds her arms across her chest. "And by 'anyone,' he clearly meant you."

Emlyn's heart quickens.

Janessa takes a deep breath. "We talked about this, Emmie. I thought we agreed you wouldn't see him anymore."

Emlyn is silent. She feels like a teenager who's just been caught scrambling into an upstairs window after curfew. "About that . . ."

Janessa raises an eyebrow, waiting.

Emlyn adjusts her position in the pool, nervous. "Well, you told me not to see him. You said I shouldn't. But technically, I didn't agree to anything."

"Emmie."

She knows she must be brave. "The thing is—you don't get to do that. You don't get to tell me who I can date, or not date. What to do or not do."

Janessa rolls her eyes. "I don't. Tell you what to do."

"You do. A lot. It's like, who you are."

"Well, if I do, it's only because I care about you and want what's best for you, you know that. And the thing is—Tyler is no good for you."

"I know, I know. His charm wears off, he's trouble. But I need more than that to just walk away from this." She looks at her friend. "I really like him, Janessa."

Janessa seems to contemplate this. "Of course you do. And I wish I could be happy for you. I really do. But—" She props her sunglasses on her head and rubs her eyes. "How do I put this? Right now you feel like you're Tyler's everything. Like you're all that matters. And that feels . . . amazing, right?"

"Well, yeah."

"That's how it is with him. He fixates, obsesses. It'll be like that for a bit. But after a while, it won't be."

Emlyn bristles at this assumption. "You don't know that."

"I do. I've known Tyler since we were babies. We went to preschool together. Camp, a thousand summer afternoons, New Year's Eve, everything. And for over twenty years I've seen it enough times to know. In third grade, it was baseball. In eighth grade, it was Lydia Ferrer. Ninth grade, Valerie Tobias. Tenth grade, soccer, first half of the year. Jenny Shultz, second half."

Emlyn shakes her head. "Nobody's in high school anymore, Janessa."

"Fine, I won't get into Tyler's past. That's his story to tell. What I'm saying is that at some point he'll . . . move beyond you. You'll no longer be enough."

Janessa's words set fire to every emotional pain receptor in Emlyn's body. They strike up every insecurity, light up every ugly thing about herself she has ever believed. Is there any other thing her friend could've said that would be more heartbreaking?

"I won't be enough," she whispers, and when she says it aloud, she hears it more as a statement than a question.

Janessa seems to recognize her misstep, and she reaches for Emlyn's hand. "That came out wrong. It's not what I meant."

Emlyn sits silent for a moment. She seems to float away from her own body, upward. From on high she looks down. There is a bubbling stream. There is a very pretty girl, vivacious and bold, and a less pretty girl, timorous and unsure. For a long time, that very pretty girl has gripped that less pretty girl tight with her allure. She has prompted and prodded; she has molded and formed. This is who they are. They've not been unhappy, this way. But, all at once Emlyn sees: in the end, that less pretty girl is still quiet and mousy and subordinate, and that's how things will always be.

Unless she decides, *No.* Unless she pulls away.

The stream swirls and sings, the steam rises between them.

Emlyn tugs her hand free.

"I'm sorry, Emmie. I don't know why I put it that way. That was dumb, it was out of line. What I meant is—getting involved with a guy like Tyler, that's not who you are."

That assured, high-handed response pushes Emlyn over the edge. She feels her self-control lashing away from her, her anger welling up. "Not who *I am*? Did you really just say that? You've got a lot of nerve, trying to tell me about who I am or am not."

Janessa's jaw falls open. "What's that supposed to mean?"

"I mean I never know which flavor of Janessa I'll get. Feisty, vindictive Janessa? Bubbly, flirty Janessa? Cool, mysterious Janessa? It's hard to keep up. And which one are you, anyway? Who are you?" She picks up a rock from the stack behind them and sets it next to her, diverting more cold water into the pool. "The sad thing is, I don't think you know the answer to that any more than I do."

Janessa winces, but only for a second. "Oh, please. You're one to talk. You've followed me around like a dog since the minute I saved you from those creeps at Bumpy's, hanging on my every word, waiting for me to tell you what we're doing and where we're going, everything."

"And what choice did I have? 'Don't cut your hair.' 'Wear this dress.' 'Give this guy a chance.' 'Don't get involved.' You've always kept me under your thumb, just like you do anyone else who dares to get close to you."

Janessa's eyes grow wide. She blinks, taken aback. "How can you say that? That's not true at all."

"It is. You might not like it, you might not even see it, but it is. You use your money, your looks, your—" She searches for a word. "—*allure* to manipulate people, to control everyone around you. You always have." Emlyn can't help it: she's angry, still pulsing with the pain of Janessa's cruel words. Somewhere deep inside her, she knows she is pushing into perilous territory, that she will look back on this conversation and regret so much of it, but there is a strange, seductive appeal in recognizing that she, too, can exact pain, and this is what she latches on to. "It's not just me, either. Tyler said the same thing."

Janessa's lips part, but she is quiet. Something unfamiliar flashes across her face. Surprise? Unease? Hurt? She tucks her hair behind her ears, her cheeks growing red. "Is that how it is now?"

There. That's it: the wound Emlyn was hoping to inflict, searing and raw.

Janessa folds her hands across her lap. For a long time she sits still, head bowed. A gust of wind picks up, and the aspens shimmer overhead. Emlyn's shoulders stipple with goose bumps. A tear slips from Janessa's eye and falls down her cheek. She tucks her head to her shoulder and wipes her face. Later, Emlyn will remember this moment, so remarkable, so singular: Janessa chastised, quiet. Emlyn has never seen her friend so diminished, and for a moment she considers backpedaling.

But then Janessa takes a deep breath, and in a moment she is herself again. "This was never about me. I wish you could see that. I wish—I wish you could accept that I have always looked out for you, always stood by your side." She rises from the stream, her long, tan legs at Emlyn's eye level. Emlyn sees at once that the tables have turned again, that each of them has resumed her rightful place: Emlyn below and Janessa above. "But you don't see that. You can't. Because you are jealous and nihilistic and suspicious, and, sad as it is, you will probably never be happy. Tyler will break you. And one day you'll understand what I mean." In her red swimsuit she scrambles across the stream to the rock and grabs her towel.

Emlyn watches Janessa storm across the dirt road to the Porsche. For a moment she wonders if Janessa will drive off and leave her stranded at the hot springs, but Janessa just sits in the car. She does not leave, but she does not say a word to Emlyn the whole way back to town. She drives too fast, spinning gravel at each bend, the Porsche holding tight to the curves, Emlyn lurching and leaning. By the time they pull into her parking lot, she's carsick.

She reaches into the back seat and grabs her backpack. Janessa stares straight ahead. Emlyn opens the door. "I'll call you tomorrow, okay?"

Janessa does not look in her direction as she climbs out. As soon as she shuts the door, Janessa drives away, peeling out as she tears onto the street.

Panic strikes Emlyn's heart. She stands in the parking lot, towel wrapped at her waist, hair dripping down her back. The sun has begun its quick descent behind the mountains, and she shivers.

Has she just made a terrible mistake? The two of them have never had a fight like this. Small disagreements, tiny skirmishes, yes. But this was more than a tussle. This was a blowup. What if Janessa is so upset with her that they never speak again? The thought terrifies her. Should she call her right now? She could take back her words, apologize, admit she was speaking out of anger. She could agree to Janessa's request; she could never see Tyler again.

No.

Emlyn spins toward her building. She climbs the steps, backpack slung over her shoulder. Friendships hinge on honesty and trust. Friendships allow each person to be who she wants to be. Janessa has no right to ask her not to see Tyler. All the vague references to what is best for her and how Tyler will ruin her are probably just another ploy to control her. Emlyn can date who she wants; she can handle the consequences, if there are any. She's twenty-three, a grown woman, a college graduate, magna cum laude. She is tired of bending to all of Janessa's whims and requests. She must forge her own way.

She pulls open the heavy door to the building and climbs two more flights of stairs to her apartment. She tugs off her wet swimsuit and takes a hot shower, the sulfur smell rising from her body. She dries herself off and heats a can of soup. She picks up her phone and types Tyler a message: *Want to come over?*

FIFTEEN

"SO, now what?" Tyler asks.

They've finished getting water and are all packed up.

"We have to go back to those traps."

Dread flickers across his face.

"I know, I don't want to, either, but we have to assume Janessa and Bush were there. So we need to take a closer look." Emlyn hefts the backpack onto her shoulders. "We have water, we have food. Hopefully we can pick up their trail and make a big push, close the gap a bit."

Tyler lifts his eyes to the treetops and nods.

As they walk, Emlyn keeps thinking of her friend. Their terrible fight at the hot springs, its painful lessons. That some things you say cannot be taken back. That friendships can shatter over a single argument. That no relationship is immune to ending.

But also, Janessa, hair dyed pink, tugging Emlyn into the icy cold water of an alpine lake. Janessa punching that guy at a party, years ago. Janessa sinking her teeth into a ghost pepper from a stand along Route 66 in New

Mexico, tears streaming down her face as she laughs and screams and fans her lips. That glimmering boldness that Emlyn simultaneously feared and envied.

Soon, though, Emlyn's mind veers into the hazardous territory of her imagination: Janessa being forced into the woods. Janessa trying to fight off a raging Bush. Janessa in a heap in the wilderness.

So many unfortunate facts, so many vexing statistics, and as they trek back to the traps, Emlyn thinks of all of them. That if a man wants to overpower a woman, he usually can. That sometimes, it only takes one tiny mistake to put a whole party in danger. That eighty-five percent of people who go missing in the wilderness are found in the first twelve hours. Ninety-seven percent in the first twenty-four. That when a person goes missing for longer than that—well, it's because they are going to be very hard to find. Emlyn pictures the thawing chicken on the countertop, the bananas, the unfinished to-do list, all the signs that this trip into the wilderness was not part of a well-laid plan.

How quickly fear and panic can flash their teeth. How easily her imagination can get the better of her. Emlyn's tired of hauling the heavy pack, she's hot. She can feel the start of a blister forming on her left heel. She knows from experience that even the smallest pain can heighten her anxieties; that, out here, despair is always just a few steps away from discomfort, and she must keep her emotions in check. She has to remain optimistic. ("Hopeful and confident about the future.") She remembers memorizing the definition in the crook of the tree, back when she was a kid. It's a word that has always felt slippery to her, impossible to hold. A word she would never use to describe herself.

But there are ways around this, when optimism eludes: tricks she has taught herself over two decades of heartache and misanthropy. She forces herself to focus on what they do know. That both Bush and Janessa are fit and competent. That according to every single record of their life together, the two of them are in love and happy. That Janessa is strong and smart and confident. That she has always been able to fend for herself. That whatever they run into, whatever they find, Tyler has requested help. A search party is on its way. They are not alone out here.

A half a mile back to the valley of traps. The two of them exit the woods and step into the field, vultures scattering at their arrival, rising and flapping upward. Emlyn hears the rush of their great wings. She circles back to their starting point, the place where they encountered the first trap. She walks beyond that, weighing the scene. In their panic she and Tyler had tramped back and forth, footprints going in every direction, making a mess of any discernible pathway. But, as she stands back and assesses, there are two possible routes that someone could have taken from this point. First, the main trail. Second, the path she and Tyler made as they pushed into the woods. Grass bent, a skinny walkway right where they went. She squats, searching the dirt for sign. Footprints everywhere: too messy. She follows the trail, hurrying past the assortment of dead animals. The stench makes her gag, and she tugs her sleeve over her hand and holds it to her nose.

Tyler stands and stares at the doe, and she skirts around him, picking up the trail. Again she squats, looking. There. And there. Human footprints, but animals, too. Mule deer, elk. Coyote. All crisscrossed, a maze. She rises, considering what lies ahead. The trail cuts through the valley's center for another quarter mile; then, where the valley narrows, the steep mountains folding close, it veers to the right and disappears. At that point, she remembers from the map, the trail begins a steep ascent up and over a mountain to an alpine lake. They could get there tomorrow if all goes smoothly. She steps to her left, just off the trail, takes a few steps forward, then kneels again.

There. The Danner print from before, back at the van. The larger Kenetrek print as well. No Merrells that she can find. Beside one of the footprints, she presses her palm into the dirt. She slides the pack from her shoulders, leans close to the ground, compares the handprint to the footprint. The edges are similar, not worn or eroded. This tells her what she needs to know. They were here, and not that long ago.

PEOPLE tend to have a rhythm when they walk, and if you're looking for it, you can usually find it. Emlyn walks to the right of the trail, studying the frequency of the tracks, working to gauge that rhythm. Not surprisingly, the larger tracks indicate a slightly longer stride than the smaller ones. Taller person, longer legs, bigger stride. But, as far as she can tell, no sign of struggle, nothing to suggest that the person with the smaller tracks is being forced along. She looks up, walks, tries not to think about forcing her own rhythm. Tyler lags behind.

They come to the point where the trail bends right, swinging into a different valley. At first, the ascent is barely noticeable, cutting through the valley and up the hillside. But it quickly changes to more challenging terrain. Emlyn stops, takes a drink. The backs of her legs burn.

Tyler pauses beside her. "That way?" he asks, pointing to the steep trail ahead.

"Unfortunately, yeah, I think so." She looks at him, does her best to appraise his state, both physical and mental. "Have a granola bar." She fishes through the pocket at her waist. "And here." She unwraps an energy chew and hands it to him. "Electrolytes." She eats one, too, then reaches out and squeezes his elbow. "Come on, we can do this."

The trail is a thin path worn into the grass, and it switches back and forth up the hillside. Into another copse of pines. The terrain is so steep her hips and knees pinch. Again she laments the overpacked backpack, the additional weight, the long, treacherous tumble she would take if she were to lose her balance. She looks straight ahead. One step, two. The sun catches a strand of spiderweb, white and glistening, and she stops. The web has been broken, and it hangs in a tangle of thin filaments.

She turns and waits for Tyler to catch up. "Look." She points at the web. "It's been broken. Something—someone—walked through." She steps closer and finds the spider, at work. "There, see? The spider's rebuilding it."

"I never would've even seen it," Tyler says, leaning closer. "I mean I would never think to look."

"'Aerial spoor.' That's the term. Broken branches, bent grass."

"You're incredible." He shakes his head.

Emlyn runs a pine branch between her finger and thumb, the branch rough, the needles smooth. "Thanks," she mutters. She's ashamed to realize how much this compliment pleases her, and she turns away before he can see her face.

On the trail, elk scat, elk prints. Emlyn again remembers her hunting license, tucked in the drawer of her Airstream. The Mathews bow in the storage compartment beneath the bed. Her push-ups. Varden, last summer, standing behind her, breath on her neck, showing her how to shoot. Where is Varden right now? She pictures him tending to his work duties. Fielding questions from kids at the visitor center, trekking into the backcountry to check a trail camera and hoping to catch his beloved wolves, cutting back an overgrown trail. What did Rev tell him? Is he upset? Worried? Most importantly, does her being out here jeopardize everything with him? Those fanciful imaginings of Christmas mornings and storybooks on a couch—is the possibility of those fantasies slipping through her fingers? This question is quickly followed by doubt: Does she even stand a chance with a guy like Varden? Is there such a thing as real, lasting happiness? She steals a glance at Tyler, who trails a few steps behind. A more troubling thought emerges: What is it that she really wants, anyway?

EMLYN and Tyler set up camp. They are even faster this time, anxious for rest.

"Dinner?" Tyler asks.

"I'll go for the risotto," she calls from inside her tent, unrolling her sleeping pad and letting it inflate. She gives her sleeping bag a good shake, fluffing it.

Tonight, she gathers the sticks and gets the fire going. "Your tent," Tyler says, pouring hot water into the risotto. "How much does it weigh?"

Emlyn shaves pieces of cedar bark with her pocketknife. "Four pounds, maybe a little more." There are better, lighter models out there, but they cost more, and for the most part, hers works fine.

Tyler stirs the risotto and seals the bag. "My tent sleeps two. You could stash yours here. We could grab it on our way back through." He clicks on the hot water again. "Just an offer."

She piles the shavings into a small pile, holds Tyler's lighter to it, and ignites the tinder. The first piece catches fire, and she leans close to blow lightly. She props up a few small sticks into a tepee. She's trying to seem occupied, but her mind whirls at the prospect, rolling between angst and desire. "Thanks," she says, then raises her eyes. "I'll think about it."

"I'll be a gentleman."

She raises an eyebrow. "Oh, I have my doubts about that."

"Okay, fair enough. I would *try*. But—you know what they say about old habits . . ." He hands her the meal, flashing a smile. The flames lick up and up.

She feels a flush crawling up her neck.

"You still reading poetry?" Tyler asks, and immediately Emlyn thinks again of Varden: his bookcase full of poetry and his Moleskine notebook.

"Some," she says, propping a small piece of wood onto the fire.

"I always liked that about you, you know. One minute you were helping me change out a bad spark plug, the next minute you were reading Mary Oliver."

She opens her chicken risotto, the steam pouring out.

"I didn't really get it," Tyler says. "The poems. You know I'm not smart like that. I didn't . . . connect. I liked the way you did, though, and I liked to listen to you when you'd read."

She pulls her fork from her backpack and blows on a bite of food. She's made these rehydrated meals for herself back home, and she understands they're not actually as delicious as they taste in a moment like this, after a long day of hiking. The fire pitching warmth, the night's cold pressing in. But right now, she's sure she's never tasted anything so good. The salt, the calories. She finishes quickly.

"You ever think about it?" Tyler asks, crossing his legs. He has swapped out his trucker hat for a blue beanie.

"Think about what?"

"About all the what-ifs."

Emlyn takes a deep breath and pokes the fire with her stick. "Let's not do this."

"I'm just asking a question here."

At first she remains quiet, but finally, she answers. "Of course I think about it."

"Me, too." Tyler unlaces his boots, slips them off, places them by his side. "Do you ever think—do you ever think maybe there's still a chance for us? After all we've been through. We've both obviously changed. We've both grown. I don't mean right now. But someday?"

She thinks of Varden, standing in the snow last winter, hauling wood to the cabin. Snowshoeing up an old logging road to show her where he'd seen a wolverine the week before. Varden baking an apple pie, his mother's recipe, for Thanksgiving.

She can hardly believe that after just two days with Tyler, it not only feels possible, but desirable: getting back together, starting over, trying. That quivering in her chest, that sense of want—she doesn't like how it seems to be growing in intensity with each passing hour. But she also can't deny that it's happening.

She doesn't answer Tyler. She can't.

For years the questions flogged her, a flock of birds, hungry and hostile. She fought them off and then, eventually, buried them, because there was no way to get answers, not with her commitment to cut ties, and because the questions were too perilous to be let loose, to soar and flap their ugly wings. But now, in the wilderness, with her heart tiptoeing closer and closer toward Tyler and all that they used to be, Emlyn understands: no matter how this pans out between them, there are things she has to know, and things she needs to say.

She takes a deep breath. "How long had you been using, before that day in the woods?"

Tyler tilts his head skyward. "A month, maybe. I don't remember."

"I didn't see it." She bites her lip. There were signs, of course, and with time she got better at looking for them. The locked bathroom door, the anxiety. The odd shifts in sleeping: Tyler wide awake at midnight, sleeping well past noon.

"I got very good at hiding it."

She pokes at a log, even though the fire's burning just fine. She rolls up her meal and tosses it into the flames. "Why didn't you come after me?" she whispers, at last. "I mean, once you were better. Why didn't you reach out? Why didn't you find me?" A tear slips from her eye. Another and another. This, Emlyn realizes, is the central question. The hang-up, the thing that has haunted her, and now that she has finally said it, more words shake loose. "Do you know how many times I heard a car pull up and thought it was you? Months and months. I waited. I hoped. How pathetic is that. But the thought that you could just—be done, be over me, us, just like that." She shakes her head, her whole body trembling now, her voice a fraying wire. "Two years we were together. You never said sorry. You never even said goodbye. Didn't you want to know where I was? Whether I was okay?"

"I knew you were okay."

She raises her eyes.

"That's the thing. I drove up, one day, that first summer. I was clean by then, I was different. I had fantasies that I was gonna win you back, somehow. Show you I'd changed. That I could be better." He swallows hard, his mouth tightening with pain. "There was some event at that inn where you were staying. A wedding, maybe? I saw you. You were with an older woman, and a guy. You were wearing a blue dress."

That day: Emlyn knows it. Not a wedding but an anniversary party. Oliver and his wife, Janet, had renewed their vows along the banks of the Salmon. But for a moment Emlyn is confused. She sieves through her memories, both real and invented. All the times she'd imagined it—Tyler rounding the bend in the river, slipping out of sight; Tyler ducking away from her at a music festival; and now this, Tyler walking through the field in defeat, a bouquet upside down at his thigh. Could it be? That one time, it was real? "I don't understand. If you came to find me, why didn't you?"

Tyler stares into the fire. "There was this look on your face." He swallows hard, the words catching in his throat. "That look. I almost didn't recognize it because—" Here, his composure skids away from him, and he chokes up. "Because I hadn't seen it for so long. It was happiness. Peace. You were happy." He wipes his eyes. "And I knew in that moment that *that* is what I had taken from you, those years we were together. You'd gotten it back, somehow, and I sure as hell wasn't gonna take it again."

She pulls her sleeves over her fingertips and buries her face in the soft fabric. "And now?"

"Now? Now, well. I always promised myself I would tell you I was sorry, if I ever had the chance. So I guess you could say that was planned." He shakes his head. "The rest of it. Well, I didn't expect it to be like this, between us. I didn't expect to feel . . . all of this."

For a long time they sit together, watching the fire burn down to coals.

At last Emlyn rises from her seat. "I think I'm gonna turn in," she says.

Tyler stands and steps closer, blocking her way. "Em, I just want to say—I wasn't over you, then." He reaches for her hand and squeezes tight. "I'm not sure I ever will be."

A warmth swells through her. Tyler's words, but also his closeness. Their waists touch. His face is just a few inches away, and she looks up at him. For a moment their eyes lock. His eyes drop to her lips. She won't inch closer, she knows that, but she also knows that she wants him to do it. Make that move, kiss her. So much about this feels right.

Tyler leans close and kisses her forehead, and the two of them stand like that, bodies pressed together, and she is shuttled backward, to their first date, the parking lot of her crummy sublet, that feeling like she'd brushed wings with something glittering and gorgeous. Something surges between them. Not just desire. Not just the old chemistry, but a whole atlas of feelings and memories. All that they've weathered. All that might lie ahead.

Emlyn isn't a person who believes in a soulmate, in the idea that there is just one person out there who can complete you. But she knows she and Tyler shared a connection that was deep and unique. And there's no denying it: that connection still exists.

The fire pops, and a litany of sparks hisses toward the sky. Emlyn takes a small step back, squeezing Tyler's hand and then letting it go. "We've got a big day ahead of us," she says, her voice hoarse. She unzips her tent, slides out of her hiking boots, and crawls inside. She slips into the sleeping bag, the nylon cold and smooth. A tingle rolls along her skin. Has she just made a mistake, in stepping away? Because things are different, she is different, Tyler is different, and maybe the universe is saying, *You two really are meant to be.* When Rev said "trust," is this what she meant?

FIVE YEARS AGO

TYLER and Emlyn have just come back from a day of fly-fishing on the Big Wood River, and Tyler is in the bathroom of her apartment, trying to scrub the smell of fish from his hands. Emlyn sits in the living room on the ugly couch and looks out the window at the parking lot. Midday in the summer, it is nearly empty, but a car pulls in, and Emlyn recognizes it right away: Janessa's Maserati. She rises and darts to the window. It's been two days since her awful conversation with Janessa at the hot springs.

Tyler comes out of the bathroom. He sniffs his hands and arms. "I think I still smell like fish guts, sorry."

Emlyn stares out the window. Janessa pulls in next to Tyler's truck and climbs out. She's wearing a baseball cap and sunglasses. She walks over to Tyler's truck and stands in front of it for a moment, hands on her hips; then she turns and looks up at where Emlyn is standing. Emlyn gasps and steps back.

"What is it?" Tyler says, walking toward the window.

Emlyn grabs his shirt. "Don't." She dashes over to the door and slides the lock, holding her finger to her lips. "It's Janessa. She's here."

Tyler grins. "Good. Maybe she'll know how to get this smell out."

"No!" Emlyn whisper-yells. Two stories below, she hears the loud screech of the main door opening. Thud, thud, thud: Janessa climbing the stairs. Emlyn flips off the light and gestures for him to hide in the pantry. Tyler pretends to yell and carry on, but slips toward the kitchen.

A knock at the door. Emlyn peers through the peephole. Janessa, distorted through the fisheye lens, arms folded. Silence. Then she knocks again.

"Em?"

Emlyn ducks away from the peephole.

"Emmie, let me in."

Click, click, click, click. The door handle crunches left and right.

"I know you're here."

Emlyn sneaks over to the pantry and presses herself close to Tyler. He tilts his head toward the door and gestures, hands open, *Why*? Emlyn shakes her head. She hasn't told him about the fight with Janessa. Tyler waves her off and acts like he's going for the door. She grabs his wrist. He wraps his arms around himself and wiggles, middle school style, like two people hugging and kissing. Emlyn stifles a laugh. He mimes a robot. He walks like an Egyptian, he does the Macarena. Emlyn covers her mouth to keep herself quiet. She tugs at his T-shirt and holds her pointer finger to her lips, and he stops and steps closer. A thrill, wild and rancorous, rushes through her. It's not just Tyler, so close she can feel his breath on her cheeks. It's that, for the first time ever, Emlyn is the chosen; Janessa is not.

Janessa thumps the door with her palm. "Emlyn? Open the door."

They've been seeing each other almost every day, but Tyler hasn't kissed her. Emlyn worries that maybe the "chemistry" she feels is all in her head. Maybe they're just friends. She's never been good at reading social situations, and she's far too shy to make a move to test the waters.

Tyler's eyes are locked on hers. He leans closer. "Yes?" he whispers.

In some cavern of Emlyn's brain, she sees Marlene, hauling groceries from the Subaru into the workshop and stopping to offer one of her rare tidbits of motherly advice. *Never kiss a boy you don't love.* But here against the pantry, Emlyn nods. "Yes."

Tyler presses his lips to hers. He tastes faintly of bubble gum and when he holds her face in his palms he smells like fish and lemons, but somehow, there is nothing revolting about this moment at all. Her heart thumps so loudly she is sure Tyler hears it.

"Emlyn!" Janessa hollers, slamming her palm against the door with a loud thud.

The kiss breaks, the spell ruptures. She pulls away, but Tyler finds her hand and holds it.

Emlyn hears the sounds of Janessa's footsteps fuming down the stairs. She hears the quick chirp of the car door unlocking, the slam, the roar of the Maserati as Janessa peels out of the parking lot. She'll call her later, Emlyn tells herself, but when she does, Janessa doesn't pick up.

TEN days later, Emlyn resumes Sunday brunch with Janessa's grandmother. The week before, she'd lied and said she had another commitment—she was nervous about seeing Janessa and wanted to give her some space. But this week, Betts herself called and said, "Listen, I know the two of you had a little tiff, but that's no reason to ruin an old woman's Sunday, so you better work it out."

At brunch, Janessa is all smiles. She has dyed her hair dark brown, and it's been snipped into a sharp and startling lob, shiny and straight. To highlight the cut, she wears a gorgeous matte lipstick in a deep red. Janessa was adorable with her stringy, long blond hair, but she is stunning as a brunette. She looks older, more refined. Confident.

"I'm moving to D.C.," Janessa announces, as she bites into a croissant.

Emlyn's heart drops.

Betts raises an eyebrow. She taps a manicured fingernail against her champagne flute and coughs out a small laugh. "Darling, don't joke."

"I'm not."

Overhead, the Idaho sun is deliciously warm.

Betts tilts her head, and her diamond earrings catch the light. She gestures toward her luscious green yard, perfected by sprinklers and two gardeners, toward the grand ski slope that stretches high beyond the hedge. "Why on earth would you ever want to leave heaven for that hellhole?" She shudders for dramatic effect. "Truly, Janessa. You know the entire East Coast is a vampire. It'll suck the life right out of you, mark my words."

Janessa sighs. "I need a change." She reaches for her sunglasses and slides them on. "I need to turn over a new leaf."

Emlyn can hardly believe what she's hearing.

"Oh, Janessa," Betts huffs, "you're being impetuous, as usual. Dramatic. Take a vacation. Go to Europe. And then come home. Everything you need is right here, in Idaho."

"Not everything." Janessa plucks her cloth napkin from her lap and dabs her lips, then turns to Emlyn. "Not anymore."

Emlyn feels the sting Janessa intends. She knows this is about Tyler. She knows it's about the mean things she said at the hot springs, she knows it's about ignoring Janessa at her apartment, and she hates the possibility that maybe she has derailed Janessa's life and sent her friend in an entirely new direction. Guilt boils in her throat. She knows what it's like to have someone you love and trust set you adrift.

For a moment, she considers reaching across the table, grabbing her friend's hand, and apologizing. She could beg Janessa not to go because, deep in her gut, she knows this friendship has ruptured, or is about to, and she isn't sure she can tolerate such a sudden and absolute denouement. Can she survive without her friend? Who is she, without Janessa?

But.

Another part of Emlyn cannot shake the suspicion that she has been a pawn in Janessa's life for the past three years, compliant and convenient. She doesn't have to defend her romantic choices to Janessa; she doesn't need her approval. She doesn't have to answer every door, every phone call, every time Janessa decides she needs her. She doesn't have to acquiesce to every whim and demand. Maybe, Emlyn tells herself, this is a gift. Maybe some space and distance are exactly what the two of them need.

"I'm happy for you," Emlyn says, raising her glass, though even as the words come out, she knows they aren't true. She's sad, devastated, afraid.

Betts's jaw drops, and her shock quickly transforms to a scowl.

Janessa stares. She presses her red lips tight together and reaches for her own flute. Betts leans back in her chair, arms folded across her chest, refusing to join in.

Emlyn holds Janessa's eyes. "To turning over new leaves."

SOON Emlyn is with Tyler all the time. She sees him every day, she thinks of no one but him. They sketch plans for overland camper vans. They dream of three children, a golden retriever, a tabby cat.

Over the course of the summer, Emlyn occasionally presses letters into her phone, brief messages that gesture toward reconciliation: *I'm sorry. I miss you. Can we talk?* She never sends any of them, because the truth is—and this is what she must remind herself of, when that feeling of grief threatens to consume her—the very first time she tried to stand up for herself, push back, claim a tiny bit of autonomy, Janessa showed her true colors, storming out of the hot springs, and then pounding on her door like a lunatic. This is better, Emlyn tells herself; this is healthier. That dynamic of theirs may have worked in college, but it wasn't working anymore. Emlyn was different, then. Everything was. It's time for her to forge her own way.

Tyler is a poultice for the loss. A distraction.

"She's always been my number one," he says, by way of explanation. "And now she's not. It's hard on her, but she'll get over it."

Then, with little more than a perfunctory kiss on the cheek at her going-away party, Janessa is gone. Emlyn is sad, she continues to feel the great abyss of her friend's absence, but now she is deep in Tyler's orbit, held steady by his pull.

This is long before Tyler chases a high and leaves Emlyn in the woods. Before his accident in the Gila Wilderness, before the guilt that tethers her to him for years to come, before all that Janessa tried to warn her about turns out to be true.

SIXTEEN

A distant rumble. Not thunder, but something consuming, something more. It's everywhere. Emlyn and Tyler are heading downhill again, and a gray-white cloud rises from the valley below. Her first thought: Smoke? The skies have cleared today, and an endless swath of Idaho blue stretches overhead.

Tyler stops. He reaches out, grabs her sleeve. "What is it?" he asks, nodding toward the noise.

She shakes her head. "I'm not sure." People sometimes haul their ATVs and motorbikes out here. Rules exist that govern where, exactly, this is permitted, and technically, no motorized vehicles are permitted in any federally designated wilderness area. Still, that doesn't mean people always adhere to the guidelines. After all, the likelihood that you'll get caught—that anyone would even be around to see you breaking the rules, especially this far out—is slim. Emlyn stops, listening. No *vroom vroom vroom* of a dirt bike or four-wheeler. A herd?

She has watched videos of the great migrations of caribou trundling across the tundra, the elephants lumbering across the savanna. But what could possibly be rattling through a valley this deep in the Idaho wilderness?

They continue their descent, pressing closer to the noise and dust. After weighing out the pros and cons, she has left her tent behind. She's now four pounds lighter, but still, her knees pinch, her hips ache from the weight of her pack.

Soon, new sounds emerge. A cacophony of animal sounds. Hooves pummeling the dry earth, cries and moans and baas. Sheep!

The trail hugs the side of the mountain and veers north, toward that alpine lake, but Emlyn wants to see this, up close, and without explaining her intentions to Tyler, she heads toward the racket. At the edge of the woods, she and Tyler drop their packs and clamber onto a huge boulder. The sheep scuttle past, all hoof and wool, a thousand tufted humps as one shivering unit. A hundred yards away, a tall Great Pyrenees stops in its tracks, eyeing them with a wary look. It takes a step closer, chin lifted high, and barks. Then it trots off, redirecting a sheep that has pulled away from the flock, chasing it back into the fold.

"I've never seen them this close," Emlyn yells, her voice drowned by the thunder of hooves.

Every summer, thousands of sheep are herded north from Snake River farms, up into the mountains to graze in designated forage allotments, before heading back south to their farms in the fall. She's seen them from the roads. Once, she watched them from the Salmon, water swirling at her thighs. But this is different, this is transcendent. She slides off the rock. Tyler calls her name. She takes a cautious step, another, another. Slow. Soon she is in the midst of it. At first they halt and veer left, right, but then they simply lumber past, close. They graze against her knees; they press into her shins. She reaches out a palm. A sheep rushes beneath, its back, scratch and fluff, brushing her fingertips. She gasps, the joy of it, the thrill, sweeping through her like some dangerous magic. Dust rises up; the sheep throng closer. She looks at Tyler. He holds out a hand, and she reaches for it, grabs tight. He pulls her toward him, and in three quick leaps she is back on the rock.

She slumps onto her rear. Her pulse gallops hard, pounding beneath her jawline. Only now does she consider the foolishness of her move. She conjures headlines: WOMAN, 28, TRAMPLED BY HERD OF SHEEP. WOMAN, 28, TROUNCED BY LONG HISTORY OF BAD CHOICES. "You gonna tell me I shouldn't have done that?" she asks when she's caught her breath.

Tyler shakes his head. "I'm not gonna tell you what you should or shouldn't do." He reaches out his thumb and brushes dirt from her nose. "Besides, I know why you did it."

"Yeah?"

He nudges her. "You always liked a good rush just as much as I ever did. Only difference is, I was willing to admit it."

FIVE YEARS AGO

MUSIC booms from the parking lot, the bass rattling the windows of Emlyn's apartment. She tries to ignore it, leafing through a magazine. "Intergalactic," by the Beastie Boys, one of Janessa's old favorites. She rises from the couch and walks to the window to close it, and when she looks down, she sees an astronaut dancing on the sidewalk below. The astronaut moonwalks for a bit. They step forward in slow motion, feigning weightlessness, then turn toward the window and raise an arm. Emlyn waves back. The astronaut points to a heap of white clothing on the ground—a second costume—and motions for Emlyn to come down.

"Emlyn Anthony," Tyler says, when she gets outside, "we have a mission."

"Yeah?" She wrinkles her nose and squints in the bright light.

"I'm gonna take you to the moon."

She can't help but smile. "Is that your spaceship?" she asks, pointing to Tyler's truck.

"Come on, it's 'one small step for man, one giant leap for mankind.'" Tyler tugs the helmet from his head. "Cheesy?"

She laughs. "A little."

"Good." He steps closer and wraps his arms around her. "I promise you'll be over the moon."

She presses her face against his chest.

Tyler gestures toward the sky. "We'll aim for the moon. Even if we miss, we'll be among the stars."

"Please stop."

"Oh, I'm just getting started. You haven't even seen the full range of where I'm going with this. I'm gonna light up the night." He points to the astronaut outfit on the sidewalk. "That's for you."

She gathers her things quickly and then hops into the truck. They head south, to Craters of the Moon National Monument. Tyler loads a playlist of every song about the moon that he could find. "Moon River," "Dancin' in the Moonlight," R.E.M.'s "Man on the Moon."

Emlyn has never been to this place, even though it's not far away. At first, they drive around and explore the park, Tyler swinging the truck into every pullout.

They walk the skinny paved path that cuts across an endless sea of lava flow, hand in hand. "Two astronauts walked on the moon, back in 1969," Tyler says, "Neil Armstrong and Buzz Aldrin. They got all the glory. But there was a third one, did you know that?"

Emlyn tells him she's never really given it much thought.

"Someone had to stay behind and man the ship. Someone had to get them home. Michael Collins. They call him 'the forgotten astronaut.' He orbited alone, for twenty-two hours." Tyler stops and snaps a photo. "I've always thought, how incredible would that be, going to the far side of the moon, alone? I mean truly alone. He couldn't even connect with NASA, for part of the time. Imagine the grit it would take to do that."

Cinder cones punctuate the landscape, stretching tall. They scale the biggest one, the wind whipping around them at the top. In every direction, the black moonscape stretches on. The two of them clamber down into a large cave, headlamps on. Here, the air is cool. Emlyn runs her fingertips over the rough edges of the rocks. She leans close and studies the bright yellow and orange lichen peppering its surface. Tyler was right: it really does feel like they're on the moon.

Later, at the campground, Tyler insists they put on their astronaut costumes. The hot air has cooled now, though the rocks retain their warmth.

Fully costumed, Tyler purses his lips for a kiss, leans close, and bonks his helmet against hers. The plastic clinks. He tries again and again: *clink, clink.* He twists his head back and forth; he feigns desperation. Emlyn doubles over in laughter.

A lilac twilight settles over them.

They snap dozens of photos, smiling, leaping, posing with a tall American flag Tyler brought from home. When they get back, Tyler prints a giant picture of the two of them that they eventually hang in their living room. She prints a small one for herself and places it on her dresser in a fluorescent frame.

YEARS later, when Janessa sends Emlyn her things from Tyler's apartment, she will include the small photo. In those early days at Rev's, Emlyn will stare at it, sometimes, filled with an alarming mix of familiarity and strangeness. How is it that this day could feel so vivid to her, so real that she can remember an inordinate amount of detail, and yet, at the same time, feel so out of reach? *I was there,* she will think. *That was us, that was me. I was in love. We were happy, once.* But she will look at the photograph, and the people in it—decked in their white astronaut outfits, heads tipped close, with a purple sky stretched behind them—will seem like strangers.

SEVENTEEN

VOICES, a shriek floating up.

Emlyn freezes. Tyler, following too close, walks into her backpack. She presses a finger to her lips, holds her breath, but she hears nothing, the stillness returned.

"What is it?" Tyler whispers, leaning close, breath on her neck.

Silence.

"I thought I heard something."

She looks up, searching. A crow, maybe, throwing its squawk, high up in the treetops? Funny how the mind can play tricks when you're wanting to hear a certain something. It's happened when she's hunting, too. A twig breaking, leaves rustling. She'll convince herself it's a deer, heading her way, she'll be sure of it. Then it turns out to be a squirrel.

The lake is ahead, just beyond the trees, and Emlyn catches bright flashes of blue gleaming through the pines. The plan is to make camp there, clean up, fill their hydration bladders. Today's trek has been grueling, and she knows both of them need the rest. And, frankly, also a bath.

She continues walking. But there—again, voices.

"Did you hear that?" she says.

Tyler nods, eyes wide.

They sneak toward the lake, off trail now, the branches scraping their arms.

Emlyn tugs the pistol from the pocket where she stashed it, back in the valley of traps. She takes off her backpack and leans it against a tree, then motions for Tyler to do the same. She pulls her bear spray out and hands it to Tyler, who looks at it with a frown, as though trying to figure out what to do with it. She demonstrates, sliding off the orange safety, pointing out the trigger. He nods. "Follow me," she whispers.

They duck, running half bent out of the woods and into the open, tucking themselves behind a lone pine. Sand and rocks beneath their feet now. Emlyn's pulse pounds. Sweat slides down her hairline. She tilts her head toward the lake, and they make another run for it, pressing closer to the sound. They come to a rise. Here they can see the water, here there are no more trees. Bellies to the ground, they army-crawl forward, rocks jabbing their elbows, then slowly poke their heads up over the rise.

Voices again.

Tyler swears under his breath. He pushes himself up, he stands all the way. Still on her belly, she looks up at him. "Wait—"

But he's off, sprinting toward the water.

Emlyn scrambles to her feet and chases after him, because whatever it is Tyler sees, she has no choice but to follow him. They're all in, now.

And then Emlyn sees her, rising from the water like some Mediterranean goddess, blond hair wet against her chest, body glistening in the sun.

Janessa.

From deep in the recesses of her memory, Emlyn unearths Janessa's word: *alluring.* The word still fits.

Janessa stops dead in her tracks, mouth open. She is too far away for Emlyn to read her face, but soon she is smiling, dashing toward them, arms high in the air, sprinting the whole way up the beach. She brushes past Tyler and throws herself around Emlyn, wet face against hers, wet body soaking Emlyn's shirt. She holds her tight. Emlyn, awkward with the pistol in her right hand, hugs back with her left arm.

For a long time they stand there, close. Relief floods through her. "You're okay," she whispers. Emlyn smells the lake in Janessa's hair; she thinks of all the things she has missed about her friend. For years she's wanted to say, *I'm so sorry I ruined things between us. I've missed you.* Also: *You were right.* And she will say those things, things they've been tiptoe-ing around for years, she decides. Later. Maybe even tonight.

For now she relishes the moment, the feel of her old friend, not only safe but also happy to see her. Janessa plants a lake-wet kiss on her cheek, and Emlyn turns her head to do the same, but—a shift. Janessa's body grows taut. She holds tightly. Too tightly. Her skinny arms surprising and fierce and all at once drained of any warmth.

She presses her fingertips into Emlyn's shoulder blades, and, lips against her ear, whispers, "You shouldn't be here."

FOUR AND A HALF YEARS AGO

EMLYN and Tyler have been together for less than a year, but already she has transformed into a happier, more vibrant version of herself. She sings in the shower, she smiles at strangers. Tyler whisks her away for weekend getaways. He comes home with bouquets of Indian paintbrush. He scrawls messages on sticky notes and presses them to the bathroom mirror.

But, it's in the moments where Tyler does not know she's watching that she falls for him. At the supermarket, he helps an elderly woman load her groceries from her cart to the trunk. Each Saturday, he continues to buy Jorge a sandwich. He delivers clothes and groceries, too. And, though Tyler has never shared this himself, their neighbor, Rita, told Emlyn that Tyler helped her eight-year-old learn how to read. These small kindnesses, acts done for no audience, no credit, are what really make Emlyn feel sure that she has indeed stepped into incredibly good fortune.

Janessa has been gone for months. And, though Emlyn regrets the way their friendship splintered after their fight at the hot springs, she also believes she made the right call. She couldn't live there in her shadow forever, trailing behind and accepting whatever crumbs Janessa allowed. More importantly, Janessa had been wrong, completely wrong, about Tyler. The discrepancy between her warnings and the reality of Tyler's goodness fuels Emlyn's suspicions. Janessa did have feelings for Tyler.

On this spring afternoon, the aspens spin green, quivering at the window. When her lease ended, Emlyn gave up her crummy apartment and moved in with Tyler, and she is cooking a grilled cheese when Tyler comes home. He is elated, buzzing with that contagious excitement she loves about him.

"There's something I need to tell you," he says, leaning against the counter.

She turns to look at him. "Okay?"

"I'm leaving." He steps close and wraps his arms around her.

She feels the breath being sucked from her lungs, because it's happening, just like she has feared it would. The inevitable departure, the heart-wrenching farewell. She pulls back. "What? When?"

"A trip I've been planning for a long time. I'm taking the truck and doing an epic camping trip through the West." He darts over to the desk and plucks a map of the United States from a drawer. He unrolls it, placing mugs on the upper corners so it lies flat. A black line marks the route: from Idaho to Wyoming, Colorado, New Mexico, Arizona, Utah, back to Idaho. "Four months, maybe five."

Her heart sinks. She stares at the black line, silent.

"I know the timing seems bad. But I've been dreaming about this for years, and I can feel it, it's time. The weather will be great in Wyoming right now. Colorado, too. New Mexico and Arizona will be warm . . ."

Emlyn tries to listen. Afraid her face will reveal her devastation, she turns away. With the spatula, she flips the grilled cheese.

"Listen, I know we haven't been together that long," Tyler says, grabbing her hand, "and I know it's maybe a lot to ask, but I've been thinking—do you want to come with me?"

SIX weeks into their trip, they are in New Mexico, the truck heaving its way up the longest, most winding road Emlyn has ever seen. Route 15. Her stomach lurches as the vehicle rises and dips; her back slides along the seat with each bend.

"Here," Tyler says, swinging into a gravel pull-off. "Let's get you some fresh air." He turns off the truck. "I'll grab a ginger ale from the cooler. You want a Dramamine, too?"

She steps out of the truck. He climbs into the back and rifles around the Yeti, then returns with a green can. "I'm sorry," he says, cracking it open and handing it to her. "Was I driving too fast? You should've said something. I'm sorry. We don't have to do this today. It can wait." He turns and takes in the view: rolls and rolls of brown, speckled with dark green, as far as the eye can see. "Wow."

She takes a sip of the ginger ale. The night before, when they were camped at an RV park and waiting on their laundry, Emlyn had read aloud to Tyler that the Gila National Forest spans nearly three million acres of rugged mountains and thick evergreen forests. "The Gila Wilderness was the first designated wilderness area in the world," she'd recited while they folded clothes.

She thinks of those facts now, as she scans the horizon. She knows that, huge as it is, what she is looking at is just a portion of that acreage.

The vastness, the desolation: it's sobering, and it's a thing to behold. Not a person in sight, not a building. They passed one vehicle all morning.

The fresh air helps. Emlyn takes another swig of ginger ale and follows the turnout to where it dead ends: a fire ring made of rocks, with old coals in the middle. A wide, cleared space, one of the many designated dispersed campsites. It would be a perfectly fine place to spend the night.

The two of them have found a good rhythm. They move every three days, buy groceries once a week, find a campground with a laundromat every ten days. Mostly, though, they stay in places like this: free campsites provided by the Bureau of Land Management or a national forest. Before they left for this trip, Emlyn hadn't known such places existed. Their first night, in Bridger-Teton National Forest, she'd hardly slept. The silence and space, the darkness—she could barely stand it, and she felt sure she'd made a terrible mistake, agreeing to come along. Now, though, she finds that the campgrounds that, just a few weeks ago, felt safe and familiar have become claustrophobic, suffocating. She does her laundry, uses the Wi-Fi to send photos to her mom. When the sun rises, she packs quickly, ready to move on.

Here in the Gila Wilderness, Tyler has his heart set on searching for some cliff dwellings he's heard about. There's a national monument maybe twenty miles away, but that's not what he's after—he wants to find the place nobody knows about. He's been talking about it for weeks, scouring the internet when they have reception, leafing through stacks of Forest Service maps.

He reaches out and rubs his palm down her back. "Feeling better?"

She leans close and pecks him on the cheek. "Yep. Let's get going." She smiles. "You have some ancient dwellings to find, right?"

"If you don't feel well, we can just stay here."

"It's not even nine in the morning. I don't want to lose the whole day. I'll be fine," she insists, and she climbs into the truck to prove it.

MORE miles. At last they come to the place where Tyler has dropped a pin. There is a small pull-off, covered in brown pine needles. It's barely big enough for the truck to fit. They top off their waters, grab their backpacks, lock the doors. This will be an overnight trek, eight miles of rugged terrain each way, if they've calculated correctly, and they're breaking it up into two days.

"Ready?" Tyler asks, holding out a hand.

She nods, and they begin walking. A trail of sorts, though not quite. A pathway through the wilderness. Wildlife, cattle, maybe both. This is public land, and ranchers make use of the opportunity to graze their livestock here. Tyler studies his phone, squints, tilts his head. They stop for lunch, see a mule deer and her young. They hike and hike some more. The terrain grows steep, rocky, riddled with tufts of grass. They're slower than they'd estimated, but Tyler hums with excitement, certain they are close.

He digs his binoculars from his backpack and begins to glass. "There," he gasps. "I think that's it."

Emlyn crunches on a granola bar. He hands her the binoculars and points. On the far side of a steep ravine, an outcropping of peach-colored rocks.

"I'm not sure," she says, looking.

"Let's head over. We can get there in less than an hour, I bet. Best-case scenario, we can camp in the actual dwellings—how cool would that be, getting to sleep in the same place where people slept, thousands of years ago—and worst-case scenario, it's just some rocks, and we sleep there and keep looking in the morning." Tyler grins. For weeks he's been reading about the ancient Mogollon culture, admiring their pottery, memorizing facts.

"Okay," she agrees, finishing the granola bar and tucking the trash into a pocket of her pack.

She takes out her hiking poles, and they begin the trek down the steep ravine, deliberately and carefully. The sun remains high in the sky—they have time, no need to push. She is tired, and slow, and she tells Tyler it's okay to press ahead. She watches his orange hat bob through the brush, his blue backpack wobble back and forth. She can see him, but she looks down, mostly, focusing on her own footing. Her ankle pinches, resisting the angle of the terrain.

And then a scream.

The backpack and hat have disappeared. "Tyler!"

Another agonizing scream.

Her mind battles for clarity. Bear spray, she thinks, and she plucks it from her side pouch. She unlatches the clips at her waist and chest and slips the pack from her shoulders, racing down the hill, which is even steeper now. She halts just in time. All at once the ground disappears, dropping into a ravine. Her pulse pounds. Carefully, she peers over the edge, searching for a flash of color. "Tyler!"

Twelve, fifteen feet below, she sees the blue backpack, calls his name again. "I'm coming! Stay right there. I'm coming!" He doesn't answer. She searches for a safe way to reach him, scanning to the left and right. There. A hundred yards to her right, the rock face ends, and the land returns to its usual slope. Steep, but passable. She runs back up the hill to grab her pack, then shimmies down through the break in the rock. "Stay where you are!" she yells to Tyler, though she's not sure he hears her.

At last she reaches him. Her stomach roils at the sight: Tyler on the ground, backpack still on, and his leg, his left leg, covered in blood, the white shards of a broken tibia protruding from the mess. She rushes forward. He is unconscious, and she says his name over and over, trying to wake him. She presses two fingers to his neck, checks for a pulse, finds it. She remembers a wilderness-first-aid class from outdoors club: *Sometimes, a patient may faint from the pain or blood loss from a compound fracture.*

"Okay," she says out loud. A sob tears from her throat. She wants to curl into a ball and cry because this is bad, very bad, and they are very far from help. She closes her eyes and takes a deep breath. "Okay, Emlyn," she says out loud. "Focus. Don't panic! You can do this. He will be okay, it'll be okay."

She grabs the first item she finds in her backpack: a merino-wool T-shirt. Cringing, she applies it to the wound, pressing it tight, palm against the bone. She nearly vomits at the feel of it. The blood soaks in, staining the shirt red, and she reaches for another piece of clothing. A pair of hiking pants. At last the blood slows, then stops. *You know what to do,* she tells herself. *You memorized this procedure for a test, once. You know the steps, just remember them and do them, one two three.* This is easier said than done, but—first, clean the wound. There. She grabs a baggie of antiseptic wipes from the kit and begins peeling the wipes from their wrappers, dabbing the wound. After this she rises, rushes over to a bush, and vomits up the granola bar from earlier.

Next, something for the splint. She searches for a sturdy stick. Not a simple task in the sagebrush, but after several moments, she finds two. She darts back to the backpack, pulls out two shirts. Unsure if they are sturdy enough, she takes her pocketknife and cuts the padded straps off Tyler's backpack. She holds these against each stick, then wraps the shirts around both. She places one on each side of the leg, bolstering it. Round and round she wraps the first-aid tape, forming a makeshift cast, until the tape is gone.

Infection. This is the primary concern of not being able to get medical attention quickly. They are on the clock. But also—how in the world will they ever cover the six miles of treacherous terrain back to the truck, with Tyler in agony, unable to use his leg?

He wakes, screams, eyes bright with pain.

"Tyler," she says, speaking loudly, holding her hands at his cheeks. Her voice is firm and confident. "Tyler, listen to me. You have a compound fracture. We have to get you out of here, you need help."

He shakes his head, words escaping him. He begins to pant.

"We can do this, Tyler. One step at a time. We'll get you out of here in no time." She pours three ibuprofen from the bottle and opens his palm. "Here," she says. "Take this. We're gonna give it twenty minutes and then we have to move."

He takes the ibuprofen and closes his eyes again. "Yes, rest," she whispers, running her fingers through his hair. She stifles a sob.

When the time comes, she grabs the walking poles from the outside of his pack. She hefts him up, he cries out in agony, she slides her shoulder beneath his. "Okay, let's do this." She can barely carry her pack, with Tyler's weight against her side. She remembers the words of her grandpa, years ago. *One step, two. As long as you're moving forward, you're not losing ground.* She's not sure she really believes that in this moment, but she tells Tyler anyway.

THEY cover a mile, and Tyler begs her to stop. He rests, and she races through options. She could leave him, get out as fast as she can, go for help. But this is risky, given his state, and she will never forgive herself if something happens to him, deep in the wilderness and defenseless, while she is gone.

And then a new thought. A good idea, somewhat risky but not unreasonable, with the sun beginning to drop below the ridge, and miles to the truck, and Tyler soaked with sweat from the pain. She digs deep into her pack, fingers feeling around the very bottom, where she has tucked a ziplock bag. A last-minute addition, an afterthought. The brown bottle of pills they'd given her after her appendectomy. Oxycodone.

Tyler moans in agony. She twists the white cap, tips the bottle on its side, stares at the small round pill in her palm. Light blue. She remembers that day, nearly a year ago, in her apartment. The pain of her surgery, the relief of the medicine, swift and consuming. The lightness of it, the release. She remembers, too, Janessa's warning. How she'd snatched away the bottle. But with Tyler's pain, he will never make it out, and Emlyn pushes away the thought. She wraps her fingers around the tablet, replaces the lid, and tucks the bottle back into the backpack.

This is the moment Emlyn will play over and over in her mind, the moment where her life swivels from its course and heads in an entirely different direction. Life is full of these moments: little points like those connect-the-dots activities from grade school, each speck building on the next to form the shape of a person's story. Her dad's departure, meeting Janessa at Bumpy's diner, this.

"Here," she says to Tyler, "open up." She places the pill on his tongue, puts the Platypus nozzle in his mouth.

It works. After thirty minutes Tyler is alert and motivated, cheerful, almost, and they begin moving again, the long trek up the hill, down, up another. Four miles left, three. They stop for the night; she forces him to eat a few bites. They huddle close, the night air cold. At midnight she gives him a pill, and he's able to rest. In the morning she gives him another. With two miles left, he insists he cannot go any farther, and she hands him her last pill. Miraculously, they make it to the truck. She drives him back through the curves and dips of Route 15, to a clinic in Silver City. They helicopter him to the nearest hospital, where a surgeon pieces Tyler's leg back together with titanium plates and screws. No infection, another miracle. The surgeon assures her she has saved his life.

She doesn't know then, nine months into her relationship with Tyler, that he started on painkillers when he was sixteen, a "gift" from a buddy, at the time just another fix for him. She doesn't know that he overdosed at seventeen, was in rehab at eighteen, then also at twenty, and at twenty-one. That oxycodone has always been his drug of choice. That there, deep in the Gila Wilderness, she has reignited the addiction that held him in its claws for years before she met him.

They cut their trip short and return to Idaho, but by the time they get back to their apartment, Tyler has phoned his old friends. Within weeks he is a different person; within three months she is calling 911 because he is laid out on the bathroom floor and she cannot wake him. She contemplates packing her things and leaving, but what holds her back is the unbearable knowledge that this is her fault, what has happened to him. She is to blame. He was clean for four years before she fed him that blue pill in the wilderness; he was fine.

Emlyn visits him in rehab, waits for his return. She lies to the neighbors when they ask questions, spinning stories to explain his long absences. Work trips, family stuff. For the next year and half, the two of them grind through a terrible cycle, good seasons always punctuated by relapse. Anchored by an amalgam of love and guilt, she stays by his side; she walks through it with him. Time and again. She will not leave him, she will not be her dad, she will not exact that kind of pain, she will not be that person who jumps ship when the going gets rough. But at last, one weekend when they are camping in the wilderness, Tyler leaves her.

EIGHTEEN

BUSH emerges from the water and trots up the beach, a deity in his own right, tan and muscular and sparkling. He snags two towels from the ground and approaches Emlyn and Janessa, smiling. Emlyn thinks of the word she assigned him back at the cabin at Patten Lake: *charismatic*. Somehow, he is even more attractive in real life than in his videos.

Janessa pulls away but loops her arm through Emlyn's. "Look what the cat dragged in!" she calls to Bush, a wide grin on her face. She still hasn't looked at Tyler, who stands to the side, jaw slack, bear spray at his thigh. "Honey," Janessa says, grabbing Bush's hand, "this is a very dear friend of mine, from way back. We were"—here she looks at Emlyn, still with a broad smile, blue eyes bright—"bosom friends, once, weren't we? Sisters. A long time ago."

Emlyn flinches at the mention of their old term. Her face is wet, her shirt damp from Janessa's embrace, and although the sun is high in the sky and the sand on the beach radiates heat, she shivers. This unsettling dichotomy. Did she mishear before? Is this about the dropped call from a week ago? Is Janessa mad at her? What, exactly, has she stepped into out here?

"Bush," Janessa says, stepping away, sliding her hand down Emlyn's arm to take hold of her hand and extend it toward him, "I'd like you to meet Emlyn Anthony."

"Pleasure," he says, and he reaches out with a thick, weathered hand. Then, unexpectedly, he pulls Emlyn in for a hug. She's swallowed in his arms, her face pressed tight against his wet, bare chest. "Anyone who's a dear friend of Janessa's is an automatic friend of mine," he adds as he steps back. For a moment he studies her face. "I've heard all about you." He holds a towel out to Janessa.

Emlyn tries not to stare. Face, body. She looks toward the lake. "You have?"

"Sure. The two of you met at some diner in college, right?" He drapes a towel over his shoulders.

"That's right." Emlyn looks at Janessa. "Janessa rescued me," she says, trying to catch her friend's eyes.

"Well, that makes two of us, then," he says, running his hand through his wet hair, loosening the waves and spraying droplets of water in her direction. He bites his bottom lip. "J," he says, raising his eyebrows, "you never mentioned she was such a knockout."

"I'm sure I did."

"No, I'm sure you didn't." He flashes a wide, teasing smile. "A man deserves a warning, just saying. A backdrop like this, two beautiful women on a beach."

Emlyn feels a flush burning its way up her neck.

Janessa gives him a playful punch. "Stop," she says, rolling her eyes.

Tyler steps closer, sliding himself between Emlyn and Bush. "Bush," he says.

"Tyler! Man—this is a surprise." He grins and folds Tyler in for a side hug. "A good surprise. I like surprises, don't I, Janessa?"

She wraps the towel at her chest and smiles sweetly. "You have to, with a girl like me."

"Never a dull moment."

The beautiful people. The high school banter, the innuendo. Also the tension. (Or maybe she is misreading?) Emlyn feels like she has wandered into some weird movie set. She's been asked to play a part, but no one's given her the script.

Janessa looks at Tyler, then at Emlyn, and again at Tyler. "Really?" she says, her eyes landing on Emlyn.

Emlyn has forgotten what it feels like to have Janessa disappointed in her. She feels herself rumpling under the weight of her friend's scorn; she has the urge to explain.

"I was worried," Tyler answers. "Both of us were."

"Oh, Tyler."

"I was! I thought something terrible happened. You know, an injury, something bad. I feel responsible. I made the itinerary, I mapped the route. You're using my van. If something went wrong, if something *happened,* you know—I'd feel like it was my fault."

Bush folds his thick arms across his thick chest. "We do all right out here, you know," he says. "I know a thing or two."

"I know, I know. It's just I didn't hear from you. And—one mistake, one bad step, and things can change, fast." He nudges Emlyn. "Tell them, Em."

She doesn't want to tell them. After all her worry, after fifteen miles of trekking through the wilderness, she feels foolish to have stumbled upon a perfectly fine Janessa and Bush, who were obviously never in any trouble at all, and who clearly weren't expecting or wanting visitors. Emlyn's embarrassed, she feels duped. She wants to go home. "It's true." She clears her throat. "But, obviously, in your case, we were wrong to be concerned."

"Hey, I'm just giving you two a hard time," Bush says, breaking into a smile. "And we owe you an apology, Tyler. I told Janessa we should just tell you we needed a little time, I really did. But you know how she is." He turns to look at Janessa. "Once she gets something in her head, there's no changing her mind. 'Let's go off-grid,' that's what she said. 'No Instagram, no YouTube, no cell phones. Nothing electronic at all. Just the two of us.' Truth is, I kind of liked the sound of that, so we dropped everything and packed up and left. What did you call it, babe? A trust-something."

"A trust-build," Janessa says. She leans against Bush. "I wanted an adventure. A real adventure. No crutches to help us along, no internet, no itinerary. Just the two of us, trusting ourselves. And each other." She squints in the sunlight, and Emlyn again feels the burn of Janessa's first words to her. *You shouldn't be here.* Emlyn could understand that frustration, if what Janessa was really after was some space and quiet. Having two people crash your romantic getaway would be annoying. Especially if you'd worked this hard to get it.

Still. Janessa's reaction felt a little overwrought, even for her.

Janessa continues. "It's hard to explain, but all this time, the incredible places and the amazing things we've gotten to experience—it's been wonderful, but it got to the point where we were just, I don't know, building a story, and after a while, it was starting to feel like that story wasn't ours at all. I couldn't do it anymore. I just couldn't."

Bush kisses her forehead. "I know, sugar." He waves his hand toward Emlyn and Tyler. "Well, look. Friends are here, the sky has cleared. How's that for going off script? Who knows how the story might turn out, once you let life write itself. Now that you're here, I hope you'll join us for dinner. I caught a lake trout earlier, big fat one. I'm putting together a feast. We're happy to share."

Janessa lays a hand on Bush's arm. "I'm sure these two want their own space."

"Yes," Emlyn says, "thank you, but we don't want to intrude."

"Oh, don't be ridiculous," Bush says, wrapping one of his bear arms around Emlyn's shoulder. "You're here. The least you can do is join us for dinner and stay the night. Really, I insist." He smiles and Emlyn notices he has dimples.

"Of course we'll stay," Tyler says.

Emlyn looks at him, but he isn't looking at Bush. Her eyes follow his, and she sees that Janessa is staring right back at him, that the two of them are locked in some impenetrable union. Emlyn's heart angles into its old terrain. Jealousy, inferiority. The sense that she is wandering the fringes of a neighborhood she cannot enter.

"Perfect!" Bush says, letting go of Emlyn's shoulder. "All right, you guys set up camp. Make yourselves at home. Take a dip if you want. The water's cold, but it looks like you two could afford to clean up, no offense." He winks and rubs his palms together. "I'll make dinner."

Emlyn and Tyler walk back to the woods where they stashed their backpacks. The sun gleams overhead.

"Well," Tyler says, picking up his pack, "what a relief."

She turns and glares at him. "A relief?"

"Yeah. They're okay, they're safe."

"Right. They're fine. They needed a break, just like I said." She heaves in disgust. "I can't believe I let you drag me all the way out here. I can't believe you convinced me to worry *that much*." She thinks of all the scenarios she played, all the terrible images that crashed through her mind. "I feel so stupid."

Tyler stops. "Wait, are you mad?"

"I'm not mad. I'm just—" She shakes her head. "I just feel stupid, like I said."

"Listen," Tyler says, stepping close. His blue eyes catch the light and take on a turquoise hue. He grabs hold of her hands. "I'm the one who should feel stupid. I assumed the worst, I freaked out. You shouldn't feel stupid. The last thing from it. You were being a good friend. You were being brave. Dauntless, intrepid." His face breaks into a smile. "How's that for some good dictionary words?" he asks, eyes twinkling. "I know you didn't want to do this. Not with me—well, *especially* not with me—but you did it anyway. Because you're brave. Because you care."

Emlyn bites her lip. She wants to be mad at him, she wants to regret the past two nights: Tyler's words, the tiny waves of static that have flickered between them. But the truth is it has felt good to be with him, the old Tyler, the real Tyler.

She bends to pick up her backpack. She clips the straps and looks out at the lake, shimmering and teal. Bush was right: the evening has turned splendid. She could embrace the opportunity, sink her teeth into the moment and enjoy it for what it is: an evening with peers, way back in the wilderness. (She's hesitant to use the word "friends" at the moment.) A gorgeous backdrop. Fresh lake trout. A campfire, a meal under the stars. It's everything she would want from a good night, and yet—something isn't right. Janessa's heart-stopping words. That Instagram post that said they were in Wyoming. Janessa and Tyler, eyes locked.

"I'm leaving first thing tomorrow morning," she tells Tyler. "With or without you."

EMLYN assesses the camp that Bush and Janessa have set up: their tent and belongings on one side, a fire ring where Bush kneels, striking flint. Towels and some clothes hang over a clothesline made of paracord, strung between two scrawny trees. A hammock sways in the breeze. Should she set up her tent opposite theirs, or will that block their view of the lake and mountains?

Janessa steps out of the tent, dressed in black leggings and a worn gray T-shirt that slips off her left shoulder. "Over there is good," she says, pointing to where Emlyn stands. She twists her long hair and wrings out the water.

Emlyn looks away. It is now that she remembers she stashed her tent at the base of their last hill climb, and that she'll be joining Tyler in his two-person tent for the night. Just five hours ago, that had seemed reasonable. It had seemed wise. Well, not wise, but not as imprudent as it now feels.

Janessa rises from the campfire and watches as Emlyn unrolls the tent. She folds her arms and tilts her head to the side, and when Emlyn's eyes meet hers, Janessa gives a look that could only be described as scornful. *Nothing happened,* Emlyn wants to say. But instead she just picks up a rock and pounds a stake into the ground.

After the tent is set up, Emlyn grabs her bottle of castile soap and a towel from her backpack and heads down to the water. She ducks behind a bush, tugs off her top, and slides out of her hiking pants, which cling to her sweaty legs. Bush was right: she is definitely due for a cleanup. She gathers her clothes to rinse off, then raises her head above the bush to confirm nobody is looking. In her underwear, she darts for the water and dives in. There is no other way: a slow approach only prolongs the pain. The body doesn't adjust, you don't get used to it. Not at this altitude, with this water, fed by snowmelt. The cold blasts through her, a mind-numbing gust that flares all the way from her toes to her head. She holds her breath, goes under, bobs up.

Tyler dashes into the water and swims close, three feet away. The water is crystal clear.

"Are you naked?" she gasps.

"Is there any other way to bathe?" he retorts with a grin.

She rolls her eyes and kicks away from him. Hands shaking, she quickly lathers herself with soap and dips under again. Good enough. She emerges and runs out of the water to her towel, wrapping it around her shoulders. She dries her face, wrings out her hair.

Higher up the beach, she sees Bush emerging from the woods with a fistful of greens, freshly foraged. He raises an arm in a wave, and she waves back and heads toward the campsite.

She ducks in the tent and changes into dry clothes, then strings a line of paracord between two trees and drapes her underwear and towel over the top.

Janessa has walked down the beach, where she now sits, looking out at the water.

"What'd you find?" Emlyn calls to Bush, who is cutting his foraged food on a slab of wood with a pocketknife.

"Just some wild onions," he says. He raises his eyes to hers and smiles. "I like to cook, especially out here. There's just something about it. Building what you eat from start to finish."

"I know. I watched a few of your videos."

"Did you? I haven't done one for a while. Not since—" He waves a hand. "Not since we started all this. I mean, I'm still doing those things. I just haven't recorded anything."

"Do you think you'll start up again, once you're done traveling?"

He stops cutting. "Oh, I think maybe not." He flashes a glance toward Janessa that Emlyn cannot discern. "I have a feeling I'm done with that."

FOUR YEARS AGO

EMLYN has just gotten home from work. Tyler greets her at the door, smiling, freshly showered. He folds her in a hug, and she breathes him in. "I got stuff at the store," he says. "I'll make supper."

She changes out of her work clothes and settles onto a counter stool with a seltzer. Tyler buzzes around the kitchen, gathering ingredients. Music hums from a speaker in the corner. Fresh mozzarella, prosciutto, olive oil, romaine. He knows she loves his sandwiches. He pulls out a fresh baguette from the local bakery and sets it on the table.

He looks at her and smiles and asks about her day, slicing the baguette down the middle with a long bread knife.

She's just picked up a new job, running the register at a local outdoors shop. The items are overpriced; the clientele are unbearable. But it's a paycheck, and, she must remind herself, it's definitely better than summer camp. She takes a sip of her seltzer and then she sees it: blood.

"Tyler—" she says, but Tyler keeps on talking. He met with their young neighbor, Ben, to help him with his reading. He stopped by the store. "I delivered those cookies you made for my parents," he says. "Mom was super grateful. I think she's fallen for you just as hard as I have," he adds with a grin. Blood oozes from the wound. It slides down the back of his hand in a thick red stream.

Emlyn stares. She doesn't interrupt him.

"Oh, I dropped off your library books, too. And!" He stops, spins, remembering. A drop of blood sails from his hand, landing on the white countertop. He shuffles through a stack of papers behind him. "I got you this! It was on display at the front." He holds out a copy of *The Carrying*. "Ada Limón's new collection. You like her, right?"

She takes *The Carrying*. She's already read this book. Tyler bought it for her and gave it to her last month, for her birthday. A line spins to her: "Sometimes, he drowns. / Sometimes, we drown together." Blood on the library book, too. A smear across the cover.

Tyler returns his attention to the sandwich, piling on ingredients. Now there is blood on the thick, beautiful bread; blood on the wooden cutting board.

A whimper ruptures from Emlyn's throat.

Tyler keeps working and talking. He doesn't feel the wound, he doesn't see the blood, and Emlyn knows what this means. Tyler is too high, too numb to register that he has cut himself.

"What's wrong, love?" Tyler coos, when he looks up and sees that she is crying. "What's the matter?"

He walks around the island and pulls her head against his chest. She listens to his heart beat, loud and strong and perfect. She feels the back of her shirt go damp against his palm. More blood. Emlyn cries harder.

"What is it, Em?"

She shakes her head, her forehead still against his chest.

This is the way of it, now. A Tyler who is a bewildering mix of good and sweet and ugly and terrifying. Four months have passed since his last stint in rehab.

"Your hand," she says, once she collects herself, and they wash it and wrap it with gauze and tape.

On this night Emlyn can't bring herself to confront him. They've had this fight before, and it always ends the same way, with Tyler denying everything, and eventually accusing her of not loving him enough to trust him. And tonight, she simply won't get into it; she can't. She thanks Tyler for the sandwich but tosses it in the trash. (This, too, escapes Tyler's notice.) Later, as he sleeps on the couch, she takes cleaner and wipes the blood from the counter, the book, the floor.

The real agony of this new life of hers is not signing Tyler into rehab or hearing an ambulance wail as it carts him away. It's not watching him lie and disappear and keep her up late into the night, worried sick, though those things, of course, are heartbreaking. The real agony, she now understands, is this. It's good things—the book of poems, the sandwich, both kind and thoughtful—speckled with carnage. It's seeing someone you love splinter away from you, shard by shard. Knowing there are parts of him left, but never being sure just how much, and at what point a person is so far gone that you won't ever really get him back.

NINETEEN

THE sun slips behind the mountains, a quick and humble plunge. In its wake: the silhouetted peaks, jagged and black against an auburn afterglow. Their campsite is high up—7,800 feet, according to Emlyn's mapping app—but the looming mountains are much higher, and they tower over the water, casting long shadows across the blue.

With the sun gone, the air turns crisp and cold, and Emlyn adds two more layers, a fleece and her packable insulated jacket. Her hair is still wet from her swim, and it clings to her neck and sends shivers down her back. She tugs her beanie over her ears. At the fire, she settles down in front of a log and tugs her knees to her chest. Janessa sits across from her, Tyler to her right. He looks at her, sees her shiver, then heads to the tent and comes back with his sleeping bag. He smiles and drapes it around her shoulders. Sits closer, their hips touching.

Janessa stares at the lake.

Bush plucks a Stanley flask from his bag of cooking utensils and hands it to Emlyn. "Here," he says with a smile, "this'll help you warm up."

She rarely drinks, but she takes a swig, the liquor fiery and sharp as she swallows. She tries not to grimace as she hands back the flask, throat still burning. Bush takes a drink and passes it to Tyler, who passes it on to Janessa without taking a sip. Janessa drinks, wincing, one mouthful and another. She holds the flask on her knee and the metal glints in the firelight. From across the fire, she stares at Emlyn. An indiscernible gaze. Not angry, not happy. Emlyn stares back. She's not sure if they're communicating something, the two of them, but if they are, she isn't sure what it is.

The orange sky grows dark, the shadows on the lake fade. Bush lets the flames burn down so he can cook on the coals, promising they'll get the fire going again when he's done. He kneels next to her, placing his lake trout on a thick piece of foil. He dots the fish with olive oil he's hauled into the backcountry in three layers of ziplock bags. With his bear-paw hands he rubs the oil into the fish, then sprinkles the chopped wild onion he harvested across the top, adds salt and a pinch of dried parsley, also hauled in. He folds the foil over the top, pinches the edges, and places it on the coals. Emlyn thinks of the videos she watched, Bush chatting easily, explaining each step, adding a self-deprecating comment here and there. Flashing a grin at the camera. He's very good, on-screen. Likable, charming. Just as he seems to be in real life. Watching him work, she feels herself beginning to relax. Janessa passes her the flask and she takes two more guzzles.

"I assume you found the van?" Bush says. He tears open a bag of instant mashed potatoes with his teeth, dumps the contents in a pan, and pours boiling water on top.

Emlyn nods. The liquor burns its way down her chest. "Yes. And the bananas. And chicken." She takes another sip of the liquor before passing it on. "We really were worried." She remembers, suddenly, that she has Janessa's red beanie, stashed in her backpack. "Which reminds me," she says, rifling through her stuff, "I also found this." She hands Janessa the hat.

"We thought of the food like four miles in," Bush says, stirring the potatoes. "There was no turning back." He shakes his head. "Anyway, we've gotta be, what? Fourteen, fifteen miles from there, am I right?" He settles on his haunches.

"Fifteen," Emlyn says.

"Impressive." He hands the flask back to Emlyn, and she takes another sip, the warmth too hard to pass up.

With two sticks Bush reaches for the fish, and gingerly removes it from the fire and onto a folded towel on the beach. He opens it, poking the flesh with his fork. Steam rolls off. "Perfect," he says.

Everyone has brought their own plate, and Bush divvies up the fish into four portions. He scoops generous heaps of mashed potatoes, and, miraculously, produces a baggie of bacon bits, which he sprinkles on top. Not equal sizes, Emlyn notices. He gives himself the smallest serving.

"Are you sure that's enough for you?" Emlyn asks, gesturing toward his plate.

He waves her off. "I'll have a protein bar if I need one. This is for you guys." Then he lifts his flask toward the fire, and says, "Bon appétit."

"Looks great," Tyler says, and Janessa murmurs agreement.

Emlyn dives in, manners out the window. The fish is tender and sweet, the potatoes buttery and salty. All of it hot and delicious. The rehydrated meals of the past two days have been pleasant enough, but what Bush has prepared is an entirely different story. She devours it quickly. "Sorry," she mutters when she has scraped the last food from her plate.

Bush grins. "Don't apologize. Please. I live for this. I love to see people enjoying my food."

Aside from their initial expressions of gratitude, Tyler and Janessa eat in silence.

Overhead, the sky bleeds Idaho dark. A deep blue-black, studded with stars. Emlyn leans back against a log and stares. The Milky Way smudging the darkness. A wide blur of pink, purple, and white. Turquoise tingeing the mountaintops. So much color, and all of it doubled, reflecting on the lake. "It's really something, isn't it?" she says aloud.

Tyler leans back next to her. "Yes."

"Magnificent," Bush says. As promised, he props up two more pieces of wood on top of the coals. "This is magnificent country. Rugged, unforgiving. Dangerous if you're not careful. But also magnificent." He pulls a pocketknife from the darkness and unfolds it.

Emlyn recalls the definition: "impressively beautiful, elaborate, or extravagant; striking." She's never assigned this word to any person, but she has to agree. It's the perfect word to describe this place, this night.

Bush continues. He flips the knife in his hand, twirling the handle between his fingers, the metal catching the light. "And the four of us, way out here. This beautiful night. I mean, what are the odds? It's almost—" He pauses here, holding Janessa's eyes, and Emlyn is certain she sees some shift toward malice in that glance. "Well, it's almost unbelievable. In fact, I would go so far as to say it's *impossible*."

Emlyn looks at Janessa, who blinks and swallows, her clavicles pronounced in the firelight.

"I mean, really," Bush says, "the trek alone, that's remarkable. Following us all the way from the van. You're good, Emlyn. You truly are." Here, Bush squints and purses his lips, as though mulling all of this over. "But the thing I can't quite wrap my head around is this: We're supposed to be in Wyoming right now. We blew off Tyler's itinerary and went in a whole different direction. We cut off all communication with

the world to venture out on this—what did you call it, J?—'trust-build.'"
He looks hard at Janessa. "At least I thought we did. That was the agreement." Now he turns to Emlyn. "So, without someone basically *telling*
you where we are, how on earth did you find us? How would you even
know where to look?"

Emlyn is caught off guard, trying to track Bush's sudden change in
attitude. She opens her mouth to try to explain, but before she can speak,
Janessa interjects. "I told Emlyn where we were," she says quickly. She
grabs her long hair and twists it around her thumb, sweeping all of it onto
her left shoulder. Emlyn immediately recognizes the gesture: their secret
signal. *I need to get out of this situation; help me.*

"I asked her to come," Janessa says, looking at Emlyn, eyes wide. She
runs her fingers over her hair again. "Didn't I?"

Emlyn nods slowly. "Yes." She's growing more confused by the moment,
but something tells her she can't ignore Janessa's cue. She quickly engineers
a lie. "For the fishing."

Relief washes over Janessa's face. "Yes. For the fishing."

"Janessa knows how much I've always loved it. And she knows I've
been a fan of yours for a long time." Emlyn forces a smile. "I've been asking
her to connect the two of us for months."

Bush frowns. "I thought you came out here because you were worried."

Emlyn realizes she must navigate her way around the lie. "Yes, that's
true, too," she says slowly. "Janessa told me where the van was, and she knew
I could find you from there. What threw me off was the stuff we found at
the van. The chicken and bananas, the hat. That's when I got worried."

Bush makes a noise: a slight, soft sound, a cross between a murmur
and a clearing of his throat. He bobs his head. "Well," he says, looking first
at Emlyn and then at Janessa, "I guess that explains everything, then."
Emlyn gets the sense that Bush doesn't believe them. He hasn't touched

his food, the plate balanced on his lap, and he turns to Janessa. "How long have we been at this, now?"

Janessa, now finished with her meal, slides closer to Bush. "Eighteen months."

"Eighteen months. What a journey, am I right?"

She nods.

The pieces of wood, dry from months without rain, catch quickly, and the flames shimmy and swirl. The four of them huddle close, faces illuminated. Tyler has barely said a word all night.

"Trust," Bush says. "That's what it really comes down to. This is true in any partnership, anywhere, but especially out here." His knife glints in the darkness. "You have to trust your own instincts, you have to trust that you can make your way." He turns to look at Janessa. "And you have to trust the people around you. Not just that they're capable, but that they've got your back. That they would never do anything to . . . compromise your well-being." He holds the knife in his right hand and pokes at a log with his left hand, harder this time. A rush of embers floats into the dark. "Or their own."

The whiskey isn't sitting well. Emlyn's arms and legs feel heavy, and in her stomach she feels a trace of nausea.

Bush turns to her. "Emlyn, am I right about this?"

She unzips her jacket, the fire now feeling too warm. "Um . . ."

"For instance," Bush continues, "if I understand things correctly, you saved Tyler's life, years ago. You did everything you possibly could've done to keep him alive. That was in the Gila Wilderness, if I'm not mistaken. Gorgeous country. Rugged, remote." He takes a swig from the Stanley flask, finishing it off. "And yet, Tyler, on the other hand, left you. That was what, a year or so later?"

The words slit at Emlyn's heart, gashing it open. The meanness of it.

All at once she is shuttled backward, to those early days in Varden's cabin, the snow piling up, the depth of her loss nearly drowning her.

"Bush, please—" Janessa says.

Bush waves her off. "It's fine. Look at them." He gestures toward Tyler's tent with his knife. "By the looks of things, they've patched things up, they've moved on. You must be a forgiving person, Emlyn; good for you. Truth is, I envy you for that. Forgiveness—well, let's just say it has never been my strong suit."

Tyler squirms. Beneath the sleeping bag, he finds Emlyn's hand and squeezes tight. She doesn't squeeze back. "Bush, I screwed up," he says. "Big time. I own that."

Bush doesn't seem to hear him. "Trust doesn't come easily for me. Some people, they trust too much. They don't make a person earn it, they just give it out. Like candy on Halloween, like stickers at the doctor's office." Here he turns to Emlyn, and, though she wants to look away, she makes herself hold his gaze. "Which is . . . well, I was going to say 'tragic,' but maybe that's too strong of a word. So I'll say 'unwise' instead." He shakes his head and again spins the knife.

Tyler shuffles nervously.

Janessa continues twisting her hair over her left shoulder, watching Bush, eyes wide.

Bush rambles on. "Not me. Trust must be hard-earned. Without trust," he continues, eyes on the flame, "you've got nothing." He presses his lips tight, wipes his eye with his sleeve.

No one agrees, no one disagrees.

"Emlyn," Bush says, closing the knife. He clears his throat and rises to his feet, apparently having shaken off the gloom of the previous moment, "what do you say you and I head down to the water? See what we can get into."

"Oh, I dropped my gear back at our last campsite," she says, grasping that her lie has again caught up with her. "My tent, too. I needed to off-load some weight." She looks at Janessa, trying again to read her. She has no desire to be alone with Bush after his disquieting little speech. The whiskey churns in her belly. She's tired. She resolves that first thing tomorrow morning, she is packing up and hauling out of here.

Janessa rises to her feet and lays a hand on his arm. "Bush, I'm sure Emlyn's tired—"

But Bush ignores her, pulling out a packable fly rod and unzipping the case. He slides the rod together, piece by piece. "It's early," he says.

Janessa drops her hand to her side and flashes Emlyn a look.

"I don't night fish," Emlyn adds. Tyler, still holding her hand, presses her fingers in his. "It's just not something I do." This is not entirely true. She and Varden have gone twice, and once, at a client's request, she took a couple, recently engaged, out on the Salmon at midnight.

"Oh, come on," Bush taunts, flashing her a smile. "That's why you're here, right? For the fishing. So, let's fish."

She realizes her mistake. She can't really refuse, not now. Not with that whole story about coming out here to fish with him.

A second rod, used earlier, leans against a fallen tree, and Bush grabs it. He kneels next to the fire, now bright and warm, and opens his fly box. He slides a large fly out and holds it to the light. It dangles from his fingertips, black and bushy, swaying back and forth. "I've got a rat on my hands," he says, and he looks at Janessa. "And I've been waiting for just the right moment to put it to the test."

THREE YEARS AGO

IT'S a Friday, and Emlyn and Tyler are hauling their things from their apartment and loading them into the truck. It doesn't take long. This is a frequent adventure for them, a weekend in the woods, and most of their gear lives in the truck, each necessity stored carefully in its designated space.

The bed of the truck has been converted into sleeping quarters. Tyler built a plywood platform across the wheel wells, with ample storage below for the four long, skinny plastic bins that hold their belongings. Their pads and sleeping bags are already in place on the platform, and Emlyn tosses in the pillows. She slides the loaded Yeti into the back seat and climbs into the front.

They drive to the Hemingway-Boulders Wilderness, which isn't far from home, but still gives them the chance to be in the woods. The first night, the temperature dips low, crystals of frost blooming across the window. She and Tyler huddle close in the truck bed and dream about the perfect camper van. Small shower, tiny sink, a bed that can be converted into a dinette. Solar power. Emlyn reads *The Captain's Verses* aloud with the light of her headlamp. Tyler lies on his back and listens, eyes closed. In the middle of the night she wakes and stares at the blurred white of the Milky Way streaming across a great and endless sky, and she is certain, despite the challenges she and Tyler have navigated, that she has never been happier.

The next day is warm and bright and gorgeous, and she wants to head to the stream to fish. Tyler says he'll run to town, sixteen miles away, and pick up lunch, Margherita pizza. It's an old ritual of theirs, an unnecessary trip to the closest town while out in the woods, just for pizza, nothing else—a waste of both time and money and therefore a treat. At first Emlyn hesitates. She'd rather they stay together, and the peanut butter and jelly they've packed will do just fine. But they are happy, this weekend, a condition she knows to be tenuous, and she doesn't want to deny him; she doesn't want to be a killjoy. So she agrees. He'll be back in maybe an hour and a half, and in the meantime, she'll fish. She grabs her case of flies and tucks *The Captain's Verses* in the chest pocket of her waders.

"Can you leave the pack with me?" she asks, meaning the small yellow backpack stocked with emergency supplies. First-aid kit, solar blanket, a water-filtration system, multitool, electrolyte powder, waterproof matches, flashlight, protein bars. She's thought of everything. "It's in the back seat."

Tyler closes the truck topper and over his shoulder says, "Sure."

Emlyn slides her legs into the neoprene booties of her waders. "Just tuck it behind that tree," she says, gesturing toward a pine. She wiggles her feet into the boots and pulls the straps over her shoulders.

He steps closer and wraps his arms around her.

"Don't break my heart and forget about me, okay?" she says, reciting his line from the night they met. She says it every time they part.

He lifts his orange trucker hat and leans down to kiss her. "Never."

* * *

ON the stream an hour slips by, and she doesn't notice. The fish are biting, and she is rapt, and in the way that nothing else can, the water holds her, the world and its hours disappearing. But then three hours pass, four. She is hot and parched, and she finishes her water. The sun slides across the sky, and she begins to worry. She scrambles to a boulder on the stream's edge and hefts herself up. She unzips her chest pocket and pulls out her phone. No missed calls, no messages, but also, she realizes: no reception. Something has happened, she determines at this point. A flat tire, a dead battery. Darkness mills closer.

She breaks down her rod and slides it into its case, then climbs through the alders to the campsite. She heads for the tree where she asked Tyler to leave the backpack. She can filter water from the stream and add a packet of electrolytes. She'll have a protein bar, and she'll perk right up.

But. The backpack isn't there.

She circles the tree, checks another, searches the whole area in widening circles. A ripple of rage at this unthinkable oversight. That's why they have that backpack, after all. For emergencies. That's why she asked him to leave it for her.

Her thirst becomes disconcerting. She looks at her watch and guesses that it has been maybe three hours since she last drank. In her chest waders she begins to walk the forest road, rutted and pockmarked. It's five miles to the paved road, eight more to the ranger station, but what else is there to do? She can't sit by the stream and wait. Soon the headlights of Tyler's truck will appear, bouncing in the distance as the truck toils over the potholed road. He'll regale her with the woes of his misadventure; he'll hand her the cold pizza and apologize over and over.

The air grows cold. Emlyn's breath is white when she exhales.

Her mind wanders into more treacherous ground. The wheel of Tyler's truck dipping over a steep ledge, the vehicle tumbling down a gorge. The handful of people who would've driven on this road today, trundling past without noticing. She pushes herself to walk faster, makes a note to check each ravine for headlights, a flicker of metal in the moonlight.

The darkness grows deep and palpable. She has walked, what, maybe two miles, maybe more. Three miles to the paved road. This will be hard, but it's not undoable. *You are fit and strong,* she tells herself. But she is slow in the waders. Tired, hungry. Her toes are pinched, the sides of her feet forming hot spots. Waders are not made for such endeavors. She attempts to calculate the hours until, God forbid, dehydration or hypothermia will begin to chink away at her ability to think rationally. To her left, some large animal crashes away through the woods, and her heart leaps in her chest.

Her foot catches on a stone, and she stumbles and falls, her palms landing hard in a pothole, where they crash through a thin layer of ice that has begun to form. The urge to weep rises up from her chest and she catches it in her throat before it escapes her mouth. She wills herself to get up, to keep moving, because it is not just her circumstances, being alone in the woods and unprepared, but also the foul, menacing thought that has been rearing its head and feeling more and more likely with each step.

Is Tyler using again?

He's been clean for five months this time. At least this is what she's believed.

Emlyn pushes herself up and wipes her hands on her waders. She tries to force from her mind a dozen memories that swarm her. Tyler not coming to pick her up after her spin class at the YMCA; Tyler with a cut hand, bleeding on a sandwich; Tyler forgetting their date at a coffee shop. But also Tyler pale and unconscious on the bathroom floor, the paramedics assessing his vitals as she stands in her nightgown in the corner. Tyler slumped in the back seat as Emlyn drives him off to rehab. The forgetfulness, the mood swings, the lies. Time shuffled away from him; he became someone else. Is he chasing a fix, is he high, right now, as she trudges through the darkness?

The sense that her situation is bad, dire, becomes apparent. She is so thirsty and now she is wet, too, and cold. She stops to rest along the side of the road, pulls her knees to her chest and tucks her chin. *The Captain's Verses* presses against her chest. The awful thought that just twenty hours earlier, she was viciously, delectably happy.

Memories of her father swim to her. Those kind blue eyes, the wrinkles at the corners. The skin leathered from too much sun. She had been his world, hadn't she? And yet—he had left. He promised it wasn't about her; this was adult stuff between him and her mother. He would keep in touch, he would still see her. And he had, for a while. But he'd also moved on. The old chorus returns, its bitter music so familiar: You are forgettable. You are a person others leave behind.

It begins to snow. No, not quite snow. Snow mixed with rain. It pelts her shoulders and neck, stinging her skin: a thousand tiny, relentless daggers. She tugs her hood over her head. The night grows loud, rumbling with the noise of the ice pellets hammering every surface.

Pathetic. "Pitiful, particularly through tragedy or weakness." And "miserably frail; feeble; useless." In the dark Emlyn drafts a new definition: *a person who is so blinded by love that she refuses to accept the truth about someone.* And another: *a person who willingly allows herself to be duped into being left behind in the wilderness by an addict.* This is Emlyn's word, and curled up along the side of the road, Neruda's love poems zipped in her pocket, the dark and the cold pressing in and wrapping around her, she knows that word has never felt more accurate. The ice amasses around her. Head, shoulders, legs. She will rest. Just close her eyes for a few moments, and then she will get up and move. Or she won't. And maybe that would be okay.

TWENTY

AT the lake, Bush ties the mouse rat fly onto one rod. He hands Emlyn his fly kit and tells her to pick something, so she cracks it open, the flies illuminated by the light of the fire. She selects a sculpin streamer with bright silver angel hair that flashes in the dark. She ties it on, her fingers shaking, even though she has done this a thousand times. Her breaths cut the darkness in white poofs.

"Good choice," Bush says.

Janessa has resumed her spot at the fire, and she stares into the flames. Tyler rises and walks toward them. "I'll go, too. I'd like to watch."

"No," Bush says, "you stay here. We'll be fine. I'm sure the two of you have some catching up to do."

Tyler seems unsure what to do. He looks at Bush, then at Emlyn. He runs his hands through his hair and then heads back to the fire.

Emlyn straps on her headlamp, and Bush does the same. They grab their rods and head toward the water. The moon hangs above the jagged peaks, a tiny crescent, stingy on light. At the water's edge she presses on her headlamp. "Okay if I go this way?" she asks Bush.

"Sure, you pick."

She walks down the beach, careful with her footing. Fist-sized rocks, worn smooth over millennia of water, dot the ground. She pictures them being loosened from the mountaintop, stuttering downhill, collecting at the lake. She scrambles over a log and then looks out at the water. Here. She glances to her left and sees that Bush has already cast.

She looks down to unhook her streamer. She wiggles the rod back and forth, letting out line. Then she begins to cast. She lifts the rod, tilts it backward, the line whipping behind her. Forward, backward again. This is Bush's rod, so the feel is different from her own, but still the rhythm is natural and easy. A sureness in the cold. She reels in, picturing the streamer wriggling through the water just like a minnow, a sleek and shiny thing shimmering in the darkness. You have to keep a streamer moving in order for it to work. Nothing, not a bite. She casts again.

Her eyes have adjusted to the dark now, and she turns off her headlamp. There are no trees behind her, no bushes, so she can back-cast without the hassle of getting snagged. Way back, way out: more and more line. She reels in again. Her stomach, still enraged about the whiskey, gurgles and moans. She glances over her shoulder toward the fire. Janessa is standing now, gesturing wildly. Tyler remains in his spot but also throws his arms up in the air. Arguing. About what? That Emlyn and Tyler have crashed the party? That the #vanlife commitments were getting to be too much? Something deeper, more complicated, more tangled up in their long history than Emlyn could ever possibly understand?

She casts again, reels in again. She holds the streamer in her palm, pretending to examine it, stealing another look at Tyler and Janessa. Maybe it's the alcohol, softening her edges. Maybe it's the fatigue of the long hike, or the fact that she came all this way, only to be greeted with *You shouldn't be here.* Maybe it's all the years she spent wondering what secret, or secrets, simmered between Tyler and Janessa. Emlyn can't be sure. What she is sure of is that she wants to know what the two of them are saying. She deserves answers. She *has* to know.

She reels in, sets the rod against the log. "Hey," she calls to Bush, walking closer to him. "I need to go to the bathroom."

He looks in her direction, the light of his headlamp flashing her in the eyes. He seems to be considering his answer, and she realizes it feels like she's asking permission. She squints and holds her hands up to shield her eyes, and he flicks off his light. His body now a large, dark silhouette in the night. "Okay," he says, after too long a pause. "Sure."

In the darkness she walks quickly up the beach, veering left, angling away from the fire, avoiding its pitching light. She glances over her shoulder for Bush, but he never turned his headlamp back on, and she can't see him. She comes to where the woods begin and stops, pressing her back against a pine. She can hear their voices lifting and floating, but she can't make out what either of them is saying. Her pulse pounds and her head thumps. Nerves, whiskey. She takes a deep breath and, tucked in the trees, sneaks closer.

Tyler's voice: "Why did you post that you were in Wyoming?"

"Why did you put us on CNN?" Janessa retorts.

"Like I said, I was worried."

"Oh come on, Tyler. Don't lie to me. You did it to back me into a corner. You did it to flush me out. But I told you before I left, I had everything under control. I told you to trust me. And now I think—I think Bush might be onto me. I think he knows."

Tyler swears.

Emlyn squats, her back to them, tucked tight against a tree. Beneath her left foot, she feels a branch snap, the sound cracking through the night. She freezes, holding her breath. The voices cease. She imagines Janessa and Tyler catching each other's eyes, craning their necks toward the sound. Someone coming toward her, investigating. A flashlight is turned on; it flares back and forth over her head. She compresses her shoulders, making sure she's hidden by the tree.

Finally Janessa speaks again. Quieter, now, but still angry. Emlyn can barely catch the words. "And why on earth would you bring *her* here?"

Emlyn's heart lurches, her stomach tumbles over itself again.

"I needed her—"

"Of all the stupid, selfish things you've ever done, Tyler, this has got to be the worst."

"I know, okay. I see that now."

"I don't think you do. You have no idea how much is at stake. You have no idea the kind of danger you've put us in."

Danger?

Emlyn waits and waits for more words. Still tucked behind the pine, she can't see Tyler or Janessa, but they're done talking. The fire pops and hisses. Her knees protest the long, overextended squat. Now what? Her reconnaissance mission has provided nothing but more anxiety. Her belly snarls and rolls. She rises slowly and makes her way back to the beach. When she's close to the water's edge, she flicks on her light and finds her rod.

"Bush?" she calls.

She raises her headlamp and flashes down the beach where she left him. Not there. Maybe he moved up the lake, searching for a better spot. She pans left, right. Hollers again. No sign of him, no rod. Did he circle back to camp? Had she passed him in the dark and not seen him? "Bush?" she calls a second time, louder now, and then she flashes her light toward the water. "Bush!"

Janessa appears at her side. "What is it?"

"I left to go to the bathroom, and when I came back, he was gone."

Janessa reaches into her pocket and pulls out a headlamp. She turns it on and straps it to her forehead, then grabs Emlyn's hand and pulls her along. Janessa's fingers, still warm from the fire, grip Emlyn's cold palm. They jog quickly up the beach, toward where Emlyn fished with her streamer. Then back again.

"Bush!" Emlyn yells again, but Janessa reaches out her warm hand and presses it over Emlyn's mouth.

"Shhh! Don't."

Now Tyler appears. "What's going on?"

"Bush is gone," Janessa hisses. "Gone!" She drops Emlyn's hand. "As usual, you've ruined everything, Tyler."

A heat rushes through Emlyn, and the taste of metal rises in her mouth. Her body has finally said: *Enough.* She spins away and vomits on the rocks.

Tyler is at her side, hand on her back. "Are you okay?"

"Yeah, just give me a minute." She stumbles away from him and heaves again.

Tyler hands her a water bottle. "Here."

She takes it and swishes out her mouth. She spits to the side. "Sorry, guys. This is embarrassing. I think it was the alcohol on an empty stomach." Had she really had that much to drink?

"I don't feel so well myself," Tyler says. "And I didn't even have anything to drink."

Janessa swears under her breath. "Same." She flicks off her light and steps away from them. "Which means we might be in for a long night."

"Why? What do you mean?" Emlyn asks. Her throat is parched now, crackly and painful, and she takes a tiny sip of water.

"It might not be the alcohol," Janessa says, so quietly that Emlyn can barely hear her. "I think maybe we've been poisoned."

TWENTY-ONE

"POISONED?" Emlyn croaks. Her throat burns, and her teeth tingle. Her legs feel weak as she stumbles up the beach toward the campfire. Tyler offers his elbow, and she accepts it, looping her arm through his. A pain blooms at the back of her head and jolts its way to her temples. "You can't be serious."

"We'll see how the next half hour goes. If all of us get sick, then we'll know."

"I don't understand," Emlyn says. "Why would Bush poison us? And where is he, anyway? What if something happened? Aren't you worried?"

Janessa doesn't respond. She runs ahead to the campsite and ducks inside her tent. She reemerges quickly, and Emlyn sees that she is close to tears. "Gone. He took it."

"Took what?" Tyler asks.

"My makeup bag. It had a flash drive, inside a compact. Bush has it." She runs her hand through her hair and begins pacing back and forth.

"He knows," she whispers. She looks at Tyler, her eyes wild with desperation. "He knows!"

"Knows what?" Emlyn asks. She eases herself onto a log. The fire seems to double, triple. There are four fires, now; they are moving, they are stuttering left, then right. Same with Janessa: she seems to split herself, she has a clone. Emlyn's salivary glands are on overdrive. Is she drooling? She wipes her mouth with her sleeve.

The meal, she thinks. Whatever is making her sick—if Janessa's right and it isn't the alcohol, it has to have been the meal. She racks her brain for answers. She knows her wild edibles; she knows the threats. This is not a thing that should be out of reach for her—she committed various lists to memory, long ago, that summer when Marlene cleaned out Grandpa's workshop—but her mind, at the moment, feels like the mud pots at Yellowstone. Brown, mushy, bubbling hot. *Think, Emlyn. Focus.* Mushrooms are always a hazard, and, back home, they grew in abundance in the damp Pennsylvania woods. Giant hogweed. Dangerous because it looks like Queen Anne's lace, and its roots resemble carrots. It can cause the skin to bubble in painful blisters; its sap can make a person go blind. Buckeye, nightshade. Pokeberry, deep purple with its gorgeous pink stems. They grew on Grandpa's land. But Bush hadn't served berries, they hadn't eaten anything like carrots. Nothing fits.

Emlyn raises her eyes and stares at the Idaho sky. Her belly ripples with rage. She knows she isn't done vomiting, and she isn't confident she has the strength or balance to stand up and dart away from the campsite to do so, a thought she finds deeply depressing in this moment. She forces herself to sift through the names and pictures of plants, sewn into her brain, all those years ago. Moonseed, with its grape look-alikes, only discernible from wild grapes if you slice them open and count the seeds. Horse nettle. No.

Overhead, a rare jet winks across the dark. The stars shimmer white. And then Emlyn pictures it: a six-petaled flower, white, with green heart-shaped glands painted in the center. Unpretentious but lovely. Death camas. The green leaves, the simple white bulbs. Just last summer, a group of kids had mistaken them for wild onions on a camping trip. They'd chopped them up and eaten them on hot dogs, and the whole lot of them had ended up in the emergency room with nausea, vomiting, and cramping. She'd read about it in the *Idaho Statesman*. Beware, the article had warned: it's an easy mistake to make. It could also be fatal. Your blood pressure could drop, your temperature, too.

Bush, sauntering out of the woods. Bush, dicing those wild onions. Were they wild onions? Or were they death camas? And if they were death camas, had Bush made an honest mistake, or had he intentionally fed them the toxic plant? The former seems unlikely, given his knowledge and experience. Emlyn looks to her left, where Bush's plate sits balanced on a log, his food untouched. How much of it had the three of them ingested, really? How much is lethal? "Is he trying to kill us?" she says aloud.

"I don't think so," Janessa says. "That would be too obvious. All three of us, dead from a wild edible, no." Her brow is furrowed, and she bites her lip. "He would do something more subtle. Something . . . that looked like an accident. He's trying to slow us down, deter us. I think. I hope."

"Deter us? What does that even mean? Deter us from what?" Emlyn asks.

Tyler runs his hand through his hair and shakes his head. He pivots, looking behind him, left, right.

"Tyler," Janessa says, "you're the one who hauled her out here. Why don't you see if you can bring Emlyn up to speed?"

Tyler bites his lip. He shoves his hands into his pockets, kicks a rock.

Janessa folds her arms and states, matter-of-factly, "Bush has been funneling drugs through the Rocky Mountain West for over a decade. Oxy, fentanyl, you name it."

The world sways, Emlyn's pulse thumping at her neck. "I'm sorry, what?"

"He's been running drugs—"

Tyler steps forward and interrupts her. "I mean, seriously, did you really expect me to just stay home, once you told me your crazy plan?"

"Yeah, Tyler, I did. I expected you to trust me."

"No way, sorry. I knew if Bush so much as got a whiff of what you were doing, you could be in trouble. Big trouble. I knew you might already be in over your head." He pauses and turns to Emlyn. "And *that's* why I asked you to help."

"You knew about the drugs?" Emlyn asks him.

"I knew who Bush was," Tyler says. "What he did, a long time ago. But I didn't know he still had a foot in that world. And I certainly didn't know that all along, Janessa had been working to, I don't know, *expose* him. At least not until last week, when she sent me an encrypted file and told me to 'sit tight.'"

"I was not in over my head," Janessa argues.

"Really? Because after Bush's little speech about trust, I think it's safe to assume you're no longer in his inner circle." Tyler glances toward the trees and lowers his voice. "For all we know, he might be tucked in the woods right now, watching our every move, waiting." He turns back to Janessa. "Does he have a weapon?"

"Of course he has a weapon. He never *doesn't* have a weapon." She wipes her palms on her pants and adds, "He wouldn't need one anyway."

"I don't understand," Emlyn says. "What about the hunting and fishing and trapping?"

"He does that, too."

"But he lives in the spotlight. His whole life is on display. How—?"

"That was part of it," Janessa says. "Hiding in plain sight, I think that was a thrill for him."

Emlyn glances toward the trees, but her vision is too blurred to be useful. Somewhere deep in her mind she understands that she should be terrified, right now. Her skin should be tingling, her heart should be pounding. But her body doesn't seem to be working right. She reaches up and tucks two fingers beneath her jaw, feeling for a pulse. It's slow and faint. The death camas.

"In the beginning, he just delivered," Janessa says. "I didn't know him, then. For a long time he had a partner, someone integral to making the whole thing work, but the only thing I could find out about him—or maybe it was a her, hard to tell—was the name Collins." Janessa shakes her head. "But whoever it was, they've gone completely quiet, for years now." She rubs a hand up and down her arm and glances toward the woods.

"They're probably dead," Tyler says, running his hand through his hair. "That's how these things go, you know. You don't just build an empire without casualties."

"I know," Janessa hisses. "Don't you think I know that?"

"And you're probably next. *We're* probably next." He glances toward the woods.

Janessa turns to Emlyn. "He has a distribution center, now. A ranch, way off the grid. That's where we were heading. I've never been there, but I know it exists, and I know where it is, sort of. They all work for him. He makes the calls, he orchestrates. I have everything, now. And I am gonna take him down."

Emlyn tries to process this, but even without her foggy brain and nausea, it would be a lot to take in. "What do you mean, you're going to 'take him down'?" Emlyn recognizes that gleam in Janessa's eye, and she's pretty sure she doesn't like it.

"I have photos, videos, phone calls, everything. And I'm gonna post all of it online. His YouTube, my YouTube, our Instagram. Altogether I can reach two million people in a matter of seconds. It will blow him up. *I* will blow him up."

"And you're just doing this alone?"

"Of course not. I have a contact, a friend at the FBI. He's been in on it the whole time. He was out here, too, at first. But we had an agreement, a signal." She dabs her forehead, which gleams with sweat. "If Bush started seeming suspicious, if I got even the slightest hunch that he was getting wary, I would set up a few traps along our trail. My guy knew that if he ever came across a trapline, he needed to turn back until I contacted him again."

The traps. The man wearing the Buff, hurrying past them.

Tyler jumps in. "There is something deeply wrong with you, you know that? Setting those traps. Being okay with that kind of suffering. You crossed a new line. There was a doe, half dead. I had to put her out of her misery. And the rest of this, all of it. I'm not joking, J: you've completely lost your mind."

"Oh, please, Tyler. You're one to talk about crossing lines."

"Does he go by the name Oscar?" Emlyn asks. She thinks back to that starry night on the patio at Patten Lake, scrolling through messages while Tyler washed dishes. She's slowly piecing the story together. "As in, @ozkerwild?"

"How did you know?"

"I dug around your account," Emlyn says. She remembers the single response from Janessa. "You replied to him, once. Numbers, mixed with letters—they weren't typos, were they? They were a code. Or something."

"GPS coordinates to the van." Janessa's eyes twinkle, and a small smile plays at her lips. "Emmie, you are brilliant."

Tyler's shoulders slump. He looks young and forlorn, a chastised kid, his blond hair a mess, beanie propped high on his head. "So, now what?"

Janessa looks at Emlyn. "I'm staying the course. Until the toxins make their way out of our system, it's gonna be rough. But I have no intentions of just throwing in the towel. Not now. I've devoted years of my life to this, and I am not about to give up. In the morning I'll reassess."

"Reassess?" Tyler hisses. "Are you insane? He's one of the most skilled outdoorsmen in the country. He could probably live out here indefinitely. We'll never find him, not unless he wants us to, and in that case, well—we have a whole different problem on our hands. You need to call it." He jabs at the fire with violence. Sparks flutter high. "Before it's too late."

Janessa shakes her head slightly. Or maybe it's a shiver.

Tyler grabs Janessa's elbow. "You need to end this. Things have gotten out of hand. If you want to blame me for all that's gone south, fine, I get it. But you know I'm right. Now that he's onto you, there's no telling what he'll do to stop you. Please, Janessa, it's not worth it. Let it go. You need to go home."

Janessa stumbles to her feet and dashes into the darkness. Emlyn hears her retching.

"I'm sorry," Tyler says to Emlyn. "I never should've dragged you into this. I knew what he was capable of, and what he might do, if he got backed into a corner. That's why I was worried." He reaches for her hand and squeezes. "But I should've just told you all of that from the start." He spins suddenly, bolting away from the campfire to be sick, too.

Janessa returns and slumps against a log under her sleeping bag. Tyler stumbles back, pale and sweaty.

"Someone needs to stay awake," Janessa says. "Six hours until daylight, so if we split it up, we can each do two hours."

"I'll take the first shift," Emlyn offers.

"I'll do the last one," Tyler says.

"Good. I'll do the middle." Janessa waves Emlyn closer and pats the ground beside her. Emlyn crawls next to her. Janessa lifts the sleeping bag and covers Emlyn. "I've really missed you," she whispers.

Emlyn is so tired. The fire's glow, her exhaustion. Somehow, in all of the night's mire, a tiny diamond of joy at these words. She rests her head on Janessa's shoulder. "I've missed you, too."

THREE YEARS AGO

EMLYN wakes to a room that is dark and warm.

In the corner, a black woodstove hisses and pops, its door open, spilling heat and light. She squints, pain blazing its way through her head. Where is she? The place is unfamiliar, the shapes a blur. Not the makeshift bed in Tyler's truck, not Tyler's apartment, not her old bedroom back home with Marlene, not a hospital. A log cabin. Tyler's family cabin at Patten Lake? No. Different wood, different furniture. Plain and modest. Pine walls, a tidy kitchenette with a small round table, an antique wardrobe on the wall opposite the bed.

Also, she realizes, and panic seizes her heart: a man. He sits beside the woodstove, writing in a small black book. "Hey," he says, raising his eyes to meet hers, and his voice is soft and deep. He tugs a pair of glasses from his face, tucks a pen inside the book, and closes it.

Emlyn struggles to gain control of her senses, to sift through the details. Where is she? What happened? And who is the strange man?

She is so thirsty.

The man places his book on a small table next to his chair. "I'm gonna stand and get you a drink. Is that all right?"

She nods. He rises slowly and walks to the kitchenette. He is tall and thick and wears jeans and a blue flannel. He pulls a mug from a cabinet and fills it with water, then walks toward her, his movements slow and deliberate. "Here you go," he says, setting the mug on a nightstand next to her. He takes two steps back and, seeming to realize that he is towering over her, kneels. "I can help you sit up if you need a hand."

Does she need help sitting up? The thought is foreign and alarming. But then, she realizes, her body does ache, her limbs feel heavy and not her own. Her toes tingle and burn. She wriggles them, does the same with her hands. Slowly, she pulls her right arm from beneath the quilt. It is then that she looks at the red plaid sleeve and doesn't recognize it. She is wearing someone else's clothes, she is in this strange man's house. All at once the heaviness leaves her, and she sits up quickly, tucks her legs to her chest, and pushes away from him.

"Easy now," the man says, and when Emlyn looks at him she sees concern in his face. Decency, kindness.

"Who are you?" she croaks, her throat so parched the words barely come out.

"I'm with the Forest Service," he says. "Name's Varden. Varden Thompson."

The room stutters and blurs, it rolls upon itself, it moves even though she sits still. She squints, hoping to halt the movement.

"Like the fish?" she whispers.

Her eyes are nearly closed but she can hear a smile, a breath. "Yeah, like the fish." The stove crackles. "I'll hand you your drink if that's all right."

She nods.

She can feel him inching closer. She opens her hands, holds them out, and he places the mug against her palms, their fingers grazing. Eyes still closed, she wraps her hands around the porcelain. Varden stays close, help-ing her raise the cup to her lips. Emlyn drinks, the water sweet and cool. She tries not to gulp, though the water tastes so good she could cry. With caution she opens one eye, then the other. The room still spins. When she is done, Varden takes the mug and places it back on the nightstand for her. He rises, backs away. At the foot of the bed, there must be a bench or a trunk, because he sits on something.

"Your clothes are there," Varden says, pointing. "I washed them." He looks away, out the window, the light from the fire catching his beard and showing flecks of gray she hadn't noticed before. He rubs his palms over his knees. "You'd taken them off."

She bites her lip. A sign of hypothermia, she knows. As a person inches closer to succumbing to the cold, they feel hot, and sometimes remove their clothes. She's read about missing people being found by search-and-rescue teams, stretched dead in the snow, stripped down to their under-wear, despite freezing temperatures. Is it possible she'd tiptoed that close to death? She remembers the freezing rain, pelting white through a pitch-black sky, determined and hard.

"Where am I?" she asks.

"Heart, Idaho."

She pictures it on a map. Maybe an hour and a half north of her apartment, even closer to Tyler's family cabin. "What happened?"

Varden leans over, elbows on his knees. "Not sure, exactly. I was deep in the backcountry, setting up a series of trail cameras—we're keeping track of a pack of wolves out there. Snow was coming and I was on my way home." He seems to struggle with the words, as though it pains him to relate this to her. "You were near the road, alone. You had waders."

Emlyn remembers the rest of it, now. Tyler leaving to get pizza. The hours slogging past. Running out of water, hiking out in the waders, her foot catching on a stone. Alone. *Pathetic*. The word slinking toward her, teeth bared. A whimper escapes her.

"I need to ask you something."

She manages a nod.

"What's your name? You didn't have any ID on you."

She tells him.

Varden nods. "Good. That's good." Relief seems to wash over him, and he runs a palm across his brow. "I didn't know if we were dealing with one case or two." He rolls up one of his sleeves. "Few hours after I found you, a woman called the Forest Service office, said she went out to where you should've been fishing, and you weren't there. She was distraught."

Emlyn had lain there next to the road. She'd realized that Tyler was using yet again, that he had abandoned her. The cold had crept up her legs, sinking deeper and deeper. The numbness and its allure. "You should've left me there," she says quietly. She isn't sure if Varden hears her, but he looks at her, holding her gaze.

He rises and disappears into a room she hasn't noticed, then returns with a box of tissues. "Quite a friend you got there. Snow was already inches deep by then, and somehow she'd gone out that Forest Service road looking for you. She could've gotten stuck back there herself. Way I see it, that girl's either nuts or she loves you an awful lot."

Now Emlyn is crying hard. She is in a stranger's house, wearing a stranger's clothes, alone. She isn't sure what day it is, but she understands: two significant events have transpired, and they are intricately linked. Tyler left her in a heap in the woods; Janessa came to her rescue yet again. She's back in Emlyn's life. Maybe for good, maybe not. Emlyn wipes her eyes with the sleeve of Varden's red shirt, blows her nose. "Both," she manages to mutter, and then she lies down, fatigue overcoming her. "She's a little bit of both."

* * *

THE next time Emlyn wakes, the room is teeming with light, the sun spill-ing in through two great windows that she hadn't noticed before. She im-mediately closes her eyes.

"Don't fret, young lady, don't fret now." A sweet, comforting voice rises from the corner.

Emlyn opens her eyes again, squinting hard. In some nook of her memory, she remembers that black woodstove, a man with kind eyes, a blue mug and sweet water. Was that a dream? Some cruel game her mind was playing? Or is the dream now? Or is all of it a dream?

A woman with long white hair sits in that same rocking chair, bathed in light. She eases back and forth, knitting, the needles sliding together as she works. In her lap, a skein of blue yarn.

Emlyn tries to respond, but again her throat is parched and tight, and she can't speak, and besides, the words seem to dance in the air in front of her, teasing and elusive, just out of reach. She closes her eyes.

"That's right," the woman says. "You take your time." And then she is at Emlyn's side, in front of the window, the sun behind her so that light haloes around her. "Here," she says, setting a blue mug on a table beside the bed. "Can I help you sit up?"

Emlyn eyes the drink and nods.

The woman leans close, her long, white hair brushing Emlyn's fore-head. She slides her hands behind Emlyn, one at her neck and one between her shoulder blades, and gently lifts. Her strength is surprising. She reaches for a pillow and stuffs it behind Emlyn's back. "There." The woman hands Emlyn the cup. "Careful, it's warm."

The tea is sweet and familiar: elderberry, honey. All at once Emlyn is transported back to her youth, the convertible workshop where she lived with her mother after her dad left, Marlene cooking elderberries on the stove, Emlyn suffering through math problems at the old table they'd picked up from the curb.

"I'm Ruth," the woman says, resuming her knitting. "But everyone calls me Rev."

"Emlyn."

Rev nods. "It's good to meet you, Emlyn," and Emlyn has the feeling Rev means it when she says it.

"There was a man here, before?" Emlyn pictures the man from the night before—the kind hazel eyes, the shy smile—but she can't remember his name.

"Varden. Yes. This is his cabin, actually." She tilts her head toward the door. "My place is across the way. He's hauling up some wood just now. Asked me to sit with you in case you woke up. Which you did. He'll be back soon."

"Has anyone called my mother?"

"Yes, sugar. That friend of yours did."

"Is she coming to get me?" Somewhere deep inside the fog, Emlyn knows that Marlene is two thousand miles away, that, quite likely, nobody is coming to get her. That she herself doesn't even know exactly where she is. But she knows this isn't home, and that surely these strangers won't take care of her for long.

The woman reaches out a warm hand and places it on Emlyn's arm. "Not in this snow, young lady. All three roads into this valley are closed. Ain't nobody getting here anytime soon."

Emlyn turns to the window. She hasn't noticed, or hasn't registered, that the world outside is dazzling white: a wide valley, tall mountains beyond it, everything glimmering.

"Listen," Rev says, "I need to check your feet again. Is that all okay?"

"My feet?"

Rev nods. "You got some frostbite. Mild, so we can work at it. Your fingers, too." She reaches for a brown glass bottle on the nightstand and gives it a shake. "I've been at it. Other times, you weren't awake, I don't think. You opened your eyes, but I could tell: you weren't really aware, so to speak. Anyhow, you're due for a treatment here, all right?"

Emlyn nods, and Rev slowly lifts the quilt from the bottom corner of the bed and folds it onto Emlyn's knees. She unscrews the lid and pours lotion into her hand, sets the bottle back on the nightstand. She rubs her palms together, then reaches for Emlyn's feet. "This is cypress," she says, and the scent lifts to Emlyn's nostrils, warm and pungent. "It helps with circulation. Bit of horsetail in there, too. And a little witch hazel to fight any infection." She massages Emlyn's feet, working the lotion onto her toes, squeezing each one between her fingers. The intimacy of this moment, the sense that this woman is positioning herself as servant. A wave of self-consciousness pitches through Emlyn. She wants to refuse, she wants to pull away, but Rev holds tight.

"There," Rev says. "Now for your hands." She folds the quilt back into place. "It isn't too bad," the woman says, pressing both hands over Emlyn's. "What you have. I've seen worse. Ranchers out after cattle. Neighbor was on the cross-country skis and stayed out too long, once. Sometimes, it's beyond me, but many times, I can help. The Lord has provided quite a bit of healing, right here at our fingertips. Roots, berries, oils. So long as a person knows how to use them." She works the lotion over each of Emlyn's fingers. She tucks her white hair behind her ear. "Do they burn, your toes or fingers?"

The tenderness of the woman's touch, the warmth of the oils, the elderberry tea. Emlyn tilts under the combined weight of her exhaustion and the kindness of this stranger. She can barely keep her eyes open.

"No," she manages to say, though the top half of her left ring finger tingles. "It doesn't burn."

TWENTY-TWO

EMLYN hears the sound of ospreys bickering close by. Squawk, screech. More than one bird. Two? She hasn't yet opened her eyes, but she lies still, listening, thinking through the possibilities of what these birds might be saying. A small happiness in this imagining. A marital tiff, perhaps. Responsibilities to be sorted out: babies that need feeding, a nest that needs cleaning. Or perhaps it's something else. Another bird infringing on the territory. Complicated creatures, birds.

She opens her eyes to a dome of bright orange and for a moment is confused. This is not her tent. She looks down. This is not her sleeping bag. And then she remembers. The headache from the night before lingers, and, now that her eyes are open, discomfort begins to throb at the base of her neck. She vaguely recalls growing cold in the middle of the night. Tyler's hands gently guiding her past the fire, scrambling into a tent. She blinks and, for one brief moment, blazes through the previous night's events. Devouring Bush's feast, fishing in the dark, getting sick, resting against Janessa. What transpired after that? Nothing happened between her and Tyler, right? She turns on her side, half expecting to see him there, but next to her, Janessa is fast asleep, her blond hair covering half her face.

Emlyn sits up slowly. Her Crocs are in the corner, and she crawls from her sleeping bag and slides her feet into them. She unzips the tent and steps out. Though she expects to find Tyler asleep near the fire, he isn't there. The sun is high. The air is crisp and sharp but quickly warming in that way it does in the mountains. Smoke wisps from the fire pit, though all that remains is a hunk of charred wood. The ospreys continue their quarrel, and Emlyn looks for them, raising her hand to shield her eyes. There, in a tall pine along the water's edge, high up. Just as she suspected, a nest. One bird comes in for a landing, fish in its talons. The other shrieks at its mate's arrival. Maybe, all along, there has been no quarrel, just joy.

She walks to the second tent and slowly unzips it. Tyler isn't there, either.

She turns around. Maybe he needed to go to the bathroom, maybe he took a walk. Her eyes scan the beach, the lake's edge. Nothing. She looks around the campsite. Her backpack, Janessa's. The plates from Bush's meal, her boots. She spins left, right. Takes another look inside the tent to confirm—yes, Tyler's backpack is gone.

She dashes toward the orange tent, and it's then that she notices a piece of paper, rolled like a scroll and tucked in one of her boots.

She squats and grabs it, quickly opening it up.

Em—

This was a mistake, bringing you out here. I've put you in danger, which of course I've done before, and for that, I am truly, deeply sorry.

I love you, Emlyn, and I think maybe I have since that first time I saw you, hiding on the deck at my parents' house. I swear, from that day forward, my world hasn't been the same. But here, in the dark on this terrible night, I am facing the painful realization that even now, I still don't belong in your life. You deserve better. You deserve someone who puts you first.

I messed up. Again. It's what I do. Mess things up. But I dragged you into this, and I will give you a way out . . . this time, I can fix this. Please take Janessa and go home. Please let me make things right.

All my love, Tyler

A noise escapes her, an animal sound, not quite a sob. She slumps to the ground. A herd of emotions gathers inside her. Like the sheep from the day before, it seethes and murmurs; it threatens to trample. She believes now that Tyler loves her, but she's also filled with a strong, terrible sense that he will not survive whatever it is that he plans to do. That she will never see him again, that there are too many things left unsaid between them.

Where is Tyler? And how, exactly, does he believe he can "make things right"?

In the tent, Janessa is still fast asleep.

"Janessa."

Janessa stirs. Emlyn repeats her name.

Janessa's eyes slowly blink open. "What is it?" she rasps, squinting.

"I need you to get up. Tyler's gone."

"What?" She rolls onto her back.

"He's gone. And so is his backpack."

"No." She holds her palm to her forehead. "Oh, no."

"I know." Emlyn squeezes Janessa's knee beneath the sleeping bag. "He left a letter. He went after Bush without us. Come on. You have to get up."

Janessa sits up and then squeezes her eyes tight.

"You okay?"

"Yeah."

There's no time for coffee, but Emlyn remembers: in her bag, she has chocolate-covered espresso beans. She goes to the other tent and digs them out, grabbing two protein bars as well.

Janessa has climbed out of the tent and is sitting on a log. Emlyn takes a few beans and gives her the rest of the bag.

For a moment she contemplates whether to show Janessa the letter. It's her letter, after all. Tyler didn't address it to both of them. And there are private, precious words there that maybe Emlyn doesn't want to share. But there could also be clues. Emlyn hands her the letter.

Janessa reads it, squinting in the morning light. She pops an espresso bean in her mouth and shakes her head. "Idiot." She waves the letter. "I mean, what's he gonna do? Does he really think he can even find Bush? He's much more likely to get lost. Or injured. Or die of starvation." She eats another espresso bean. "And if by some chance he finds Bush and confronts him—what's his plan, then?" She shakes her head and crosses her arms. "You know, my whole life, this is how it goes. He's always . . . wanting to be a hero. And also always overreaching. That ego of his. That confidence. I swear, of all his irritating qualities, that's probably the worst."

Emlyn sits down beside her. She realizes it's that confidence, that pluck, that she's always loved about Tyler. About Janessa, too. She nods, hands Janessa one of the protein bars, and sits down next to her. "It's probably his most endearing quality, too."

"I know." Janessa puts her face in her palms. She massages her temples and then rests her chin on her fists. "I wish you could've known him, before. He was so smart. And funny, and kind. Even in middle school, when no one is kind, Tyler was. He just had this way of, I don't know, pulling people in. He was always just—"

"Captivating."

"Yes, exactly. He could've done anything, been anything." She shakes her head. "By the time you met him—he was still Tyler, but he was already different. He was, I don't know, something less than he'd been."

Emlyn understands what Janessa means. Her mind shuttles backward, years ago, when Tyler made her a sandwich and cut himself, so high he didn't even feel it. He was there, and he also wasn't. She places her arm on her friend's shoulder.

"You know who gave him the first pills?"

Emlyn shakes her head.

"Bush. There were plenty of people at our high school who wanted to dull their pain, or chase a new high, or whatever, and all of them had the means to pay for it. At that point, he was just small-time, but he had a pretty good little setup, even back then. Tyler met him skiing. They partied, sometimes. I tried to help." She looks down, bites her lip. "But by the time I found out he was using, I don't think he could've stopped even if he wanted to."

"So—you knew? From the start, you knew who Bush was, what he'd done?"

"Of course I knew."

"But you pretended? Not to know?"

"For a while, yes. But once I got him to trust me, I started asking questions. I told him I wanted in on it."

"And you pretended to be in love with him?"

Janessa wrinkles her nose. "Don't say it like that. Like I'm some kind of phony, or jerk or something." She shoves two espresso beans into her mouth. "I had a mission. I *have* a mission. And I decided from the get-go that I would do whatever it took."

Emlyn stares at her friend. Janessa has always been full of surprises, but this feels extreme, even for her. The Instagram account, all the photos of their travels. Emlyn thinks back to that fight at the hot springs and feels a flicker of sadness, because even now, Janessa still seems to be throwing herself headlong into someone else's life.

"What?" Janessa says, chewing. "Listen, he ruined Tyler's life. And in turn, he ruined yours. I'm sure there are plenty of others." She holds Emlyn's gaze. "I saw the way he looked at me, when I came back to Idaho. The first time I talked to him, I knew. I knew I could make him fall for me." She tugs a hunk off her protein bar. "And that's exactly what I did."

Emlyn plucks another espresso bean from the bag. Her mind turns to Rev, with her warmth and light, and Varden, with his quiet steadiness. "My life," she says at last, "isn't ruined. It's different. But it's not ruined. I'm okay. I really am." And she is. She's okay. Better than okay, maybe.

"I know. I can see that. And I'm very, very glad that you are." Janessa leans against her, their shoulders pressed tight. "Sometimes I think about when you first told me, about you and Tyler. I wish I would've just told you everything, right then and there, why I didn't want you to get involved with him. I was trying to protect you, I was trying to protect him, and in the end, I lost both of you."

"You didn't lose me," Emlyn whispers. "Not forever."

For a moment they sit there, the sun warm on their faces, the ospreys bickering in the treetop. They finish off the espresso beans, and Emlyn feels the coffee's bright buzz hit her veins.

"You know we can't leave him out here, right?" Emlyn says. In her mind she's estimating when Tyler might've left, how far ahead he'll have pressed, how they'll go about trying to catch up with him.

Janessa takes a bite of a protein bar. "I know." She pushes herself up and stands. "We have to pack up and go after him." She holds out her hand and helps Emlyn up.

"Good," Emlyn says. "I was hoping that's the way you'd see it."

THREE YEARS AGO

DESPAIR licks at a door of Emlyn's heart. It flashes its teeth and whispers its mean words.

You are pathetic, you are forgettable. You have wasted your life.

Three days in, the snow has stopped falling, but now a bitter wind assaults the valley. It barrels down the hillsides, scooping snow, cycloning white in the parking lot. It piles at the door and hammers at the cabin window. Varden shovels and shovels. Rev fills mason jars with water in case the power goes out. Emlyn is at Rev's house now, where she has her own bedroom, and she spends long hours staring out the wide window at the world of white. Beyond the basic courtesies of yes, please, and thank you, she doesn't speak. She has no words, she's an empty room. Tyler calls and calls. He sends messages with abundant question marks. She reads them and does not respond.

Janessa, with some reluctance, has assumed the role of liaison, and it's through her that Emlyn patches together the story. Tyler showed up at Janessa's parents' house, high and delirious, and Janessa, home for her dad's birthday, drove him to the hospital. Somewhere in the midst of this, she realized Emlyn had not been accounted for, and immediately set about trying to track her down. Tyler is in rehab. Emlyn asks Janessa to tell him it's over.

But pulling away is easier said than done. The happy moments of her old life—Sunday pizza, sandwiches for Jorge, cozy nights in their truck camper, weekends at the cabin at Patten Lake—they beckon and sing. They take on greater prominence, they subsume all the bad. She watches happy videos on her phone and constructs a narrative of her life, a patchwork of truths. In some moments, she nearly convinces herself that she was happy and healthy with Tyler. That he will get better, that they can work things out, that all the things that are broken about both of them can be fixed.

ON her first Sunday in the valley, Emlyn sits at the long wooden table in Rev's kitchen, completing a crossword puzzle from an old *New York Times* left behind by a summer renter. Rev fills a bright blue kettle with water, then turns to look at her. "Well, young lady," she says, "figure you might want to get dressed. Church starts soon."

Emlyn is wearing an ankle-length nightgown from Rev's closet with Varden's flannel on top, a pair of knitted wool socks pulled to her knees. She isn't quite sure whether her last shower was two days ago or three. She fills in a series of small blocks: *parkour*. She looks up and forces a smile and says, "I don't go to church."

"No, maybe not. And that's all well and good. But church is here, in this living room, and of course you're more than welcome to wear my nightgown as long as you'd like—nobody here's gonna hold that against you—but they'll start pouring in any minute. Just wanted to give you a heads-up."

Emlyn retreats to the bedroom that has become hers for the time being. She keeps the flannel but swaps out the nightgown for a pair of blue velour sweatpants Rev has set out for her. She washes her face, and, because she is unsure whether it would be rude to stay in her room during church, returns to the main room.

The band of Sunday misfits begin their boisterous arrival, stomping snow off on the porch, shuffling in and peeling off scarves and heavy coats. This first Sunday, Emlyn knows none of them, and her finger tingles through the entire service. Later, she will learn their names. Oliver, Roxy, Shane, Darla. Gerald with his kind eyes and his quiet wolf dog that sits guard at the door. Rev carries a tray of mugs to the living room. Varden adds a log to the fire.

This is not the Sunday service Emlyn has witnessed in movies. No stained glass and polished pews. No white-robed priest. Nor is there a snarling preacher, spinning on the balls of his feet, hollering and red-faced, like she'd seen at the little church down the road from Grandpa's that Marlene took her to, once.

Instead, Rev leads the hymns in her rich tenor, tapping her foot, nodding her head when the singers need to speed up. She inquires about Gerald's niece, who's due to deliver a baby any day. She asks Shane how he is managing his depression, which apparently grows worse each winter. She asks whether anyone else needs prayer. Emlyn stares hard at the fire, just in case anyone is looking at her and thinking she might spill her guts. Rev prays in that odd, musical way of hers, the prayer almost a song, hands raised. Emlyn opens one eye and steals a glimpse. She wouldn't be surprised if the heavens opened up and Rev floated skyward.

After the prayer, Rev takes up her Bible. "We'll continue our reading of Numbers, the eleventh chapter," she says. "And for those of you who weren't with us last week, let me recap. Moses has led the Israelites out of slavery in Egypt at this point. They're no longer under Pharaoh's thumb, but now they're in the wilderness. The people are hungry and thirsty. They're beginning to think maybe they should've stayed in Egypt. At least there they knew what they were in for, bad as it was. Out in the wilderness, there is new danger. There is fear and uncertainty." She slides on her glasses and begins reading.

When Rev finishes her excerpt, she closes her Bible and looks around the room. "Well," she says, folding her hands on top of the Bible, "what do you all make of that?"

In the weeks that follow, Emlyn will come to understand that this is Rev's version of a sermon. She reads a passage of Scripture; she asks questions. That's it. Now, the small crowd is silent. Gerald shuffles in his seat. His wolf dog raises its head. Emlyn's finger burns.

It's Varden who finally raises a hand. "Wilderness is a lonely place. It's a place of hardship and doubt." He takes off his beanie and folds it in his hands. "You don't know where you are, and you don't see a way through. And that is a real, real hard spot to be. Been there myself, on more than one occasion."

Rev murmurs and nods. "Same here, Varden, same here."

The wolf dog grumbles in the corner. The fire burns blue and orange.

Varden's words seep under Emlyn's skin. This story from the book of Numbers is new to her, but somehow she understands that she is deep, deep in a wilderness, right now, encompassed by unfamiliar terrain. Aimless, alone. *Pathetic.* She has no idea where she is, and she has no idea which way to go. *How do you get out?* Emlyn wants to ask. *How do you survive?* But she is too shy to speak. She stares at the floor, studying the lines in the wood.

"But it's in the wilderness that you grow," Varden continues. "In ways that you couldn't, anywhere else. If that makes sense. And the thing you can't forget is that wilderness isn't the destination. It's not the final chapter. It might feel that way, it might seem like you're so deep in it, you'll never get out." Emlyn dares to raise her eyes, and she sees that Varden is looking at her. "But your story—it goes on."

She stares right back. It's as though the two of them are the only ones in the room. At last she blinks and ducks her head and wipes her eyes on her sleeve and remembers she's wearing Varden's flannel.

"Amen to that," Rev says. "Amen!"

Rev prays, but Emlyn doesn't hear the prayer.

At the end of the service, Gerald reaches out a rough, gnarled hand and squeezes hers. "Good to meet you, Emlyn," he says, before trundling over to his dog and leaving without a coat.

A gust of snow scuttles in through the open door. The wolf dog turns and looks her way. Varden's words smolder in Emlyn's mind, throwing smoke and heat. Noise, nonsense, garbage, she tells herself: she doesn't believe any of it. And yet—she knows without a doubt that she wants to. She wants to believe that beyond her wilderness is better, less formidable topography. It's just that right now, she can't imagine she'll ever get there.

TWENTY-THREE

EMLYN and Janessa do what they can to consolidate. Janessa dumps Bush's pack onto the ground and the two of them rifle through the heap, Janessa grabbing a package of jerky and two dehydrated meals, Emlyn sifting through his tools. A tourniquet, a pocketknife, a small canister of waterproof matches. As she shoves these items into her pack, her fingers graze over Rev's flashlight. For a moment she stares at it, thinking of her friend and her prayer and her word, and, feeling sentimental, she tucks it into the zip pocket of her fleece.

They debate taking a tent—how long can they realistically be out here?—and ultimately decide on Tyler's lightweight double. They break it down quickly. As she begins rolling it up, Emlyn feels something small and hard in a corner, and she fishes it out of the folds of nylon. The GPS unit! She turns it on, goes to the messages. Maybe Tyler's contact at the Forest Service has reached out, maybe they are closing the distance. Either way, she'll send a message with an update and new coordinates.

She presses the small gray buttons, trying to navigate. Okay, good: Tyler's message with their initial coordinates and a request for help.

Except—? Is this right? The message was never sent. In fact, there are no sent messages at all.

An unpleasant thought bubbles up—what if this wasn't an oversight or an accident?

No, that doesn't make sense. It has to have been a mistake. Tyler's always been absentminded, and with the fatigue and stress, it's obviously worse. Emlyn tells herself not to despair. They are okay. They will be okay.

She grabs her phone and finds Varden's number, then adds it to the GPS unit. She types a brief update. *Found Janessa, she's safe. Tyler and her boyfriend, Bush, are gone. Looking for them now. XX, Em.* She checks her mapping app and adds their coordinates, too. If and when they find Tyler, they will hit that SOS button. There's no need to fret.

Janessa scrapes the remnants of food from the night before into the fire, and Emlyn fetches water from the lake and quickly rinses the dishes. The pan Bush used to fry the fish, the pot he used to make the mashed potatoes, four plates and eating utensils. Even though they're short on time, they can't leave that kind of invitation for animals to raid their site. Janessa dumps the dishwater on the coals, the fire hissing loudly, steam rising up. They filter and fill their water bladders. They leave everything else right there on the beach. If someone does come along, someone looking for them or not, they'll find the remnants of the group's night under the stars. The dumped pack and its contents. One tent, plus the lines in the sand indicating that a second tent had been there. All of this a sign that someone had left, and left quickly. If Emlyn were to come upon such a scene in the woods, only one conclusion would make sense: something had gone wrong.

THE plan is to find Tyler. Bush can fend for himself, and will. It's Tyler they're worried about. About fifty yards from the campsite, Emlyn picks up his trail, footprints in the sand, left toe occasionally dragging. She re-sumes the tracking option on her app. Whatever transpires, she still needs to be able to find her way back out of here.

Tyler was moving quickly. Worry skitters along Emlyn's skin. It's not that Tyler is incompetent. He's fit, strong, and knowledgeable enough. It's that he's never been good alone. He gets swept up—the destination; the landscape; even the smell of the sagebrush; the arrowleaf balsamroot, yellow and bright—and he gets distracted. He forgets to drink water; he convinces himself he's not hungry. Without Emlyn there to remind him, will he keep on top of those things? The trouble is, at this point in their trek, the body is already worn down. After last night, he is almost certainly starting the day dehydrated and at a caloric deficit. But she knows Tyler, and she knows he won't recognize those things in himself. He'll push ahead, he'll drive himself into the ground.

She picks up the pace.

Tyler's path hugs the lake's edge, and they follow it, Emlyn looking down, Janessa watching the treetops. There's a trail of sorts, here. Not well-traveled, but perceptible. They walk in silence for several minutes.

"I came to tell you I was sorry," Janessa says. "That summer. I'd over-stepped. And you were right: I was always overstepping. It was your choice, if you wanted to be with Tyler." She stops and stands still. "I knew you were there, I saw you in the window." She swallows hard. "Tyler's truck was in the parking lot."

"Oh—" Emlyn remembers this day with startling clarity: the mean thrill of dodging Janessa, that first kiss with Tyler. "I don't know what to say."

"It's okay, I'm okay. You had a right to be mad. You had a right to shut me out." Janessa wipes her eyes with the back of her hand. "But I also understood, that day, that you two were moving on, together. And that by trying to step in, I'd ruined my friendship with both of you. I knew there wasn't room for me, not anymore."

Emlyn wants to disagree. She wants to lie and say, *No, that's not right. Of course there was room; there was always room for you.* But she knows those things aren't true, or at least they weren't, then, and instead, she just throws her arms around her friend and whispers, "I'm sorry."

She feels Janessa nodding.

"When you told me you were leaving, I shouldn't have just raised a glass." That moment on Betts's patio flutters back to her. How flippant and callous she must've seemed. "I should've held on to you. Or tried."

Janessa shakes her head. "We both needed to go our own way for a while. That's the way I look at it."

Emlyn squeezes tight. They stand like that, hugging, for a long time.

THEY press on. The lake thins and bends into the mountains, and last night's campsite slips from view. Tyler's trail grows harder to follow. He is, Emlyn realizes, perhaps aware that they are following him, and attempting to hide his tracks. She signals to Janessa to stop. They drink water, share some beef jerky. Emlyn pulls out her phone and studies the map. The battery is now at twelve percent. Janessa leans close, and Emlyn shows her.

"Hey, something I've been meaning to ask you," she says as they resume their trek. "Last week, when you called, you said there was something you needed to tell me. What was it?"

Janessa shakes her head. "It doesn't matter now."

"Okay, but can you tell me anyway? What was it?"

Her friend rubs the back of her neck and looks away. "I was gonna say that if Tyler reached out to you, if he asked you for some kind of help, you should tell him no."

THREE YEARS AGO

ON Emlyn's eighth day in Heart, the temperature rises and the snow begins to melt. It's only October, after all, and winter is merely cracking its knuckles before the real assault. Within weeks the temperatures will plummet, the cold air from both the Obsidians and the Borahs trundling down from the icy peaks and settling in the valley. At the moment she has no plans; she has not yet formulated what exactly she will do, where she will go, or whom she should call. She only knows that she cannot stay in this cozy house with its plaid couch and crackling woodstove, with Rev and her homemade bread, and Varden and his Moleskine notebooks, forever. For over a week she has leaned into their kindness, she has basked in the glow of Rev's radiance, but of course this can't go on.

"I should be going," Emlyn tells Rev and Varden over a supper of roasted venison. That afternoon the snowplows had come through, clearing the roads, pushing black-dotted snow into high mounds on the sides of the road. The sun, bright and glorious, has melted what snow still clung to the roads, and now the vast white is interspersed with black lines.

Rev dabs her mouth with a cloth floral napkin and grips it in her hand. "About that," she says. "Young lady, I was wondering if you'd consider staying."

Varden stops chewing and looks at Rev and then Emlyn. Though he answers questions and conveys necessary information—"Tell Rev I'll check for eggs," and "Careful, the hot water is extra hot today"—he doesn't talk much, and he seems beleaguered by shyness.

"The reason I say that," Rev continues, "is because I could use the help. Cleaning, organizing for next season. It's always such a burden, and it doesn't get any easier with age. And truth is, neither one of us would mind the company. Would we, Varden?"

Varden's cheeks grow red, Emlyn is sure of it, and he shifts his gaze to his plate. "No."

Still Emlyn is silent.

"What I'm proposing is room and board for your efforts. Come spring, you can reevaluate."

"I couldn't," Emlyn says, a hunk of Rev's bread warm in her mouth. But she is thinking, she could, really. Work around the cabins, stay through the winter, avoid retrieving her few belongings from Tyler's apartment, dodge the pain of having to see him.

And also the lure of it.

"Well," Rev says, poking her mashed potatoes with her fork, "promise me you'll think on it a day or two." She takes a bite. "You really would be doing me a favor, if you can swing it."

Emlyn nods. She steals a glance at Varden, who is twisting his cloth napkin between his finger and thumb.

"Sure, I'll think it over," Emlyn says, taking a sip of water. "Thanks." She pokes at a carrot. "Varden, I was wondering, could I borrow a book?"

She knows that in Varden's cabin, there's a tall corner shelf, crammed with books. Books upright, packed tight, books backward. Books on their side on top of those. Novels, biographies, poetry collections. A range so vast she cannot possibly identify any particular taste or leaning. Henri Nouwen, Stephen King, Mary Shelley, Tomas Tranströmer. (Also, Emlyn noted yesterday, when Varden was shoveling and her curiosity got the better of her, a sizable collection of Amish romance novels, all with the spines hidden and the pages facing outward.) A book would do her good, right now, and surely there's something on those shelves that would suit— maybe even an Amish romance.

Varden stares at a knot in the wooden table before flashing her a glance. "I guess," he mutters. He rises from his seat and walks to the kitchen.

Rev rolls her eyes. "Oh, Varden." She follows him to the kitchen, where he is filling the sink with hot, soapy water. Emlyn finishes her piece of bread, watching from her seat at the table. Varden stacks the pots and pans to his right and begins tackling the plates. Rev returns, sliding a game of Scrabble from an end table drawer.

Emlyn stands and joins Varden at the sink. "I'll dry," she offers, and he nods. "Is it all right if I come over later to pick a book?"

"Why don't you just tell me what you're looking for, and I'll see if I have it."

"Well, can I browse?"

"I'd rather you didn't."

The possibility that maybe this is because he's embarrassed about those Amish romances crosses Emlyn's mind, and she can't help it: a smile plays at her lips. She plucks a dish from the rack and wipes it down with her towel. "Okay, then," she says, sliding the dish onto its shelf. "I guess just surprise me."

* * *

THE next morning, Varden comes to the door. Outside, his Jeep is already running in the little parking lot, and he's dressed for work. "Here," he says, holding out a book: *Wuthering Heights.* Sticking out from the first page is a small piece of paper, folded lengthwise, edges creased. He tugs it out, presses it tight in her palm, and for a long time he looks right at her. His eyes are a light brown, flecked with green, and his lips are full and soft. He holds his hand to her hand, then walks out the door. When he is gone she opens the note immediately and reads the words, copied in his tidy handwriting on a piece of paper torn from one of his Moleskine notebooks.

The Thing Is
to love life, to love it even
when you have no stomach for it
and everything you've held dear
crumbles like burnt paper in your hands,
your throat filled with the silt of it.
When grief sits with you, its tropical heat
thickening the air, heavy as water
more fit for gills than lungs;
when grief weights you down like your own flesh
only more of it, an obesity of grief,
you think, How can a body withstand this?
Then you hold life like a face
between your palms, a plain face,
no charming smile, no violet eyes,
and you say, yes, I will take you
I will love you, again.

—Ellen Bass

Emlyn holds the poem, the edge of the paper gripped tight between her finger and thumb. She reads it again. Something scuttles through her gut, a fish of desire and despair. Is it true? Will she hold life like a face between her palms and say, yes? She can barely fathom it, the possibility that she could love life again. And how did Varden know? How could he possibly know that a poem, *this* poem, could carve right through her and open her up?

She walks to the window on unsteady legs and looks out as Varden climbs into his white Forest Service Jeep. He closes the door, starts the engine. He sits at the wheel, then finally looks up at her. For a moment the two of them are still, eyes locked. The windowpane fogs with Emlyn's breath. Exhaust rises white from the rear of the Jeep. She presses the poem to the window, palm holding it in place. Varden nods. And, though she lacks a name for it, a feeling rises in her throat. Not love, not peace. But some strange permutation of feelings that spin and wrap themselves around each other.

Emlyn decides right then and there that she will accept Rev's offer to stay through the winter. She asks Janessa to box up her things at Tyler's and ship them to Rev.

By Christmas, the heaviness that made Emlyn want to stay in bed and never get up begins a slow and reluctant lift. By spring she'll have come up with a word to describe what it is that Varden and Rev gave her that winter, as the snow spun and twirled like ghosts off the Obsidians and Borahs. The sense that maybe she could love and be loved. That maybe Varden was right about the wilderness, that her story goes on. A tiny word, four letters, no frills. "Hope."

TWENTY-FOUR

THE terrain grows more difficult. Emlyn and Janessa scramble over rocks, struggling with their packs, which they must take off frequently to pull themselves up and over the boulders that line the lake's edge. Emlyn scrapes a knee, Janessa nearly loses her balance. The lake bends again. No, Emlyn realizes: there are two lakes, separated by a thin strand of rocks and pines that they have no choice but to cross. The name for it echoes from seventh-grade geography class: *isthmus*. The left side rises sharply, a rocky scarp, gleaming white in the sunshine.

Emlyn goes first. She hefts her heavy pack above her head and pitches it onto the first rock. Then she clambers up. Next she takes Janessa's pack, and Janessa scrabbles toward her. On either side of the isthmus, the land drops sharply. On one side, water. On the other, rocks.

"Do you really think Tyler came this way?" Janessa asks, which is a reasonable question. She is heaving from the undertaking.

"Where else would he have gone?"

Little by little, they continue making their way across the crag.

Backpack, body. Body, backpack. Up and up and then down. The sun, now high in the sky, burns gloriously overhead, and Emlyn can feel the first prickle of a sunburn on her neck and face. She thinks of the man wearing the Buff, @ozkerwild. Once they get across this thin finger of rock, she'll wrap her scarf around her head.

By the time they make it, the two of them are out of breath. Emlyn points to the trees, where they can find shade, and each of them slumps against a pine tree, relieved to be off the crag.

Janessa bends her knees and tucks her head between them. "I don't know how much more I can take."

Emlyn takes a long drink of water. "You'll be okay." This is what she says aloud, but deep down she isn't so sure. Janessa looks spent. Emlyn, too, feels the brunt of the previous days. The long, taxing hike to the lake. The vomiting, the dehydration. It's likely that they haven't fully flushed out all the toxins yet, and, even if they have, they've certainly not recovered from the stress on the body. The emotional strain, too, is taking its toll.

She closes her eyes and forces herself to breathe deeply. She rifles through her bag, looking for the scarf, takes it out, and wraps it around her neck, face, and head. "You're getting burnt, too," she tells Janessa, noting her red cheeks and forehead. "Do you have something you can cover up with?"

Janessa nods and searches through her bag before producing a Buff and sliding it on.

Higher up the hill, a twig snaps, and Emlyn spins her head in that direction. "Did you hear that?" she whispers.

Janessa shakes her head.

They hold still. Emlyn's eyes scan the hillside. No movement, no other noise. Of course there are animals everywhere—marmots, squirrels, chipmunks, mice, birds—and most likely, the noise was a critter. But there has been no sign of Bush, really, and the ugly possibility that maybe they're the ones being followed rises up in Emlyn's mind. She looks all around, searching. What if Tyler was right? What if Bush hid near their camp last night and waited to see what unfolded? What if he is following them, now?

EMLYN looks out at the water, glassy and blue-green. Remnants of last winter's snow still dot the black faces of the mountains beyond, deep pockets that only melt in the hottest of summers. Such bright colors, such beauty.

For so many years Emlyn has tried to ignore the part of her that sees everything through the gray lens of suspicion. It was a hindrance, a bad habit to be overcome. She remembers Rev's prayer, just before she left for the wilderness. Emlyn has tried to trust. Others, and herself. For the most part, she really is happier this way, giving people the benefit of the doubt, choosing to see the best in them. But right now that old tendency is gnawing hard at her mind, baring its teeth. And she can't be sure, but maybe it's not her baggage that's the hang-up: maybe it's instinct, and maybe she shouldn't ignore it. Did Tyler really forget to send the coordinates on the GPS unit? Where is Bush? And if all that Janessa says about him is true, how far will he go to protect himself?

TWENTY-FIVE

EMLYN decides they should push to higher ground, away from the rocky shore and into the trees, so they scramble up the hill and then resume their trek, their feet quiet on the pine needles. Here there is shade. A woodpecker hammers overhead, and Emlyn looks up. The pink-red belly, the stunning dark wings. White neck, red face. A rare Lewis's woodpecker. Varden has taught her so many birds. She thinks of him, the two of them looking out Rev's window, knees pressed together, watching the birds float to the feeder. She points to the woodpecker, whispering its name, turning to show Janessa.

But Janessa has fallen back. She's looking toward the lake below them, transfixed. Emlyn follows her gaze.

Through the trees, she sees a figure in an orange trucker hat standing on the rocky shore. Tyler! Relief tumbles through her. She takes a step toward him, ready to run, but Janessa grabs her sleeve. "Wait," she whispers. She holds a finger to her lips.

Tyler squats, rummaging through a small pink bag. He stands and dumps out the contents. Sunscreen, toothbrush, mascara, blush. Then he raises a foot and begins stomping on all of it.

Janessa gasps.

Tyler stomps and stomps.

Then Janessa is off, bolting toward the water, stumbling down the hill. "No!" she screams.

Emlyn, shocked, staggers after her.

Down by the water, Tyler squats again, sifting through the rubble. When Janessa reaches him, he is rising, half crouched, still looking at the ground. Janessa plows into him, hard, and he stumbles backward, nearly falling.

Emlyn arrives on the beach and grabs Janessa's arm. "Stop! What are you doing?"

Janessa points to a hundred shiny pieces, shards of metal and plastic on the rocks. A canister of lip balm; a tube of mascara; blush, smashed, its pink crystals glimmering. "That's the makeup bag I thought Bush took. And somewhere in that mess is the flash drive where I was keeping everything. He was destroying it." Janessa kneels, sifting through the rubble. She picks up a small piece of blue plastic and holds it in the air. "He's the one who took it, not Bush."

Emlyn looks to Tyler, frowning. She unclips her heavy backpack and swings it to the ground.

Tyler raises both hands. "I can explain."

"You can explain?" Janessa hisses. "You're destroying the evidence I spent a year and a half collecting—and you can explain?" She clenches her fists. "You better do a lot more than that."

Emlyn feels the sun on her shoulders. She hears the lap of the water at her feet.

The CNN clip.

The unsent GPS message.

Tyler's insistence that Janessa give up and go home.

Now this.

Emlyn sees all of it, laid out before her, and at once she understands. Why they've come all this way, why they're here in the wilderness.

It was never about finding Janessa to save her. It was about finding her to stop her.

Emlyn looks at Tyler. His eyes, darting left and right, his left shoulder hunched. He's fashioning another lie, she knows it, and before he can speak, she steps in. "'Tying up loose ends,'" she says, remembering his phrase from early in their trek. She thinks of their first night at the campfire, that feeling of letting herself believe that Tyler had changed. How close she'd come to forgetting: there was always, always something Tyler would love more than her. Anger bubbles in her throat, and her voice grows thin. "Or maybe you're just 'making things right'?" She folds her arms across her chest. "Which one is it, Tyler?"

Tyler stares at the lake, gleaming turquoise in the midday light. He takes a deep breath. "Both."

Her heart drops. She'd expected a lie, but this is the truth, and it catches her off guard. "What were they?" she asks quietly, after she's had a moment to process. "The loose ends."

Tyler doesn't answer.

"Tell me," she says. "I think, after everything, you at least owe me that."

Tyler tilts his head toward the sky. He seems to contemplate whether or not to answer. "I was part of it."

"A part of what?"

"I worked for him, sometimes."

Janessa inhales sharply.

Emlyn holds the course. "When we were together? Before? After we broke up?" She wills herself to stay calm. "Don't you dare lie about it, Tyler. I want the truth."

Tyler closes his eyes, considering. "Before and during. Not after."

Emlyn lets this information sink in. How had she missed it? They'd lived together, eaten at the same table, shared a small bathroom. They'd done everything together. How had she not known?

He takes off his hat and runs a hand through his hair. "I swear, I really have been clean since we broke up. I haven't touched a thing, I haven't been involved, nothing."

Janessa steps closer to him. "But something I found made you nervous."

Tyler gives a slight nod. "I saw what you had in those encrypted files you sent me, and it would've been enough to send me to prison for years."

Emlyn's mind flashes back to a day, years ago, at Craters of the Moon. Tyler's fascination with the forgotten astronaut.

Janessa's jaw drops open. "*You're* Collins?" she says, her lip quivering.

"*Was.* I'm not anymore. That's the thing: I don't deserve . . . prison. Punishment. I'm done with all of it. It's been years." Tyler looks at Emlyn, his eyes pleading. "I had to stop her, don't you see? I knew that if Janessa took him down, I'd go down, too."

"So you lied," Emlyn says. "You used me. You convinced me Janessa was in danger, and you put all of us at risk, so you could save your own skin." He'd been so compelling. At the fly shop, at the cabin, those nights around the campfire. All those things Tyler said to her—*I love you, I'm sorry, I've never gotten over you*—were those lies, too? "I believed you," she whispers. "I trusted you."

He reaches for her. She shakes her head and pulls away from him. Whatever it is Tyler wants to say, she doesn't want to hear it. She's done.

Janessa steps in front of her. She roars and shoves Tyler hard again.

This time, he stumbles backward, stunned, circling his arms to try to stabilize himself, but it's too late. His body topples backward onto the rocks.

Emlyn sucks in a long, startled breath and lurches backward, an instinct to reel from the sight. She pushes past Janessa and rushes to Tyler, kneeling next to him, knees pressed into the rocks. She says his name, over and over. She checks for a pulse. His eyes flutter open, he squints.

Behind her, a scuffle: flesh to flesh, a thump. She turns and sees Janessa on the ground, face in the sand.

And then a terrible blow to Emlyn's back, a pain that surges quickly up her spine. Her head whiplashes badly, and she bites her tongue, a searing, sour pain. Somehow, she has the wherewithal to put her hands out to break her fall, but still, her face hits the rocks. More pain scuttles through her jaw, and the taste of blood fills her mouth. Next, hair. Someone has grabbed her by her long hair and is dragging her across the beach. She kicks her legs to move with the tow. She twists and scrambles, she reaches for the hand that grips her hair. A thick, strong mass, the knuckles rough beneath her fingertips.

Bush.

She sinks her fingernails into the flesh, presses as hard as she can, and pulls.

Bush roars in pain, and, still holding her hair, he spins her faceup. She squints. His face, so handsome, has morphed into something dreadful and hideous. He tightens his grip on her and drags her toward the water. She gulps a big breath.

The cold blasts through her, legs, belly, shoulders. Her heart feels as though it will burst. Bush shoves her head underwater. She opens her eyes, grasps for his body. She kicks her feet, trying to find bottom. There. She plants her feet on the ground and with all of her strength, she surges from the water. Air. She takes a giant breath before Bush, with both hands now, shoves her back underwater.

She reaches up and claws at Bush's arms. He loosens his grip for just a moment, and, though she barely gets her face out of the water, she manages a small gulp of air.

A baptism service. The day hot with August sun, Rev standing in the Salmon, reciting the words: "In the name of the Father, Son, and Holy Ghost . . ." Three people got baptized that day, and Emlyn swore each one emerged from the water, beaming and resplendent, radiant as Rev. Varden was one of them. She never saw him so beautiful.

Rev. Her lovely white hair, her tender blue eyes. Has she seen her old friend for the last time? And Varden? Those sleepy fantasies of Christmas mornings and hot cocoa and books on a couch. Will she even get to tell him she dreamed of those things? Is this what it feels like to be at death's door?

She has been here before. That day on the road, three years ago, the freezing rain pelting her neck, the cold overtaking her.

She twists her body, writhing. Something jabs her in the chest. Again her feet find the lake's floor, and she bursts from the water, gasping. Bush quickly pushes her back down. She can feel her strength waning.

Another jab, this time at the base of her ribs. Something heavy there, a weight. Rev's flashlight. She reaches into the pocket and tugs and tugs until it comes out. She runs her thumb over the sharp point, meant for breaking glass. She grips the light hard in her hand. She can feel Bush dragging her deeper into the lake. Soon, she won't be able to touch bottom.

But then his grip on her loosens again. His fingers are tangled in her hair, but he wriggles them free.

Now. Her feet kick down to the lake's floor, and one last time, she punches upward. Bush stands a foot away, hands over his eyes. With every scrap of strength she has left, Emlyn swings the flashlight toward his head. The glass-breaking point connects with his temple, right where she was aiming. That sensitive spot on the head. He gasps. Sways left, then right.

Emlyn wheezes, sucking in great swallows of air.

But oh—all at once a seething, terrible burn. Eyes, mouth, throat. Emlyn squints, forcing herself to hold her breath, but the pain does not subside, it is inside of her, she can feel it scorching her lungs. A dreadful, scalding sense overtakes her. Is this what it feels like to drown?

An arm appears at her chest, tucked between her armpits. Skinny, tan. "Come on, girl. You're okay. Come on." Janessa pulls her, lifeguard-style, away from Bush, who still holds his hands over his eyes, roaring in pain, the water lapping at his waist.

Emlyn collapses on the beach. She coughs and coughs, and a mouthful of lake water and bile surges from her mouth.

Janessa pats her back. "There you go."

Emlyn's ears ring. There is water all through her, in places it shouldn't be, nose, ears, throat, gut. Her head throbs. But there is also that terrible burning. Everything stings. Everything is a blur, but out in the lake, she watches as Bush's hands drop to his side. Blood trickles from his temple and down his face. His head rolls back and he tumbles into the water, a great splash, the blow from her flashlight finally taking hold of him.

At first, a sense of relief surges through her. Bush is down, he's gone. He can't hurt her, or anyone else. "Tyler," she says.

"He's fine." Janessa huffs beside her, watching the lake. "Wait here," she pants, and then struggles to her feet. Emlyn watches a smeared, foggy Janessa trudge back into the water.

A part of Emlyn wants to tell Janessa to leave him out in the lake to die. Less than a minute ago, he was trying to kill her in that very same water. Maybe he doesn't deserve to be saved. This is karma, this is good triumphing over evil.

But, though everything hurts, and nothing makes sense, a different, better part of her understands: this is not how she wants this to end. Yes, she was defending herself. Yes, he was trying to kill her, but—she doesn't want Bush to die at her hands. Monster or not, she doesn't want that on her conscience. That's not who she is.

Janessa wades out, grabs Bush by the collar of his shirt, and lugs his limp, floating body back to the shore. Emlyn crawls toward him, the round pebbles pressing into her knees and palms. She can barely breathe herself, but she rolls him onto his back. She leans her face close to his, feeling for breath on her cheek. Nothing. She places the heel of her hand in the center of Bush's thick chest. Two inches down, and then again and again and again, a hundred times, in quick succession. She's practiced this on dummies, maybe a dozen times over the years, but this is the first time she's attempted it on a person.

Emlyn is nearly zapped of strength. She bends again, her cheek grazing his lips. Still no air. She sits back up, pinches his nose, takes a breath and leans down, pressing her mouth to his, creating an airtight seal. One second. She takes another breath of her own and then exhales in his mouth again. She watches for the chest to rise, begins thirty more chest compressions. On eighteen, Bush writhes and hacks up a mouthful of water onto her arms. He coughs and gasps. She rolls him onto his side.

"You have to strip off the wet clothes," Emlyn says. Her teeth chatter. "He needs to get warm. Both of us do."

"You first." Janessa steps closer, helping her shrug out of her drenched fleece and undershirt. She unbuttons Emlyn's pants and wrestles them down her wet legs, tugs off her socks. She dumps the backpack. "Here," she says, unrolling a sleeping bag and helping her crawl in.

Then Janessa turns to Bush. She strips his clothes and dumps them in a heap. Emlyn averts her eyes. She reaches into her backpack and pulls out the GPS unit. Her hands are shaking badly from the cold, and she can barely unlatch the tiny trapdoor that protects the SOS button. She holds it down for several seconds. A question pops up, asking her to confirm that she is reaching out for help. For a moment she pauses. She shivers, her body stippled with cold. Yes, she answers. She looks at her watch. Six minutes later, she receives a response from the International Emergency Response Coordination Center. *This is the IERCC, what is your emergency?*

How to answer such a question. *My friend and I are deep in the backcountry with two men, both of them large and strong and maybe crazy, and we will never get the two of them out of here, so now we need rescuing.* Instead, she presses the tiny keys to spell out the message: *two near drownings, one concussion.*

NINE minutes later, she receives a response. *I have spoken with emergency services. They are getting help to your location and have requested you remain where you are.*

That, she can do.

She pictures the flurry of activity—phone calls, text messages, a scramble to rally a team—that she has just kicked into action. Relief settles onto her shoulders, a fuzzy blanket, a warm compress on a bruise.

She presses the arrows on the GPS unit, looking for a message from Varden, hoping he has responded, but he hasn't.

Janessa grabs Bush's hands and pulls them behind his back. He coughs some more. She takes out some paracord from her backpack and winds it round and round his wrists, cinching it tight.

"Maybe we should give him a minute," Emlyn says. Her throat still burns with every word.

"Sorry," Janessa says, tying one knot and another. "I'm not taking any chances." When she's done, she ties his feet together, too. Bush hacks and heaves. Janessa covers him with a second sleeping bag, tucking the edges beneath him.

Emlyn winces. "I don't understand why my eyes and throat and lungs feel like they're on fire."

Janessa wrinkles her nose. "Bear spray. I aimed for Bush, but you took a little, too. Sorry."

"Well," Emlyn says, coughing on her words. She remembers the first time she met Janessa, all those years ago, at Bumpy's Diner: Janessa slamming the canister onto the Formica tabletop, confessing to Emlyn that she'd always wanted to bear spray a dirtbag in the face. "I guess you can check that off your bucket list."

TWENTY-SIX

"YOU don't have to do this," Bush says.

It's been two hours since Emlyn sent the distress signal, and they are still waiting at the lake.

Tyler is awake but groggy from his concussion. Janessa gave him some ibuprofen for the headache, and Emlyn found an emergency ice pack that he is holding over the back of his neck.

"Shut up," Janessa says. She rises from her spot next to Emlyn and goes to check that Bush's hands and feet are still tied.

"I'm just saying: It's an option. You can still change your mind. We can all just put this behind us. No hard feelings."

A terrible bruise, dark and purple, has begun to spread its way from Bush's temple toward his left eye, and blood from the flashlight wound has caked on the side of his face. His eyes are bloodshot and swollen from the bear spray; the rims are red. "Think of all the good times we had, babe," he croons. "Think of the fun. You can't do this to me."

"Don't," Janessa snaps.

A few more moments of silence. "I can be done with all of it," Bush tries. "I can change."

"It's a little late for that."

"I love you. And I know a part of you loves me."

"You don't love me," Janessa says flatly, staring at her boots, and then she adds, softly: "And I never loved you."

Bush scowls. He's become hideous, Emlyn realizes, and not just because of the bruise and the blood. Gone is the charisma he'd exuded; gone is that infectious smile. In their place there is rage and hatred and desperation, and it emanates from his body and face, an unpleasant and palpable darkness. The transformation is unnerving. He glares at Janessa and begins spewing a litany of insults.

Janessa reaches for her trekking pole. For a moment Emlyn wonders if she intends to strike Bush with it, but instead, she begins to unwrap a piece of bright orange duct tape from just below the handle. A common hack for outdoor enthusiasts, a way to pack some in case of emergency without hauling the whole bulky roll. Janessa tears off an eight-inch piece of tape and walks toward Bush, who continues his ugly rampage. He swears and spits, foaming at the mouth. Janessa leans down and he leans away. He spins his head back and forth, resisting, until she roughly grabs a handful of his thick hair. "That," she says, pressing the duct tape to one side and then carefully taping it taut across his mouth, "is enough out of you."

Bush's fury is amplified now; he kicks his tied feet and thrashes at the waist. Emlyn hates to think of the damage he might do if he weren't constrained. Help, she keeps reminding herself, is on the way. It might be two hours, it might be six. But the end of this mess is in sight. They just have to wait.

Emlyn hasn't spoken a word to Tyler. She's still trying to sift through her confusion—about the past three days, about the past five years—and she's so exhausted that making sense of anything feels impossible at the moment.

Darkness settles over them. Emlyn is dry now, mostly, aside from her long hair, but she's still a little cold. She knows the acute threat has passed, but she still has that awful feeling that water has slipped into places inside her where it shouldn't be. Both ears ring, and she swears there's a pocket of water trapped deep within the left one.

She dozes off. In her dream she weaves together one vision and another, memory after memory, conflating them.

Her father on a stream, waving her forward. Her father turning to wave as he walks away.

Grandpa with his ornery grin, handing her *Brave New World*.

Bush with his thick hands gripping her by the hair, dunking her in the lake. The cold water rushing through her, the burn of the pepper.

Varden pressing the Ellen Bass poem into her palm, scrawled on a piece of paper from his Moleskine notebook.

LATER, she opens her eyes. The fire glows orange, the embers still hot. Janessa has tied Tyler up, too, now, and he and Bush lie back-to-back beneath an open sleeping bag, arms out. Janessa sleeps at Emlyn's side. There, in the distance: a light. Small, white, bright. It bobs along the far shore of the lake, flashing left, right, up, down, in uneven, jittery movements. A flashlight?

The light disappears. Maybe Emlyn dreamed it. Maybe this is a floater, maybe her eyes are failing her after the pepper spray. She closes her eyes and tries to fall back asleep.

"Emlyn?" a voice hollers through the darkness.

She bolts upright.

The rescue team has arrived.

She pokes Janessa. "Did you hear that?" she whispers.

Janessa rolls over and moans.

"Emlyn!" the voice again.

The light dances closer.

"Here!" she tries to yell, but the sound comes out as a woeful croak, a snort-wheeze, like deer make when they're spooked. "I'm here!"

She slips out of the sleeping bag and struggles to her feet. Her hair is still damp.

The light nods closer, more erratic now: the person is moving faster.

Janessa stirs, sitting up.

"Emlyn!"

She recognizes the voice, now, and her heart surges with hope and joy and relief. "Varden!" she calls. Again her voice fails her, but this time, it's because she is overcome. All at once she is a thousand streams, she is snowmelt. Tears and more tears pour from her.

The light flickers down the hillside. She can barely move but she forces herself to stumble toward the light.

"Thank God," Varden says, wrapping his arms around her.

She's crying so hard she can't speak.

"Hey, are you okay?" He squeezes tight. "I was so worried."

"I sent a message, from a GPS unit. This morning."

"Good," he says, still holding her. "That's good."

She shivers and cries some more, because she is realizing—for Varden to have caught up with them by now, he would've already been on his way, this morning. He wouldn't have had cell service to receive the message. "You didn't get it, did you?"

He shakes his head.

"I don't understand," she says. "How did you find us?"

"We synced our mapping apps, last fall, when I tagged along on your job for *Afield*. I didn't remember, honestly, but two days ago I packed up to go fishing at Tatum Lake, and when I went to map my route, I saw yours. I hiked to the lake, anyway, but I had this bad feeling, and I just couldn't shake it, so I turned around and then set out to find you." He steps back and turns to look beyond Emlyn. "What about everyone else? Did you find your friend? Is she okay?"

"Yeah, we found her, and she's okay." She realizes there's so much she needs to tell him. How and when will she explain everything?

Varden walks toward the fire behind them. "Forest Service," he says, as a means of introduction, and for a moment he stands and takes in the scene before him. A bruised and battered Bush, tied and duct-taped. A forlorn Tyler, with an ice pack propped at his neck and a T-shirt draped over his eyes, also tied up. Janessa, rising to her feet, jaw slack.

"Well," Varden says, "this is unexpected," and then he immediately shifts into professional mode. He kneels next to Tyler, flashing a light in his eyes to check his pupils. He asks him questions. *Do you know where you are? Can you count backward from twenty for me? Do you know what day it is?* When he's finished, he rises and takes a few steps toward Bush.

He seems to hesitate, but then slowly tugs the duct tape from Bush's face.

"Sir, we are being held against our will here by these two lunatics," Bush says in a grave voice. Emlyn can't help but notice that he seems to have transformed himself back into his more likable self. He looks earnest, concerned.

Varden just nods and runs him through a similar set of tests. He tugs a first-aid kit from his backpack, unwrapping an antiseptic wipe and dabbing Bush's temple.

Bush winces.

"How'd you get this?" Varden asks him. He uses a Q-tip to smear antibiotic ointment on the wound.

"She hit me," Bush hisses, lifting his chin toward Emlyn.

Varden turns and flashes her a surprised look. "Who, Emlyn?"

"Yes!"

Varden opens a large bandage and places it over the wound. "I guess you probably had it coming, then."

"Please untie us, please let us go," Bush says.

Janessa steps forward to interject, but before she can say anything, Varden carefully replaces the duct tape, pressing it taut across Bush's mouth. Bush thrashes in fury.

"Well," Varden says, rising, and turning to face the women. "I'm betting the two of you have quite a story to tell." He extends a hand to Janessa. "I'm Varden, by the way. I think we spoke, years ago, but this is the first time we've officially met."

"Janessa," she says, shaking his hand. "It's good to finally meet you." She turns to Emlyn, wide-eyed, jaw open, and fans her face dramatically.

Emlyn, embarrassed, gives her a look.

Janessa sinks to the ground next to her and leans close. "You are absolutely insane to even think about Tyler, when you've got him right in front of you," she whispers. "You know that, don't you?"

Overhead, the moon is a thin, unassuming shard of light. A piece of wood rolls from the fire, and the sparks swirl upward. Her left ring finger tingles in the cold night air.

Emlyn looks at Varden, who has taken a spot between Tyler and Bush. "I know," she says quietly. "I just hope it's not too late."

LAST SUMMER

EVERY evening, Emlyn watches Varden through the window of Rev's living room. He comes home from work, grabs his bow and target from his cabin, and carries both, one in each arm, to the field beyond the parking lot. There, he dips out of sight. Curious as she is to watch him practice, she can't muster up the courage to invite herself. But, one day in July, she grabs her ball cap, calls to Rev that she'll be right back, and slips out the door to follow him.

The sun is still high in the sky, the grass a rich honey gold that has caught fire with evening light. Varden stands a hundred yards away, feet shoulder width apart, shirtless. He seems to settle himself, a slight ripple from shoulder to shoulder, a small shuffle in his stance. He nocks his arrow, raises the bow, draws back. Every muscle in his back tenses, tight undulations of flesh. He shoots. The quick *thunk* of the release, the *whoosh* of the arrow hitting the target. Bull's-eye. He stands and looks, assessing the shot. He tugs another arrow from the quiver, spins it in his fingers, and sets it into place. This time she sees the way his fingertips brush the side of his cheek when he draws back. The curve of the muscles in his back, the lines in his forearm. Another bull's-eye.

He turns toward her, a quick glance, and she shifts her gaze toward the mountains. Flushing, caught in the act. Varden leans his bow against a rock, reaches for his T-shirt, and slips it over his head.

"I have an old bow," he says. "I can adjust the poundage for you, if you want to give it a try."

She ventures closer, the sage crackling against her legs. "You look good," she says. "I mean the shooting, it looks good. Those were good shots."

"Thanks," he mutters. He scuffs his boot in the dirt.

"Why do you do that?" Emlyn asks.

"Do what?"

"Look away when I talk to you sometimes."

He has a dimple beneath his left eye and it twitches. "I don't."

"You do."

"Well, I don't want to say."

She grabs hold of his elbow, and he flinches. "Tell me."

He rests his bow against his thigh and stares at the ground. Then he raises his eyes and looks right at her, and she sees that in this light, his eyes match the landscape, green-gold. "It's because the first time I met you, you were stark naked, and I feel a little awkward about it."

Now it's Emlyn's turn to blush. "Oh."

The dimple appears again. "Under normal circumstances, I'd at least like to buy you dinner before we get to that stage." Now he flashes his teeth, and his face breaks into folds of laughter.

"Varden!" she gasps, shocked to hear him joke like that. Her mind flashes to the shelf of Amish romance novels, pages facing outward. She's sure her face has turned bright red, splotches creeping their way up her neck, but she finds herself laughing, too.

"That's not why," he says, plucking an arrow from the quiver. "Well, that's part of it. It's because I'm awkward around women, always have been. Especially ones I like." He pauses here, then closes his eyes and wrinkles his nose. "See what I mean? Awkward."

"You *are* awkward," she says with a grin. "But I don't mind it."

He resumes his stance, draws back, and shoots again. The arrow sails over the target, missing it completely.

"Am I distracting you?" she asks.

He turns away from her to go fetch the arrow. His back is to her, but she can still hear him. "You have no idea."

TWENTY-SEVEN

AT dawn, Emlyn wakes to the sound of a helicopter stuttering through the mountains. The sun spills orange onto the water. She sits up, rubs her eyes, and looks around. Janessa slumps next to her. Varden stands vigil, leaning against a pine, arms crossed. Way down the lake, the chopper floats into sight. It circles over them, then shoots south in search of a landing spot.

Varden had removed Bush's duct tape for the night, and Bush seizes one last opportunity to persuade Janessa to reconsider. "It's not too late," he says. "You can still change course."

"It *is* too late," she says.

"Babe."

Janessa glares at him and points to the additional duct tape on her trekking pole. "Don't push me."

The EMTs scramble from the helicopter and trot up the shore. They administer a battery of tests similar to the one Varden did the night before, and they listen to Emlyn's chest and check her ears.

Varden has used his own GPS to request that at least one law enforce-ment officer accompany the chopper, and he explains that the two men should be restrained for the duration of the flight.

"Sorry," the EMT says, once they've assessed everyone, "there's only room for four of you."

After a moment, Varden raises a hand. "I can hike out."

"Me, too," Emlyn adds quickly. She knows she's not really up for such a trip, and she's sure she'll slow him down. But there's so much she wants to say to him, so much she now understands. She looks sheepishly at Varden. "I mean, if that's all right?"

"I guess," Varden answers, but he turns away from her, and dread fills her heart.

Bush and Tyler are bound and loaded into the helicopter. Emlyn doesn't allow herself to look at them.

"Call me when you get home," Janessa says. "I want to visit. Check out your Airstream, meet Rev." She glances at Varden. "I want to learn all about your new life."

Emlyn nods. She holds her friend close until Janessa pulls away and climbs into the chopper. The helicopter lifts, churning dust and debris. Emlyn and Varden hunker behind a boulder, shielding their eyes, then watch as it glides over the lake and disappears. The two of them finish packing up their gear and extinguish the fire in silence, but it's not the usual quiet they share, easy and comfortable. Agony churns in Emlyn's gut. She wants to say something—apologize? ask whether things are okay between them?—but she isn't sure where to start. And she worries that whatever she says might make things even worse.

They begin the long hike out of the wilderness. Her legs feel weak, her back aches, and her left ear still feels waterlogged. It doesn't take long for her to question her decision to attempt the hike, but she doesn't complain.

When they stop for a break, Varden looks at Emlyn and leans his head to the side. "Can we talk?"

Her heart drops. This is it. The moment she's been afraid of, the moment she knew would inevitably come. Whatever it is that was on the brink of blooming between the two of them—she's ruined it. Varden has had enough.

He takes a deep breath and then kicks at a pebble on the shore. "I know you and I are not . . . together. Technically. Although sometimes it feels like we are? Or should be. Anyway, when Rev told me what you were doing, and who you were doing it with, I'm not gonna lie, I was ticked. I kept thinking, if you went back to him, after—" He pauses here, shaking his head, choking on the words. "But also. If something happened. If I had three years and didn't tell you how I felt about you, I would never forgive myself."

Emlyn shudders. Is Varden really saying what she thinks he's saying? She closes her eyes and leans into him.

"I know I'm probably speaking more words right now than I have the whole time you've known me. But I need to say this. I like you. A lot. More than a lot. And, am I crazy, or is there something between us? Something good and worthwhile. Or could something be there, if we let it?"

"I'm a mess," she whispers. "You need to know that. I have a lot of stuff I need to work through."

"Everyone does."

"Like, decades of stuff."

"It's okay." Varden pulls back and looks at her. "I want you to hear me when I say this." His hazel eyes look deep into hers. "I'm not going anywhere."

THEY walk and walk. Emlyn is slower than usual, and more than once Varden has to wait for her to catch up. Across the rocky cape, through the trees, back to the campsite from two nights ago. It's getting dark, so they'll stay there for the night. They dig out their sleeping bags, and Varden starts a fire.

"I'll see if I can catch us some dinner," he says, assembling his rod. "You want to come?"

"I think I should rest," she says. She's so tired. "But I'll sit and cheer you on."

Perched on a boulder, Emlyn watches as he ties on a fly and casts. There are few things more mesmerizing than watching Varden on the water, she determines. He's so skilled, so at ease. He walks up the shore, his eyes on the lake.

Emlyn thinks of Rev, rubbing her sore, frostbitten hands and feet with her essential oils, back when Varden first found her and brought her to the valley. What is it her friend had said just a few days ago, when Emlyn was trying to decide what to do? *I can't say what it is you need to reckon with. What it is you need to clear up for yourself, what needs to happen in there. . . .*

When Emlyn gets home, she'll tell Rev everything. The people, the smoke, the mountain lion, the flashlight, the wilderness.

She has a feeling Rev won't be all that surprised.

The sun begins its descent, and the air grows cold. Emlyn slides into her jacket and drapes her sleeping bag over her legs. She tucks in the edges. In her mind she replays Tyler's confessions. She sees, now, that so much of their life together was built on lies. There was a short season, maybe, when this wasn't the case. The night they met and staggered through the sprinklers; that shimmering first date at the lake; a purple evening at Craters, both of them dressed as astronauts. Those things were true. And good. But for far too long she held on to them, convincing herself that they outweighed all the bad, that Tyler's problems were her fault, that she didn't deserve to move on. Now she realizes: those things she believed about their relationship and herself—they were lies, too.

Still, she should be livid or crushed or something, shouldn't she? Three years ago, when Tyler left her in the woods, she'd wished that Varden hadn't found her. For weeks she'd watched the snow whirl and heap with some deep, dreadful longing; she'd wanted to be buried in it. She hadn't wanted to go on. Later that spring, that desire faded, and in its place came fury and self-loathing that frothed in her gut, a nasty concoction worse than the desire to die. She's certain it would've done her in, if it hadn't been for Rev and Varden.

And yet.

Somehow, she isn't devastated, now. She isn't angry; she isn't crushed. With Janessa safe and back in her life, and with Varden on the water and the Idaho sky stretching overhead, she feels inexplicably serene. At peace. For the first time ever, she sees Tyler as Janessa must've seen him, all along. As he truly is. Not captivating, as he's always been to her, but broken, selfish, desperate. Tragic.

There is a strange, marvelous liberty in seeing a person for who they really are.

Because maybe—could this be right?—she can finally see herself for who she really is. And right now, even though she's exhausted and much of her body still ripples with pain, she doesn't feel pathetic. Not at all. She feels brave and resilient and loved and chosen and expectant and enough and also—well, decent. Maybe even radiant? All of those things at once, somehow. The words seem to tumble at her, an avalanche of new, glittering possibilities.

A shadow flickers overhead. Emlyn shields her eyes and looks skyward. An osprey dives to the water, swift and focused. Varden calls her name and points. They're his favorite. Fish hawks, he calls them. A splash, a split second of chaos. The bird rises from the water, defeated, empty-handed. Emlyn knows it will try and try again. One more word cartwheels her way, and maybe this is the most unexpected and gorgeous one of all. "Free."

AUTHOR'S NOTE

My titles never stick.

This is my fourth book—and *none* of my titles have stuck—so I suppose by now, I ought to know this. But when this book was mostly finished and the email with the subject line "Title Thoughts" arrived in my inbox, I knew it wasn't going to say, "Kimi, we love your title!" And I was right. We were driving through a stretch of Idaho with fields that glowed bright with July mustard. I braced myself for battle.

You see, the truth is, I grow quite attached to my titles, and it's always hard to let them go.

For a long time, *Wilderness* was this book's title. I came up with it pretty early on—because, well, it had to have a title! At first, I wasn't all that enamored with it. Over the course of many months, though, it grew on me. It became a word that I meditated on and worked to incorporate into the characters' journeys. When I was deep into this project, my pastor began

292 | AUTHOR'S NOTE

a series titled "Wilderness," which of course felt providential. I scribbled notes and continued to hold tight to my word.

When that "Title Thoughts" email hit my inbox, I called my agent and explained my hang-up. I don't come up with a title after the book is written. I don't brainstorm catchy phrases that will pop off the shelves in a bookstore. Rather, *Wilderness* was the word I'd been fixating on, obsessing about, building the book around. I couldn't just let it go!

My agent listened. She said that whatever I decided, she'd support me, and I knew this was true. But she also explained something in a new way for me.

This works great for you as a technique, she told me. It's a means of building themes and weaving the setting into the bigger matters of the book. But maybe that's all it is—a method that helps you center and focus and build. And maybe that word doesn't need to be the book's title.

I'm not sure why this never occurred to me.

I'm not sure why it feels so important to me that readers know that *Wilderness* was the book's original title, that this is the word I built the book around.

I want readers to know, also, that when I wrote this book, I tried to build a character who was strong, resilient, and lovable, even though she didn't see herself that way. I aspired to ferry the reader through mountains and valleys, fields and streams. I wanted them to experience both the beauty and unique challenges of a physical wilderness, but also the loneliness and lostness of a more metaphorical, spiritual wilderness. I wanted to craft a story that ultimately left readers—especially readers who might be in a wilderness of their own—feeling uplifted. Bolstered. If that's you, reader, I hope you'll remember: wilderness isn't the destination. It's not the final chapter. Your story goes on.

ACKNOWLEDGMENTS

I couldn't have finished this book without a daily commitment to pray over not only its contents—where it should go, what it should be about—but also that I would finish it at all. So, first and foremost, thank you, Holy Spirit, for grace and guidance and presence.

Thanks, importantly, to my agent, Amy Cloughley, for ushering this book from its initial idea (which, at the time, was "A woman who lives in an Airstream goes into the woods to look for someone . . .") to its finished product. I'm very lucky to have you in my corner.

Thank you to my discerning and intrepid editor, Sarah Grill, for believing in this book when it was in its infancy, and for challenging me to mine, build, and polish. This book is so much richer because of you.

To the rest of the team at Minotaur—Kelley Ragland, Allison Ziegler, Hector DeJean, Cathy Turiano, Lisa Davis, Benjamin Allen, Terry McGarry, David Rotstein, and all the other people who worked to mold my Word document into a finished book—thank you.

Thank you to friends and early readers Erica Young Reitz, Melissa

Morrow McCulley, Tanya Botteicher, Amy Henning, and Bethany Spicher Schonberg, who had a look at this manuscript in various stages before it was finished and who offered support and feedback to help me get it on its way.

Thank you to my doctor friends, Joshua Botteicher and Nathan Salinas, who offered medical guidance on my chapter set in the Gila Wilderness.

Thank you to Melanie Rios, for all the coffee, your Friday check-ins, and your friendship.

Thank you to my brother-in-law and pastor, Aaron Henning, for the well-timed sermon series, "Wilderness."

Thank you to Hudson Grant, for the tutorial on tying flies.

Thank you to Ellen Bass, for graciously allowing me to use your poem in this book, and for all the good work you do to support writers.

Thank you, Missy, for sending the Ellen Bass poem. I knew immediately that I wanted it to appear in this book.

Thank you to Hudson and Holt, my comrades in wandering and fellow lovers of Idaho. Your vibrance, curiosity, and love make me a better person.

Thank you to Chris, my best friend and life partner for the past two decades. You believed in me long before I ever believed in myself.

Soli deo gloria.

Holt Grant

KIMI CUNNINGHAM GRANT is the *USA Today* best-selling author of *Silver Like Dust, Fallen Mountains, These Silent Woods,* and *The Nature of Disappearing.* She is also an award-winning poet and essayist whose work has appeared in *Fathom, Literary Mama, Rattle, Poet Lore,* and *Whitefish Review.* She lives with her family in Pennsylvania.